TAHOE

—a place of tantalizing contrasts

It whispers like a breeze
*   and jangles like a slot machine.*
It offers wealth and fame
*   but leaves you broke and broken . . .*
It promises love
*   but delivers loneliness . . .*
*   . . . unless you're lucky!*

TAHOE

—where anything can happen

TAHOE

BY DOROTHY DOWDELL

PLAYBOY PRESS
PAPERBACKS

TAHOE

CHAPTER

1

So far, no one on the jetliner had recognized her. Not a single fan had shoved a piece of paper at her to autograph, and for once Lea Turner was relieved. The one-hour flight from San Francisco to Reno would give her a breathing spell, which she needed. She took off her large dark glasses, untied her Pucci scarf, which matched her blue Ultrasuede pantsuit, and fluffed her honey-pale hair.

Of course, there'd been the inevitable interview in the VIP lounge just before she embarked. Vicky, her indefectible manager-secretary, had arranged it. "You might as well make use of that waiting time," she said. "Usually you look all right before a flight; so you can be photographed." Vicky was not one to flatter.

At first, the young reporter had been obsequious; that should have put her on her guard. "Aren't you pleased with the rave reviews you've been getting here? One critic said you are the most exciting entertainer to appear here in the last decade."

"Naturally, I've been very pleased—especially since San Francisco is one of my favorite cities. The audiences were so warm and responsive, really great!"

"Any more TV specials?"

"One was taped just before I left New York. It's to be telecast in October, I believe."

"Now that the musical *Remember Me?* has closed after a long run, are you planning to appear in another one?"

"Yes. Rehearsals begin as soon as I return to New York, in September. It's called *Ms. Behaving*. Get it right—capital *M-s*-period. Sort of a fun thing on women's lib. I'm very excited about it."

The reporter scribbled his notes and continued, "You're going to be a headliner in the Celestial Room at Starr's Tahoe Resort, right?"

Lea nodded. "Yes, with a complete company. We're putting on a full production. We'll open June 10th. I'm going to Nevada ahead of the others to visit old friends."

"You were born and raised in Reno, weren't you?"

"Indeed I was. I got my start there, at a small casino called the Mardi Gras club. I'll be forever grateful to Tony Rizzi, who owns it. Be sure to mention his name. It's spelled *R-i-z-z-i*. He gave me my first break."

"You'll be seeing him, of course?"

"Oh, naturally. And other dear friends, too. I love Nevada, so I'm very happy to be going back."

The reporter rubbed his pencil on the side of his nose. "If you feel that way, why is this the first time you've returned in five years? Wasn't there some trouble . . . ?"

The color drained from Lea's face, but Vicky, bless her, burst in. "Of course not. You ought to see the schedule she's had for the last five years." She rattled off a list of shows, TV specials, and nightclub appearances, then said, "Come on, Miss Turner, you'd better get on the plane."

As they walked quickly toward Gate 14, Vicky muttered, "Nosy s.o.b.! Now, Lea, watch what you say when you land in Reno. You'll be met by a full contingent of press and TV people. The mayor and Lyle Starr—the works. 'Local girl makes good' treatment."

"I'll be careful."

"Be the last one off the plane so the cameramen will have plenty of time to take your picture. And be sure to pull your jacket down when you get out of your seat so it won't hump up around your neck. Check your hair and makeup, too, before you get off."

"Yes, Vicky. You should be going with me."

"No, you need a couple days alone with your friends. I'll see that the whole company gets on the chartered bus day after tomorrow. You know what a hassle that always is. We'll meet you at Lake Tahoe."

They arrived at the gate. "Here's your boarding pass." Vicky's hard, fortyish features softened as she kissed Lea's cheek. " 'Bye, lamb. Have a good time. By the way, here's a batch of telegrams that came to the hotel. Read them on the plane so you can thank the people."

As the plane taxied to the end of a long runway and waited for clearance, Lea thought of Vicky and what a jewel she was. Over the years, Vicky had managed her career, paid her bills, taken care of her mail, kept her on schedule, chosen her clothes, helped her with the press and coped with fans and camp followers.

It was four years ago that she met Vicky—after Lea's short, rotund agent, with ferret eyes, took a cigar out of his mouth, waved it at her and said, "Kid, you're on your way. You're about to be a superstar, and you're only nineteen. God, you worry me!"

"But I can take care——"

He snorted. "You're an innocent babe in the woods, with the wolves howling all around. And I don't mean the boyfriends you might sleep with. I mean all the leeches that'll come out of the woodwork now that you're going in the big time. You need someone to travel with you and protect you. You're valuable property, and you shouldn't be on your own."

"You mean have a bodyguard?"

"Naw, much more than that. Some older woman who's wise to the ways of this wicked world. A manager-secretary." He paced back and forth in his office. "But she should also be a combination duenna, confidante, *chargé d'affaires*, mother figure, *and* bodyguard."

"That's quite an order. But where would I find her?"

"I know just the gal. Vicky Goldring. She's a divorcée. She'll never see forty again. She's from the entertainment world, too. Her grandfather was in vaudeville, her parents were in summer stock, and her former husband plays in an orchestra at a TV studio. She's a sharp cookie. By God, nobody'd try any tricks with her around! She'll take good care of you."

It took Lea a long time to get used to Vicky's frank, abrasive tongue and her abrupt manner. During the first month she snapped, "You haven't a grain of sense about money, Lea. What are you going to do when you can't sing and dance anymore? You won't have a nickel of all that bread you're making if we don't do something, and fast."

Vicky found a prestigious financial management firm that took charge of the earnings, made investments, paid the income taxes and gave Lea a living allowance.

At first, Lea thought Vicky was a drag, a battle-ax, and was tempted to fire her. But she was afraid of what her agent might do. After a while, she realized how much she depended on Vicky. It was amazing how the phonies seemed to disappear and how the members of her troupe became cooperative when her dragon, Vicky, came around breathing fire. Also, Lea stayed out of the drug scene, drank little and smoked less. And she kept on a diet. Who wouldn't, with Vicky casting a baleful eye on a piece of pie or a hot fudge sundae?

"Where are you going to wear that, Lea? On your hips?"

For a long time she almost hated Vicky—her jailkeeper. Then, during a rehearsal, she saw Vicky knitting a sweater with her quick, thin fingers. It was a pale shell pink, in an intricate pattern as lovely as Belgium lace. When they took a short break, Lea touched it reverently and half-whispered, "Who's that for?"

"For *you*. Who else? I haven't a chick or child in this world except you." Then Vicky cleared her throat to get the huskiness out.

Lea couldn't go on hating her, not after that.

When they were airborne, Lea saw the vast San Francisco Bay below, pushing inlets and coves into the surrounding land. Wind through the Golden Gate stirred the water into whitecaps and trimmed the sails of sloops and dinghies, which bobbed up and down like a swarm of butterflies. A dozen cities blanketed the hills around the Bay, with freeways cutting through the grid patterns of streets and houses.

Soon they were over the flat, verdant valley, the heart of California's agriculture, that lay between the Coast Range and the Sierra Nevada. The Sacramento River, which for centuries had flooded and overflowed its banks to feed the rich soil but was now controlled by levies, snaked through the valley.

To the east, on the other side of the Sierra, was Nevada. A surge of anticipation ran through her. She was going home at last. If only Kirt Schroeder were still there! Kirt—handsome, sweet. Her man. An aching, a longing for him, stabbed at her.

Lea thought of the reporter, probing at a raw nerve, asking why it had been so long since she'd returned to her home. It had taken her five years to put everything behind her so she *could* come back. All those years, she'd still been in love with Kirt, although his death had done something to her. Of course, there'd been a lot of men in her life since then, but it hadn't been the same, not at all. They had met at the Mardi Gras Club, where Kirt was a new bartender, and in no time at all they had become lovers.

She tried to ignore the memories of Kirt's older brother, Otto, who blamed her for Kirt's death. So what? Otto was still in prison. She turned away from the window. Don't think about Kirt and Otto, she told herself. Just don't think about them. Remember your other friends in Reno. Think of your homecoming, with the mayor, the reporters, the TV cameramen. Isn't that why you've worked your tail off during the last five years? To come home a success? A superstar?

The telegrams! She had almost forgotten them. She hoped there would be one from Tony Rizzi.

The first one said, WELCOME BACK TO NEVADA. ANTICIPATING GREAT SHOW. BEST REGARDS. JUSTIN STARR. Well, it would be a great show. And it would be a triumph to be a headliner at Starr's, which was owned by the most famous of all the gambling czars. When Lea had first begun, at Tony's Mardi Gras Club, she could see Starr's high-rise casino across North Virginia Street and had dreamed of someday appearing there. It was known worldwide as the most luxurious of the gambling casinos. Only superstars such as Frank Sinatra, Sammy Davis Jr., and Liza Minnelli played in its headliner room.

The new Starr's Tahoe Resort, fifty miles from Reno, had been built since she left Nevada, and it would be even more grandiose. According to her agent, its Celestial Room was the very latest in theater-restaurants, with a stage large enough to hold the most elaborate productions. They'd gone all out to get together a lavish show.

She tapped the telegram against her teeth and thought of Justin Starr's grandniece, Barrett Starr, her best friend in high school. Barrett had none of her granduncle's great wealth; her father was a ski instructor and her mother a legal secretary. The two of them, Barrett and Lea, had been inseparable and were usually with Judith Davenport, whose father was a cattleman.

Barrett was working for an advertising agency in New York, and Lea had had lunch with her a few times, but she wondered about Judith. Was she happy in her marriage? Was she still living in Beverly Hills? Perhaps she'd find out. There were so many friends to see and talk to in Reno.

The other telegrams were from the mayor of Reno, the governor, her former voice teacher, and the chamber of commerce. What fun to arrive in a blaze of glory! She anticipated the headline: LEA TURNER RETURNS HOME!

She opened the last telegram. It was from Tony Rizzi, who had kept in touch all these years.

WELCOME HOME. OTTO S. IS FREE. EXPECTED HERE
ANYTIME. LOVE. TONY RIZZI.

It was a warning. Otto Schroeder was out of
prison! But how could he be free so soon? And he,
too, was on his way to Reno. Fear pooled in the pit of
Lea's stomach; then it seemed to penetrate every
organ, to work into every cell like some dread poison,
turning her blood to ice.

On another flight to Reno, Justin Starr bent his
silver-maned head toward his grandniece, Barrett,
and said with a laugh, "When I flew to New York last
week, I never expected to bring you home with me.
How lucky for me!"

Barrett turned from the window, where she'd been
looking at the endless mountain ranges below as they
flew from Denver to Salt Lake City. "You mean how
fortunate for *me*." She smiled at her uncle. "For you
to offer me a summer at Lake Tahoe just when I'd
lost my job. I still can't believe it."

The old man felt a sharp surge of pride. She was
the most beautiful girl he'd ever seen in his life. Her
long black hair curled slightly around her exquisite
face. Her camellia skin was clear and smooth, and her
dark eyes warm and intelligent. He wondered if her
thick lashes were real. Her model's figure, long-legged
and slender, was incredible.

Over the years, he'd watched thousands of lovely
girls in his showrooms—and Starr's had the best on
the supper-club circuit. His grandniece had blos-
somed into a winner beyond belief. He hadn't seen
her in five years and had forgotten how attractive she
was. Or else she'd been a late bloomer. In any case,
he could hardly believe that she was related to him.

An impulse had made him look her up in the telephone book when he arrived in New York; he knew
from her last Christmas card that she was working

there in a small advertising agency. He invited her to dinner at his hotel the next evening. When she arrived, wearing a long white dinner suit, her appearance left him breathless, as if he'd run up a steep flight of stairs; and when he took her arm and led the way into the cocktail lounge, everyone turned to watch them.

Over a drink she said, "You couldn't have come at a better time, Uncle Justin. I needed someone in the family tonight." Her chin trembled slightly. "Would you believe that I lost my job today? I'm still in a state of shock. My firm went into bankruptcy, went belly up, and I'm through. Along with the other employees. We got severance pay instead of notice."

He put his hand over hers. "Barrett, I'm so sorry. Let me write a check to tide you over."

She shook her head. "No, Uncle Justin. It's sweet of you to offer, but I'll get along fine. It's just that I'm so surprised. I knew we were having financial problems, but I expected the boss to work them out. Instead, he just called it quits."

"That's too bad."

She sipped her martini. "Now, that's enough of my sad story. I want to think about something else. Tell me about your wife and your son, and about Reno and your new resort at Tahoe."

He talked at length over their drinks, and when she was relaxed, he took her into the dining room. While they were eating their soup, Justin said jokingly, "I suppose a pretty girl like you has a man in the background. Now that you're out of a job, you'll no doubt be getting married."

"Not me!" She shook her head. "I don't want to get married for years yet. I want a business career first. I'll find another job."

Justin put his spoon down. "With your looks, you could always be a model."

Barrett grimaced. "That's not for me at all. No, I want to go into management. I'm going to rise to the top, too. It's doubly hard for a woman, but I'm going to make it. Wait and see!"

"Good for you. I like that." Justin noticed her firm chin and the forceful, determined expression in her lovely eyes. "Say, I have an idea. Why don't you go home with me and spend the summer at Lake Tahoe? You can come back to New York this fall to look for a job. I'll pay your plane fare. The change'll do you good."

Barrett fell back in her chair and looked at him. "Why, Uncle Justin, I'd *love* it. Thanks so much." Her voice rose with enthusiasm. "Besides, things are slow right now, at the beginning of the summer. They'll pick up in the fall, and it'll be a lot easier to find a job then."

Pleased with himself, Justin went on. "Fine! You can act as hostess at Starpoint for the summer. That's my home at Lake Tahoe. I built it a year ago near my new Starr Tahoe Resort."

"That sounds wonderful."

"I often invite the stars who perform at my theater-restaurant to stay at Starpoint during their engagement. Some of them bring their husbands or wives and kids. Gives them a lot more privacy. But I'd like a member of the family to be there and keep an eye on things—oversee the servants and all—since Eunice and I live in Reno."

"I could help at the resort office, too, if they need me. I've had business training."

"We can always use extra help, especially during the summer season. We'll work out a salary for you."

Barrett reached over and patted his arm. "You don't have to pay me anything. Just the trip out there, and to stay at Starpoint, will be enough."

Justin looked at her in surprise. By God, this was

one girl who wasn't on the make! They were mighty few and far between, especially in the gambling world. He laughed. "Well, we'll find a few nickels in the till to make it worth your while."

It had been surprisingly easy to leave New York, and Barrett's apartment mate was delighted with the turn of events. "Frankly, Barrett, this is great," she said. "Phil and I want to try living together. He can take your place for the summer, and we can see how it all works out."

When the jet landed at Salt Lake City, Barrett and Justin stayed on the plane. While they waited for the disembarking passengers to get off and others to take their place, Justin said, "I forgot to tell you that Lea Turner is going to appear at Starr's Tahoe. In fact, she's going to be staying at Starpoint. She'll open June 10th, but she's coming a week early to rehearse."

"*Lea?* Oh, wonderful! She was my best friend in high school. I'd love to have a real visit with her again. We had lunch together a few times in New York, and I saw her in *Remember Me?* She was marvelous."

"We're lucky to get her this summer. She hasn't been available before."

Barrett squeezed her uncle's arm. "I'm getting so excited about going home again. I've missed Nevada."

Justin chuckled as he looked at his niece with affection. "This summer will be a good break for you. Eunice and I will enjoy having you near. Lyle will, too."

"I can hardly wait to see them. I was always so fond of Lyle, and Aunt Eunice is a darling."

Justin's expression saddened. "I want to warn you, Barrett, you might see a change in Eunice. She has a little drinking problem, and lately it's gotten worse."

"I'm sorry. But don't worry about me. If she isn't up to seeing me, that's all right. I can look up all my old friends in Reno and visit my old haunts. Just to be at Lake Tahoe will be something else."

"What a breath of fresh air you'll be for us, Barrett."

She laid her head against the back of the seat, glowing inwardly. This was going to work out for the best. She'd have a glorious summer before returning to New York to hunt for a job. After all, her agency had been small. What future did it have? Actually, it was a dead end. Sooner or later, she'd have had to quit. Now she'd have more experience behind her and would qualify for a better job with a big firm that offered real opportunities.

She'd prove that she could handle an executive position. She was just as capable as any man. All she needed was a chance. She could see herself in a suite of offices, with a private secretary and with the words BARRETT STARR, PRESIDENT on the door. Nothing was going to stand in her way. She was twenty-three —where would she be at thirty-three? At forty-three? At the top, that's where.

The plane took off again, and it wouldn't be long until they'd land in Reno. Barrett could hardly wait. She loved Nevada, with its fresh, clean air, its gray desert hills that turned pink and mauve in the setting sun, and its valleys greening with alfalfa. She loved to see the great cattle herds grazing in the sagebrush and the flocks of sheep tended by Basque sheepherders with their trained dogs. Most of all, she loved the tingle, the excitement, of the crowds in the gambling casinos in Reno and Tahoe.

She turned toward her uncle. "Tell me about Lyle. How is he?"

Lyle Starr was Eunice's son, whom Justin had

adopted fifteen years before, when he married the recently widowed Mrs. Andrew Bellingham. Lyle closely resembled his partician mother, a descendant of one of the Boston Brahmin families.

"Lyle's fine. I've been grooming him to take over Starr Enterprises. I sent him through Stanford and two years of graduate school. He has a master's degree in business administration." Justin's voice swelled with pride. "I'm seventy years old, and I'm not going to live forever; I'm certain of that. I want Lyle to be ready when I'm through." He paused. "But between you and me, we don't always see eye to eye on a lot of things. I've tried and Lyle's tried, but we have some problems to work out between us."

"Isn't that true of all fathers and sons? Your footsteps would be darned hard to walk in, Uncle Justin." Barrett sympathized with the aristocratic, elegant Lyle, knowing how hard it would be to take the reins from this driving, forceful lion of a man, who had borrowed fifteen hundred dollars forty-three years ago to open a saloon in Reno—with only a couple poker tables—and had parlayed it into one of the great gambling fortunes.

There was concern in Justin's granite face. "I'm devoted to him, you know that. He's a good lad and just needs more time to get the grasp of things." He reminded Barrett of an aging Indian chief, reluctant to give way to his son.

"I always admired Lyle," she said. "When I was in high school, he seemed like the glamorous man-about-town, very suave and refined."

"He still is. Real upper crust, just like his mother. He's such a nice guy; everyone likes him. Very active in the Stanford Alumni Club. He's community-minded, too. Last year he headed the United Crusade and organized a big football game to raise money for the Crippled Children Society. Do you know he got the Young Man of the Year award from the 20–30 Club? You can imagine how proud his mother and I were over that."

"Does he still collect artifacts from the South Pacific?"

"Yep. He spent his vacation there last summer. Added to his shell collection, too. I guess that Polynesian culture will always be his first love, but now he's on a Nevada Indian kick. He financed and is helping an expedition for a professor at the university. They're unearthing an Indian burial ground near Carson City."

"How interesting!"

Justin shook his craggy head. "Beats me how anyone can get so het up over tribes that lived thousands of years ago. So what?" He drummed his stubby fingers on his armrest. "There's plenty going on in our business to absorb anybody's time. You don't have to go out and dig a hole in the ground to find something interesting."

Barrett suppressed a smile. "But it's a wonderful hobby."

Justin snorted. "*I* don't need any hobbies. I'm too busy handling all the politicians, the gambling commissioners, the racketeers, the competition—and everyone else who's clawing his way up at my expense. I tell Lyle, 'By God, you have to have some starch in your spine to deal with them. There are some tough characters in the gambling world. You can't shilly-shally when you're up against *them!*' "

"Oh, Uncle Justin, he'll learn to cope. You must be patient." She patted his arm.

"Lyle's no kid anymore—he's thirty-one. Been in the company for seven years. In lots of ways he's done an excellent job. Can't be beat when it comes to public relations and that sort of thing. And he's a good boy. He really is. I shouldn't complain."

"You were fortunate that Eunice had a son, since you never had a child of your own."

"That's right." Justin rubbed his firm jaw thoughtfully. "Starr Enterprises covers a lot of interests now —gambling casinos in Reno, Tahoe, and Las Vegas; motels; lumber mills; mines; cattle ranches; apartment houses, and so on. We own a lot of property on the California side of Lake Tahoe, too. We're quite an empire. I suppose every man who owns his own business wants a son to take over when he's getting old."

"It's too bad you didn't have a son by one of your other marriages," Barrett said. "He'd be forty or fifty by now." And one with the same guts and drive that you have, she thought to herself. Someone who would be truly interested in the gambling world.

Justin nodded. "And he'd be a chip off the old block. A real Starr."

For a long minute Barrett stared at her uncle. Excitement rose in her and throbbed against her temples. She didn't dare say a word, but she thought, You've got *me*.

A white Cadillac convertible, upholstered in red, swiftly ate up the miles on Highway 395 as it followed the eastern slope of the Sierra toward Reno. At five o'clock that morning, Judith Davenport Rosenfeld had crept out of her father-in-law's palatial home in Beverly Hills, flung her overnight bag in the front seat of the car and left for good. Her trunk was packed with all her belongings.

She'd beaten the commuter traffic out of Los Angeles, headed northeast, crossed the edge of the Mojave Desert and picked up Route 395 before she stopped for breakfast. Then she put the top down and let the wind whip her chestnut hair. It was a damned shame she hadn't left three years earlier, when her marriage had first turned sour, she told herself. Nothing had been solved by the delay; things had only worsened.

On her left was the jagged wall that was the eastern side of the Sierra, hundreds of miles long, rising abruptly from the desert floor to heights of ten to fourteen thousand feet. For two million years, rivers of ice had sculptured the great granite core of the mountains by freezing, melting and freezing again. Wind had blasted away the surface of sedimentary rock. Torrents of rain had cut deep V-shaped canyons. Then glaciers had gouged, scraped and polished, until they had rounded the canyons into valleys, carved out basins that became lakes and exposed massive domes and spires.

The granduer of the scenery calmed Judith's turmoil and put her troubles in better perspective. An eagle soared above her. Scarlet paintbrush, lupine and goldenrod colored the meadows. Pure, cold wind rushed off the scattered snowbanks, yanked at her hair, filled her lungs and whipped at her jacket. But she kept the top down. Let the wind blow away all the ugliness of her marriage! She was returning to Sage Creek Ranch, close to Reno, to get a divorce.

She drove the powerful car up the long grades and over the seven-thousand-foot Sherwin Summit. The convertible was the only good thing left from her disastrous marriage. Her father, Elliott Davenport, had given it to her as a wedding present five years ago.

Judith drove very fast, longing to get home, but dreading it, too. How could she face her father? She remembered only too well that April night when she told him she wanted to marry Murray Rosenfeld after he graduated in June from the University of Nevada.

"But, Judith, you're only eighteen. You're just finishing your first year at the university. Wait for a while."

"But Murray is going back to Beverly Hills. He wants to take me with him. I can't bear to have him go without me!"

She knelt on the thick rug beside her father's chair. He grasped her chin with gnarled, work-worn hands that had wrangled cattle all his life. She looked up at his honest, leathery face and his concerned gray eyes.

"Judith, are you sure? Have you thought this over carefully? Do you realize what it will mean?"

"Of course." Murray was the most exciting man on campus. The one with the red Jaguar. A senior. The son of a prominent movie producer. (He was a lot of other things, too, but it had taken two years of marriage to find out about them.)

"Honey, I beg you not to rush into anything. When school is out, why don't you and your mother fly to Los Angeles and meet Murray's folks? Mr. Rosenfeld can take you to a movie lot—show you around. You can meet some stars. You've never had that experience. And there's Disneyland. . . ."

Judith shook her head. "We want to get married, Dad. We want to be together all the time. Besides, I've met his folks, when they came to visit Murray one time. They're nice; they like me."

"But do they like you well enough to have you marry into the family? They're Jewish. Wouldn't they prefer one of their own as a daughter-in-law? Won't they resent you? Isn't Murray their only son? Think of the hopes and dreams they must have for him. How do you fit into the picture?"

"Murray says they think I'm great. He says there's no problem at all."

For a long minute her father studied her, then said, "I don't want you to get married while you're so young. I make this suggestion: Promise me you'll wait one year. Get another year of college under your belt. See how you and Murray survive a separation. And you and your mother visit his family a few days this summer. Then, if you still feel the same a year from now, you'll have my blessing."

Judith shook her head again. "I'm not waiting. We're getting married this June—month after next."

They argued for two hours, and his anger was terrifying. He had never been so harsh with her. Finally he bit off the words, "All right! *Get* married. But you know how I feel about marriage. It's a sacrament, a sacred vow you make to God. If you marry Murray, make a success of it. Don't come running home to me to get a divorce. I don't believe in divorce. *Never*."

He hadn't changed his mind. Five years had passed, and he was still adamant. Divorce was out. At different times she had sounded him out, but it was no use. According to him, you didn't "play around," either—not if you were married. When she came home for visits, she would meet Lyle Starr in Reno for dinner and dancing or to see the shows. She had lived in dread that her father might find out.

Over the years he had grown more prosperous, with more and more rangeland and thousands more head of cattle. He was lieutenant governor, too. But he hadn't mellowed a whit.

Judith stopped for gas at a hunting and fishing resort and saw a poster announcing Starr's headliners for the weeks ahead. Lea Turner! OPENING AT STARR'S TAHOE RESORT JUNE 10. Judith recalled the

fun Lea, Barrett Starr and she had had in high school
—and that first year of college, too, when they'd used
false IDs and made the rounds of the gambling
casinos and the entertainment bars with their boyfriends.

If she could only go back to those carefree times.
If she had only listened to her father and waited a
year before considering marriage. Getting out of the
mess now was going to be sticky. As if getting a
divorce wasn't bad enough, wait until her father
found out that Murray was paralyzed from the waist
down, with no hope of recovery. Would her father
believe her when she explained that Murray had been
in a gay bar, gotten high on cocaine and then gone
out and wrecked his car, killing his male lover?

In any case, she was on her way home. In spite of
her father, she was getting a divorce. She'd be Judith
Davenport again. What would her father say? What
would he do?

A Greyhound bus lumbered along Highway 80,
following the Humboldt River across northern
Nevada. Long ago the forty-niners, who had crossed
this same land, had loathed this turgid, sullen river
and the white, alkali land along its barren banks. It
was a land filled with mountains, range upon range,
lonely and immense; hoarding treasures of tungsten,
uranium, gypsum, and copper; dry, gray-green,
toughly vegetated, forbidding and strangely beautiful.

Most of the passengers sat in a quiet trance or slept
with their heads against rented pillows, but not Otto
Schroeder, in new Levi's and clean T-shirt. He looked
out the window hour after hour, as if he couldn't see
enough of the outside. A sandy beard hid his prison
pallor.

He had no feeling about his new freedom, no
reaction at all. It was too much to grasp so soon,

more than his emotions could encompass all at once. He had waited five years for his release, and the full realization that it had finally been granted would have to come gradually.

Instead, he concentrated on the powerful drive that had been part of him so long. Revenge. At last his time for revenge had come. Such a sweet word, *revenge*. He rolled it over and over on his tongue; then it hit the back of his throat and coursed down his gullet, giving the greatest satisfaction. Determination to get revenge had kept him going all those years in prison and had made him a model prisoner in every way, so he earned time off his sentence. *Revenge!* No one could destroy his brother, Kirt, cut off his life at twenty-one, and get away with it!

First, he'd deal with Elliott Davenport, who had brought the feds and the sheriff to the airstrip at Sage Creek. It was his fault that Kirt had been killed. If only *Judith* Davenport were still around. But she'd probably be married by now and living elsewhere. If he could only get her and *do* something to her. That would be the way to get even with her father. That would make Elliott Davenport suffer!

Then he'd find that bitch Lea Turner, no matter where she was, if he had to travel all over the country. He looked down at his powerful hands, flexed and unflexed his long fingers, and studied the calluses on his palms. He'd fix her, too.

It had all begun with her five years ago, when she was performing at the Mardi Gras Club and wanted Kirt to take her to San Francisco for her eighteenth birthday.

CHAPTER

2

As she applied her makeup for her first show, Lea could see Kirt's reflection in her dressing-room mirror at the Mardi Gras Club. A lock of his curly brown hair hung down his forehead, and there was an apologetic, pleading expression on his face. Anger boiled inside her until her hand shook.

"It's my eighteenth birthday next Sunday, you know that! You've known it for weeks!"

"Lea, honey, don't be mad. Please don't. I know I promised to take you someplace, but now I *can't*." He reached out and touched her hair.

"Someplace?" She whirled around and gripped the top of her chair until her knuckles whitened. "What do you mean—*someplace?* Kirt Schroeder, you know you promised me months ago that you'd take me to San Francisco this weekend to celebrate my birthday. You *know* you did!"

"Honest, I'm sorry, Lea. I can't. That's the truth of it. You've got to understand. I just can't."

"Why not? We both have Sunday and Monday off.

It's only two hundred miles. We can drive to San Francisco Sunday morning, stay over that night and the next and be back Tuesday before you have to go to work. That's exactly what you told me months ago. Now you want to chicken out."

"I know that's what I said. I know it's your birthday. But I promised Otto I'd help him with a job. Please understand, Lea."

"You promised me first!" She rose from her chair, glared at him and stamped her foot. "For the last month you've gone off every Sunday and Monday with Otto. What are you doing?"

"Otto is doing some special work for his boss. He needs me to help him." Kirt tried to make his voice convincing.

"By 'his boss,' do you mean Mr. Davenport or the foreman at Sage Creek?"

"Not the foreman." Kirt shook his head. "Elliott Davenport himself."

"Then, let Mr. Davenport and Otto get someone else." Lea put a hand across her chin. "I've had it up to here with your brother."

"Lea, please understand. I've got to help Otto this Sunday. I'll make it up to you later."

"But my birthday is next Sunday—not later. Either you take me to San Francisco on Sunday or I'm through with you!"

"Now, wait a minute, Lea. Just cool it. I'll see Otto first thing tomorrow morning. Maybe I can work something out—get him to postpone it. I'll try."

"You'd better." Anger still seethed in her.

Kirt grabbed her to him, pressed his mouth against hers and kissed her. Finally he let her go. "Don't be so uptight. Just relax, honey. I'll think of something. But I've got to go back to the bar now."

She watched him go. "You'd better! You'd just better!" she shouted.

She wanted to put her head on her arms and sob until she got over her fury and frustration, but it was too close to showtime. She forced the tears back, slipped out of her robe and put on the red sequin-covered costume for her dance routine. Around her waist she snapped a long ruffled net overskirt for her vocal numbers, which came first.

Would Kirt stand up to Otto? Of course he wouldn't. He was so dominated by his older brother, ten years his senior, that after one word from Otto, Kirt jumped to obey. Well, she'd had it. She wasn't going to take it anymore. He could take his choice—Otto or her.

A long row of poplars with October-yellow leaves bordered the lane that led into Sage Creek Ranch, to the large two-story Victorian house, painted a soft gray with white trim. A veranda encircled the house. As Kirt looked at the house, which reflected the bright morning sunlight, he thought of all the Davenports who had lived there for generations, passing the ranch down from father to son and gradually adding to the spread, until now there were ninety thousand acres of rangeland and lord knows how many head of cattle. Now Elliott Davenport owned it all and could pass it down to his children. Kirt felt a pang of envy. Some people had all the luck.

Kirt took a side lane, which led to a cluster of out-buildings and corrals, and maneuvered his VW between the tractors, cattle trucks, horse trailers, and pickup trucks that were parked in an open area. He leaned out the window and called to an Indian cowboy who was leading a sorrel, "Hi, Jim, is Otto around?"

The cowboy nodded and pointed east. "He's mending fences."

Kirt followed the road alongside the fence and

hoped he wouldn't get hung up on a rut. Before, he'd always ridden out on the range with Otto in his four-wheel-drive pickup. A plume of dust trailed behind him as he passed the watering troughs, salt licks, and feeding bins. Finally he saw Otto ahead, squatting on his heels beside the barbed-wire fence, and he pulled up next to him.

Otto squinted from under his wide-brimmed hat. "Hello," he said, a welcoming smile on his firm-jawed face. "Didn't expect you today."

Kirt hesitated; he didn't know how to begin. He opened the door, climbed out and stood beside his older brother. He reached in his jacket pocket for a pack of Camels and offered one to Otto. Striking a match and sheltering it in his cupped hand as he lit their cigarettes gave him a chance to screw up his courage.

For years Otto had taken the place of their parents —ever since they'd split up and their mother had married a cuss as mean as they come, who had no use for stepsons. Although he was only sixteen, Otto had protected Kirt and had taken many beatings rather than let his six-year-old brother get knocked around. From then on, Otto had taken charge of him. It wasn't easy to defy him now.

"Well, what's on your mind? I know you didn't get up this early and drive out here just to pass the time of day."

There was no easy way to start, so Kirt plunged in. "You've got to let me off this time. As I told you before, it's Lea's birthday this Sunday, and she's got her heart set on going to San Francisco. Now she's madder'n hell."

Otto took a long drag on the cigarette, leaned against the VW and let the smoke curl from his nostrils. His face was turning dark red under his hat, and his eyes were narrowing. "We've been over this before. The answer's still no."

"Can't you get somebody else this time? Give him my cut."

"No!"

"Indian Jim, for instance."

"*No!*"

"Postpone it a week."

"Are you out of your mind? When you're dealing with our contact in Reno, you don't postpone nothing! You stick to the schedule." Otto spit through the fence and turned to his brother. "*Let* the broad get sore. She'll get over it."

"She won't get over it. She's really pushed out of shape." Kirt put his hand on his brother's shoulder. "Go by yourself this time and keep all the dough. I don't want any of it."

"It's not that simple, and you know it." Otto shook his brother's hand away. "I need someone to refuel the plane the minute we land across the Mexican border. The reason we've been successful all four times is because we've worked so fast. We land, make our pickup and cut out before the border patrol gets wise."

"But Perez can refuel the plane while you get the heroin from Soria."

Otto gave him a disgusted look. "Christ, man, use your head! If I went down there alone, how long would I last? The minute I gave them the twenty-five grand I'd be done for. They'd have a knife in my ribs before I could put my wallet back in my pocket. They'd have my money and the heroin to sell to someone else, and they'd dismantle the plane and sell the parts. Don't be stupid."

Anger washed over Kirt. "I've never wanted to be part of this racket! Right from the first, I've wanted out."

"What's the matter? Is my baby brother afraid?" Otto grabbed Kirt by the jacket.

The color drained from Kirt's face. "Yes, I am. It's too damned dangerous. I don't want to go again, not ever!"

"Is that so?"

"That's so! I never wanted to be in on it, and you know it."

Otto sneered. "I don't suppose I'll have any trouble persuading you to take your share of the hundred grand we've got hidden in the mine. No, it'll be all right then. It'll be a pretty *good* racket when you get your paws on that dough, so you can buy a bar and get set up in business for yourself, won't it?"

"You keep my share, Otto. Just let me get out of it."

Otto gave him an angry shake. "What are you going to do? Work for someone else all your life?"

"If I have to."

Otto shoved him away, so that Kirt lost his balance and fell to the ground. "You make me disgusted."

Kirt got up and brushed the dirt off. "I don't want to make you sore, Otto, but I want out. You can keep all the money. Turn the plane in and forget the whole deal. I'll keep my mouth buttoned up. You know that."

He headed for his VW, but Otto took hold of his arm. "I contracted to bring in five shipments. We've only brought in four. Now this is our last——"

"To hell with it! Tell 'em you can't do it."

"Grow up, kid! I can't tell those guys in Reno that I won't bring in the last load. They've already got it set up. It's too late to back out now. They can play rough—you'd better believe it."

Kirt stood next to his car and stared at his brother. "Otto, I mean it. I don't want anything more to do with smuggling dope. You shouldn't, either."

"No?"

"Let's cut out of here today. You fly the plane back to Reno and get our deposit back. Then we'll go to the mine, get our money and head for the East Coast."

Otto sneered and pointed to the VW. "You mean, make our getaway in this tin can?"

"Hell, this is only Wednesday. No one expects us to turn over the shipment until Monday night. That gives us six days' head start. Besides, we can buy a bigger car on the way."

His brother hooked his thumbs in his belt and looked at him disdainfully. "Kid, you're not dry behind the ears. The guy I rented the plane from is part of the racket. He contacted me because he knows I've got a pilot's license and he knows I've done crop-dusting. The minute we turn the plane in, we're sunk."

The autumn wind hit Kirt through his jacket and made him shiver. Or was it fear? "Maybe we could get in the plane and——"

"Come off it! The minute we had to land for gas, we'd have the narcs on us."

"But we'd have six days' head start. We don't have to turn over anything until Monday."

Otto spit out an obscenity. "You think we could just drop out of sight and no one would get suspicious? Me from this ranch and you from the Mardi Gras Club?"

A shiver ran through Kirt again. He brushed at his face as if he had stepped into a large cobweb. He could imagine the ruckus Lea would make if he didn't show up for work that afternoon. Tony Rizzi and his other bartenders would talk, and someone would overhear them and tip off the underworld. If anyone suspected anything, they'd call Sage Creek and ask for Otto. Then, when he wasn't there, the fat would be in the fire.

If they could only take their hundred grand and get out. Would they ever be able to enjoy it? He'd had reservations about the racket right from the beginning. All along, the vibes had been bad.

At first, he was sure that Elliott Davenport would get wise to the deal, though the airstrip was a long way from the house—several miles, as a matter of fact. It was on land that had belonged to the government at one time and was used during World War II as a training ground for desert warfare. Davenport had bought it for rangeland after the war. It had a short airstrip and a hangar, of sorts, that was falling down.

It had been easy for the two of them to clear the airstrip and repair the hangar so they could hide the plane in it. They had gathered tumbleweed and stuck it in the holes in the corrugated iron walls so that anyone riding by, on horseback or in a jeep, wouldn't notice anything.

Kirt, on the flights to the border and back, had really been scared, thinking every plane or helicopter they saw was the feds in pursuit of them. But they'd done it four times without a hitch. And they'd made a profit of a hundred grand and cached it in an abandoned silver mine.

As if reading his thoughts, Otto said, "Look, kid, one more time and we can call it quits. Everything went OK the first four times, so why shouldn't the fifth? We've got it down pat."

"But Lea's really ticked off, Otto."

"That kid's getting too big for her britches. Just because people are going into Tony Rizzi's dump to see her perform, she thinks she's so great."

"Well, she *is* terrific. She's just as good as anybody on TV."

"Just don't let her dictate to you. You'll be sorry if you do."

"You know I promised to take her to San Francisco for her birthday—before this smuggling deal came up. You can't blame her for being sore at me."

Otto put his hand on Kirt's shoulder. "Kid, I'm sorry—I really am—but there's no way we can get out of this last run. I promise I won't get you into anything like this again."

Kirt kicked at a clod of dirt while Otto talked. "This was just a one-shot deal. I made that clear at the beginning. One contract for five shipments and that would be it."

Kirt shrugged. "OK, I'll be here Sunday as usual."

"Fine."

"But I've been against this racket from the beginning. I've hated it."

"It hasn't been so bad."

"Well, I guess I'm just not cut out to be a crook. I would never have gotten into anything like this if it hadn't been for you and your big mouth. Christ, I wish I'd said no right at the first."

He shouldered Otto to one side, climbed into the VW and drove off, with foreboding and dread eating like a cancer at his guts.

After he had driven the twenty miles into Reno, Kirt was tempted to swing by the apartment where Lea lived with her mother, over a dance studio. Ever since he could remember, Mrs. Turner's dancing classes had been an institution, with Lea as her star pupil. He glanced at his watch. It was only ten-thirty, and Lea and her mother liked to stay in bed until noon. Lea would be in no mood to listen to what Otto had said.

Even that night, when he went to her dressing room and told her, Lea was in no mood. She listened in disgust to his excuses and then said, "OK, Kirt, you've made your choice, and it's Otto. So we're through."

"Please, Lea, you don't mean that!" He reached for her, but she stepped back from him.

"Yes, I do. I'll see you around. Now, get out."

When she was alone, Lea felt shocked and sick. It had turned out just the way she predicted. Otto had won, as she knew he would. Well, that was that. She was in love with Kirt, and she'd carry a torch for him for a long, long time, but she'd never let on. She'd go out on that stage and sing and dance as never before.

Ignoring Kirt that evening and the next was more easily said than done. The stage on which she performed was at one end of the cocktail lounge, and Kirt stood behind the bar near the other end and watched her all the while she was on. A dozen times she resisted the temptation to talk to him as she crossed the lounge. Then, remembering her birthday and his broken promise, she turned her back to him.

It was easy to rationalize—to tell herself that it was all for the best. Where did Kirt fit in her future, anyway? She wasn't going to perform at the Mardi Gras forever. She was going on to the big time. New York, maybe. Someday she'd be a superstar. And Kirt? She couldn't see him as her manager, and he wasn't a musician or anything like that. How could a bartender go on tour with her? So it was easy to rationalize, but nothing eased the pain in her heart.

Friday afternoon, when Judith Davenport dropped by the dance studio with a birthday present, Lea was delighted. "Come upstairs to the apartment. I'm so glad to see you!" She opened the present in the living room and admired the cologne Judith had given her.

"It's what all the girls in the sorority are using,"

Judith said. "I thought you'd like it, too. I gave it to you today because I'm on my way to Sage Creek for the weekend."

Lea sniffed the cologne again. "It's luscious." She put the bottle on the coffee table in front of her. "Tell me, are you still enjoying the university?"

"Yes, I just love it. I'm pledged to a sorority, and I get to live in 'the house' next semester. And I'm meeting a lot of new guys. Speaking of men, are you and Kirt going to San Francisco for your birthday?"

Lea shook her head. Her mouth contorted, and she started to cry; then she covered her face with her hands. Judith jumped from her chair, sat beside Lea on the sofa and put her arms around her. "Lea, what's wrong?"

After a minute, when Lea had herself under control, she poured out her troubles to Judtih.

"You say Otto is doing some special work for my dad? I can't imagine what it could be."

Lea nodded. "Yes, and Kirt's helping him. They've been busy every weekend for the last month now. Even this Sunday."

"How strange."

"Even though Kirt promised me months ago that he would take me to San Francisco for my birthday, he's not going to now. He has to jump to 'big brother's' command."

"I'm so sorry."

"Well, I'm through with Kirt. I don't want anything more to do with him." She started to cry again.

Judith spent the rest of the afternoon comforting Lea and then drove home to Sage Creek. While her mother was finishing dinner and her two brothers were doing their chores, she joined her father in his study and drank a glass of sherry with him.

"Dad, I've been with Lea all afternoon, and I feel so sorry for her." She told him about their conversation and about the birthday excursion to San Francisco, which had been canceled. "What special work would you have for Otto and Kirt Schroeder that would tie them up every Sunday and Monday for a month?"

Before her father could answer, the phone rang. It was one of Judith's boyfriends, asking for a date. Then the family had dinner, some neighbors dropped in, and the subject never came up again.

Long after the others were asleep, Elliott Davenport lay in bed and thought about Otto and Kirt Schroeder. What was going on? He remembered that some weeks ago Otto had asked him for Mondays off instead of Saturdays. "Kirt has Sunday and Monday off, and we'd like to go fishing together, if that's agreeable with you, Mr. Davenport," he'd said. But every Sunday afternoon Kirt would show up and the two brothers would drive toward the east boundary. There was no fishing out there. Why didn't they head in the other direction, toward the Sierra and the Truckee River?

Davenport liked Otto, who was an excellent worker and would make a good foreman when an opening came up, but he hadn't assigned him special work. That was an outright lie. Why would they say he had? There was something fishy about this, and he didn't like it one bit. He'd do some investigating on his own, first thing.

The next morning he sent Otto to another ranch with instructions that would keep him occupied all day; then he got in a four-wheel-drive pickup and headed east. His two sons had gone on a 4-H field trip, so he didn't have to bring them along.

On the way, he checked the fences, made sure the watering troughs were full and looked over his herds. Everything seemed normal. Were the Schroeder brothers tied in with a cattle-rustling gang? Some sophisticated operation, carried on with helicopters and cattle trucks? He doubted it, for a rustler needed access roads to the isolated areas. He could imagine pulling it off on some of his spreads, but not at Sage Creek. Not here, where every vehicle had to drive out the lane and past the main headquarters. Otto was too smart to try to drive a truck full of stolen cattle off the ranch in front of all of them. That didn't make sense. Besides, the Davenport cattle brand wasn't easy to alter.

He decided with disgust that he was on a wild-goose chase. Everything looked the same as usual. Even the jackrabbits were as frisky as ever. Judith must have misunderstood Lea. Just as Davenport was about to turn around, he saw the abandoned hangar and airstrip in the distance. Well, as long as he had wasted half the morning, he might as well give them the once-over.

At least the tumbleweeds were making use of the old hangar, he thought, as he drove up to the abandoned building. Everything looked the same, but when he climbed out of the truck, he noticed tire marks near the airstrip, and the strip was slick and clean, with most of the sand brushed off. What was going on, anyway?

He walked to the sagging hangar, pulled a tumble-weed from a large hole in the wall, pushed his Stetson hat back and looked in. When his eyes got used to the darkness inside, he let out a long, surprised whistle. A new airplane was parked near the door, five-gallon gasoline cans stood along the far wall, and two rolled-up sleeping bags were stacked in a corner.

He remembered that Otto had worked as a crop duster in the San Joaquin Valley in California before returning to Nevada. A man had to be a mighty good pilot to handle crop-dusting, as it was dangerous work. As far as he knew, Otto was the only one on his ranch who could fly a plane, so he had to be the one who was connected—in some way—with this airplane. What was his purpose? Something illegal, no doubt, since the plane was hidden so carefully.

Davenport looked at the plane again. Apparently, the two brothers had come here on those Sunday afternoons, gassed it up and checked it over and had slept here overnight. Then, perhaps, on Monday morning, had taken off. Where to? Probably the Mexican border, which was not much more than five hundred air miles. They could fly down and back in one day if they left at daybreak and turned right around. If he guessed right, they were smuggling something, drugs most likely.

Davenport put the tumbleweed back in the wall, erased his footsteps and got in the truck. He backed around, trying to use the tire marks that were already there. No sense leaving a calling card and letting the Schroeder brothers know that he was on to them.

He drove back to his house as fast as he could. Because Judith and his wife were talking to each other in the kitchen, he stepped into his study and closed the door. Then he called the sheriff and reported his discovery.

The sheriff, after he had listened to Davenport's story and asked a few questions, said, "If they are smuggling drugs, we want to wait and catch them Monday afternoon when they fly in from Mexico. We want to nab them with the goods in their possession. Otherwise we have no evidence that they're doing anything wrong, except using that hangar without your permission."

"That's right."

"I'll be out early Monday afternoon with some federal boys, and we'll be ready for 'em."

"Fine. They'll have to land before dark; we know that."

"Right. Thanks for calling, Mr. Davenport. Keep all this under your hat until I see you Monday."

As they lost altitude, Kirt looked down at the folded desert hills, purple in the fading light, and relief washed over him. This was the last time, thank God. Everything had gone without a hitch, and they were almost home.

Now all they had to do was deliver the box that was stowed at his feet. As usual, he and Otto would drive to the outskirts of Reno and wait at the rear of the closed service station until the two men in the green Chrysler drove up next to them and turned off their lights. He didn't know their names and didn't want to know. Otto would take the box to the Chrysler, wait until the men inspected the contents, then return with an envelope stuffed with greenbacks. This was the last time for that, too.

Kirt looked away from the window and at the pistol on Otto's hip. It was handy to his brother's right hand, in case they ran into trouble in Mexico or when they delivered the heroin in Reno. Kirt didn't like the gun, either. He didn't have the stomach for danger and knew he was playing out of his league. From now on he'd stick to tending bar.

But he wasn't afraid to be with his brother when Otto was at the controls of a plane. Otto was a great pilot, and Kirt watched with admiration as he made a perfect landing, even though it was growing dark. When the plane came to a stop in front of the hangar, Otto turned off the engine, and they climbed out to wrestle the sagging doors open and push the plane inside.

But they never got to the hangar. Four men lunged at them from the darkness, and a powerful beam of light struck Kirt in the face. "Halt!" a voice ordered. "You're under arrest!"

"Get the truck started!" Otto shouted, pulling out his gun.

Shots rang out. Kirt ran for the truck, but as he opened the door, a bullet struck him in the center of his back.

Thursday afternoon, after the funeral, Lea sat across from Tony Rizzi in his office. She fought back the tears and said, "You can understand, can't you, why I want to get away? Everything reminds me of Kirt. I keep looking at the bar, expecting to see him standing there." She put her elbows on the desk and covered her face with her hands. "I loved him."

Tony patted her shoulder. "He was a nice boy. How he ever got mixed up in that racket——"

"Otto made him do it!"

"Yes, I guess you're right. He seemed to do whatever his brother said. But I'm surprised about Otto, too. He had a good job out there at Sage Creek. He was bound to work into something first-rate before long. Now he'll go to prison." Tony's fat, middle-aged face saddened. He reached in his desk and took out a box of tissues. "Help yourself, honey."

Lea wiped her eyes. "I want to get away. I've got to."

"I hate to lose you; you've sure pulled in the customers. But I'm not going to stand in your way. You've got what it takes and can hit it big."

"I think I'll go to New York and try to get in one of the shows."

Tony leaned back in his chair and studied her. "Don't try to hit it cold. You'll eat your heart out waiting for a break."

"Then, how?"

"You need a top-notch agent to help you—one who carries some weight in the entertainment world."

"But it's hard to get one to handle a beginner like me."

Tony made a steeple with his plump fingers. "The entertainment director at Starr's owes me a favor. He has for a long time, and I've never asked him for one; so maybe this is it. He knows all the agents. They come out here from New York a lot. I'll get him to arrange an audition for you."

"Oh, Tony, you're a darling! Make it as soon as possible."

"I'll do my best for you, you know that."

Friday and Saturday night Lea performed as usual, then spent most of Sunday in bed reading the papers of the last few days to learn more about Kirt's death and Otto's arrest. It was then she noticed with horror the "Reno Roundabout" column, which said:

It was a tip-off from Kirt Schroeder's girlfriend that sent the lawmen out to the abandoned airstrip at the east end of Sage Creek Ranch. The result was one of the biggest drug busts in this county in years. Schroeder met his death and his brother, Otto, was arrested. That was one canary who really sang!

"Oh, no! How unfair!" She didn't know that Kirt and Otto were smuggling drugs. She didn't tip the lawmen. Judith must have told her father about her conversation with Lea and he guessed what was going on.

She wondered who else had read the column and whether anyone else would connect the drug bust with her. She pulled the bed sheets around her. Was she in danger? If she could only leave Reno this very day and go someplace else—as far away as possible, where she could forget what had happened.

On Tuesday, Tony Rizzi greeted her with a smile.

"Got it all arranged. One of the top agents in the business will be in the audience tonight. Give your performance all you got, Lea."

She kissed his fat cheek. "I can never thank you enough, Tony. Keep your fingers crossed for me."

That night she gave the best performance of her life, and the agent took her on. She planned to leave for New York the next Sunday, so Saturday night was her last at the Mardi Gras Club. All her life she'd be grateful to Tony for giving her a start. Now it was up to her to be a success.

After her last number she worked her way through the crowd around the bar to go to her dressing room. Several people spoke to her and wished her success. When she reached the dimly lighted hallway that led to her dressing room, she didn't notice the man by her door. He wore a hat pulled over his eyes and dark glasses. His dark suit blended into the shadows.

He stepped forward and said out of the side of his mouth, "I got a message for you from Otto Schroeder. He says to tell you, 'Just wait!'"

CHAPTER

3

The Greyhound bus rumbled along Highway 80, and Otto Schroeder glanced at his watch. It was almost noon; they were due in Winnemucca for a lunch break. That was one of the good things about being out of stir: he didn't have to sidestep in a long chow line, past unappetizing steam tables, and be served a trayload of runny, overcooked food. He no longer had to eat with hundreds of other men, with their foul body odors and sickening table manners, crowded shoulder to shoulder in the prison mess hall. He could go to a café, sit down by himself and order from a menu.

It was Lea Turner's and Elliott Davenport's fault that he'd been so degraded—that he'd had to put up with five years of hell. Well, that was behind him, and now it was time to get even, to make them suffer the way he had. Yes, it was time for revenge at last.

When the bus stopped, he climbed off and stretched his legs. He put a coin in the slot of a newspaper rack and took out a copy of the *Gazette*. That was another pleasure he'd almost forgotten: holding a folded, unopened newspaper in his hand, smooth and virgin, and being the first one to open and read it. It was all his—he didn't have to share it with anyone. He put the paper under his arm and walked down the windy, dusty street toward a restaurant. The town looked about the same as he remembered it. Four or five thousand people lived here, he supposed —fewer than in the federal pen.

He entered a café and sat at a corner table where he could be by himself. He flung his Levi's jacket over the chair on the other side of the table, like an animal staking out its territory, as if daring anyone to intrude on his privacy. When the waitress came, he ordered a steak, knowing that it had to be cooked just for him.

For the first time he realized that at last he was free. This awareness had been coming very gradually; it was made up of many small actions and sights and sounds that had not been part of his life in prison. Slowly, he was discovering that he had the right to make choices like anyone else, that he belonged to himself again, was truly his own man, no longer at the mercy of prison guards. It was a thrilling, satisfying feeling—so new and strange that he was almost reluctant to give way to it for fear it would leave him.

He spread the newspaper on the table and glanced at the headlines of world and national news, then turned inside to the local news, to reacquaint himself with Nevada. On the last page he found a big advertisement with Lea Turner's picture, announcing the coming attractions at Starr's. She would open at Tahoe on June 10. Otto gasped and read the ad again, hardly believing his good fortune. He wouldn't have to hunt all over the country for her. He wouldn't have to waste weeks and weeks tracking her down. She was coming to Nevada—this very month.

Starr's Tahoe Resort must be a new casino, Otto decided. It hadn't been there five years ago. But he could find it easily, and Lea Turner would be a sitting duck. At long last he was getting a break!

Otto picked up his steak knife and carefully cut out the advertisement, then put it in his wallet in a plastic slot behind Kirt's picture, along with the "Reno Roundabout" column about Lea's tipping off the cops. He put the wallet back in his pocket and settled down to his steak. This changed his plans: he'd get Lea first and then go after Elliott Davenport.

He was hardly aware of the 160 miles between Winnemucca and Reno, there was so much to think about. The best thing to do was get a job at Starr's Tahoe Resort so he could size up the situation and plan the best way to get his revenge. He'd be right there, with Lea Turner, and could take full advantage of any opportunity that came along.

Of course, he couldn't ask for a good job, such as a dealer, because all employees in a gambling casino, except kitchen help, have to go through an FBI check, have their fingerprints taken, and all that. It was against the law to hire an ex-convict, he knew, but he could work in the kitchen. He'd ask for something at the bottom, where there was a large turnover of drifters, like scraping dishes and putting them in the dishwashers—something where he'd be inconspicuous yet have an employee's badge, which would give him access to the resort. He didn't care about the wages. Who needed them, with a hundred thousand bucks hid away?

He wasn't afraid that he'd be recognized by Lea, since he had a beard and was twenty pounds heavier than five years ago. Besides, even if Lea saw him, she was a superstar now and was not likely to notice a peon in the kitchen. He would change his name, too —to Owen Shulman, the name on his false social-security card. He'd been getting ready for this for a long time.

He got off the bus in Reno and, heading for the used-car lots, walked under the famous sign arching over the street: BIGGEST LITTLE CITY IN THE WORLD. The town looked about the same, with the casinos side by side, their doors always open and blasts of air keeping out the weather, hot or cold.

Bank upon bank of slot machines could be seen from the sidewalk. The crowds looked the same, too: pensioners from California, who'd been hauled in by excursion buses; summer tourists, looking a little ill at ease amid the open gambling; jaded Nevadans, who took the casinos in stride as their normal way of life.

Otto wanted an inconspicuous car that didn't look like much but ran all right. Thanks to the training he'd had in auto mechanics in stir, no fast-talking salesman could fool him. When it came to automobiles, he knew more than the next guy. And when he'd taken care of Turner and Davenport, he'd light out for another state—like Idaho or Wyoming—use his real name again, buy a little acreage and an auto-repair shop at the edge of town and start living.

He found a battered green Chevy with a good rebuilt engine. Even the retread tires were in good shape. He bargained with the salesman and got the price down to five hundred dollars, which still left him with another five hundred. He signed the papers "Owen Shulman," which he'd picked because the initials were the same as his real name and so he'd get used to it more easily. Then he drove to a second-hand store and bought a small trunk with a good lock, some old clothes and a flashlight.

It was nearly six, but he was too tense to feel hungry. Was his money still hidden safely away in the abandoned silver mine? It would be daylight for a couple of hours yet—time enough to go get it. Besides, he wanted to feel his hands on a steering wheel again and to cruise down a highway with the desert wind scouring his face.

He drove out the main highway toward Carson City, took the turnoff on Route 17 to Virginia City and the silver mines of the old Comstock Lode and carefully guided the Chevy along a barely visible dirt road that curved behind the low mountains, followed a dry creek bed through an arroyo and ended at a tumbledown mill that was used a hundred years ago to crush ore. He got out of the car and started to walk. His footsteps startled a jackrabbit, and a lizard darted along an outcropping of rock. Otto kept a sharp eye for rattlesnakes, for now that the sun had touched the crest of the Sierra in the west, the land would cool and the snakes would come out from under the rocks and bushes.

The entrance to the mine was midway up the hillside. As he climbed toward it, puffing and panting, he thought, God, I'm out of condition! I've got to get this extra lard off once this job is done. He stopped to rest and looked around, absorbing the solitude of the canyon. Not another soul; he was absolutely alone. He felt renewed—a human being again.

When he resumed his climb toward the mine, his heart pounded from the exertion and from fear that someone might have found the hiding place. But there were thousands of abandoned mines in Nevada. Why would a prospector pick this one? And why would anyone pay attention to the old overturned powder box in the black recesses of the tunnel?

Still, he hurried the last few yards, switched on his flashlight and, crouched over, entered the tunnel. Sixty-five feet inside the mine shaft, the flashlight illuminated the powder box and, within it, the footlocker, whose canvas wrappings were undisturbed.

Feverishly, Otto undid the binding and snatched the canvas from around the footlocker. Inside, snug and dry, were bills of all denominations, sorted into bundles. Each packet was a thousand dollars, and there were a hundred packets.

He dragged the footlocker to the mouth of the tunnel and, slipping and falling, carried it down the mountainside to the car. When he got to the car, he sat on the footlocker and emptied the dirt and pebbles from his boots. Then he shouted with joy and laughed at the echoes that reverberated through the canyon.

What a glorious feeling! He had his freedom, he had his hundred grand, and Lea Turner was coming to Nevada.

He assumed that Davenport was still around. He was a cattleman through and through and wasn't apt to have sold his ranches. If only Judith, his daughter, were still here. Of course, there were the two sons, but Judith was the apple of the old man's eye. But first things first. He would take care of Lea Turner, then Elliott Davenport.

Otto put the footlocker in the trunk of the Chevy, next to the secondhand trunk. Ravenously hungry, he drove back to Reno, found a restaurant and parked the car where he could see it through a window. No one would suspect that the battered car contained a fortune in unmarked bills, but he wanted to keep it in sight every minute. He ordered the most expensive filet, french fries, salad, and several bottles of beer.

His hundred grand was intact and back in his possession, thank God. He thought of all the interest it would have earned over the past five years in a savings account—thirty thousand at least. He groaned. But it would have been too risky to open an account. They would have asked too many questions. How had a cowpoke like him got his hands on that much cash? No, better be satisfied with what he had.

After he ate, he drove around Reno until he found a motel where he could get a ground-floor room and park right in front of it. Before he registered, under the name of Owen Shulman, he made sure that it had a strong security chain inside the door. When no one was in sight, he unlocked the car trunk and carried the footlocker into his motel room, slipped the chain in its holder and shoved the footlocker under the bed. He took a long, hot shower, dried himself, stretched out naked on the clean sheets and planned his next step.

As soon as it was daylight, he'd take the footlocker back to his car, wrap the old clothes around it and put it in the trunk he'd bought from the thrift store. Then, about eight, he'd drive to Carson City and put the trunk in storage, where it would be safe until he wanted it. After that, he'd eat a big breakfast of hotcakes, slithering with butter and syrup, and a side order of ham and eggs. Then he'd drive to Tahoe and wait for Lea Turner.

CHAPTER

4

Earlier that day, Justin Starr instructed his chauffeur, who had met them at the Reno airport, to drive through the business district on their way home.

"You'll notice some changes, Barrett," Justin said to his niece. "Reno's grown in the last five years. Business is real good. New people are moving here all the time."

As she looked at the city from her uncle's limousine, Barrett recalled learning about Reno in elementary school, how it had burst into prominence in 1859 with the discovery of silver in the fabulous Comstock Lode. At that time it was called Lake's Crossing, but nine years later the Central Pacific Railroad built a station there and named it after a Civil War general, Jesse Reno. The town was on the rail route between the east and San Francisco and was an important transfer point to Virginia City and the mines. Now, despite its exclusive shops and the university, it still had the aura of a frontier town and the Old West image. Even the hills on the north and east, smooth and brown, looked as if they were covered with buck-skin. She realized with a wrench how much she had missed the place.

It amused Justin to watch Barrett discover a new or a renovated building. That girl was sharp. Didn't miss a thing. She truly remembered the town in which she had grown up, and she noticed all the trans-formations. A person like that appealed to him.

When they passed Starr's Casino, she grabbed his arm. "You've got a new sign! Isn't it attractive? You've rearranged the slot machines in front, too."

"You've got a great memory." He chuckled to himself. Now, how did she notice all that so fast? She'd caught just a glimpse of the casino as they drove by. Right on the ball!

"Oh, there's a big new department store!"

"It opened a couple of years ago. It's been very successful."

"I'll have to go there sometime this summer."

"Maybe it'll seem like small potatoes, after the stores in New York." He patted her arm. "Perhaps Reno will, too, after living five years on the East Coast."

Barrett turned toward him, her face radiant. "No, it looks wonderful! I'm so glad to be home again. I can't thank you enough for making this possible for me. It's going to be a glorious summer." Secretly, she hoped she'd never have to move back to New York. This was home. This was where she belonged.

The Georgian mansion, which had cost Justin half a million dollars to build fifteen years ago, was on a rise at the edge of town, overlooking the Truckee River, which flowed through the middle of the city. At night one could see the lights of Reno and the fifty-foot-high neon sign that advertised Starr's Casino with garish red letters that spelled the name and then dissolved into a cascade of falling stars in ceaseless repetition.

The chauffeur drove between the wrought-iron gates in the wall that surrounded the ten acres of the estate. They passed carefully tended gardens and stopped in front of the white portico, supported by finely fluted Corinthian columns that were topped with handsomely carved capitals. There was a leaded fanlight above the large front door. The house was pale buff with white trim.

The butler opened the door. "Welcome home, sir. Good afternoon, Miss Starr. I trust you had a pleasant flight."

They returned his greeting, and Justin asked, "Where is Mrs. Starr?"

"In the upstairs sitting room, sir."

As they walked down the hall to the winding staircase, Barrett admired the Louis XV marquetry commode with bronze escutcheons and two Sèvres vases on its yellow Sienna marble top. Five years ago she'd been too young and unknowing to appreciate the treasures in this house.

Eunice Starr called from the top of the stairs. "It's so good to have you back, Justin. And Barrett. How wonderful to see you again."

As they climbed the stairs toward the small, elegant woman, Barrett wondered how many generations of selective breeding it had taken to produce such a true aristocrat. Eunice must have been nearly fifty-five, but in the muted light she looked much younger. She was *soignée*. Her light-brown hair was carefully tinted and coiffed; her simple blue dress, understated and chic, was graced with a string of matched pearls. It was only when Barrett kissed her that she noticed the puffiness in her face and a hint of wine on her breath.

Eunice linked her arms in theirs and walked

between them. "Come to the sitting room, and we'll have a cold drink and sandwiches. Barrett, I've ordered iced tea for us and beer for Justin, but you may have anything you want."

"Iced tea will be fine." Barrett wasn't hungry, but she was grateful for Eunice's thoughtfulness. Somehow, it allayed her uncertainty over whether she'd be welcome, for she'd always been in awe of Justin's third wife. She couldn't imagine a more mismatched couple than this blue-blooded aristocrat and her self-made uncle, whose father had been a carnival man.

The upstairs sitting room, which was part of the master bedroom suite, was decorated particularly for Justin. The grasscloth walls displayed pictures of his family, the carnival, and the original saloon, as well as a collection of chips from his various casinos and a collage of programs and sketches of the stars who'd appeared in his headliner rooms.

There was a fireplace with a gas log, a long television and stereo console, bookshelves with popular fiction and magazines, and a small bar in a corner. A figured sofa in soft greens, oranges, and gold matched Eunice's high-backed armchair, and a huge black leather recliner, especially chosen for Justin's ample frame, dominated the room. By its side was a tray-lamp with a light that could be adjusted to just the proper angle. A humidor with cigars, a jar of macadamia nuts and a large ashtray rested on the tray. A rack of newspapers, with the *Gazette*, the *Wall Street Journal*, and the *San Francisco Chronicle*, was within easy reach. The room faced south and was gay and cheerful, with direct sunshine and a garden of hanging plants.

It was Justin's favorite room, where he could take off his suit coat, put on his slippers and relax in his recliner. He could be himself—the saloonkeeper, the gambling-casino owner. Eunice never objected if he

dropped cigar ashes on the carpet or otherwise dis-
arranged this room. He never felt completely at ease
in the rest of the house—not with Eunice's rare
antique furniture that she'd brought from her Bellingham home in Hillsborough, on the peninsula below
San Francisco, or with her butler, her French chef,
and her personal maid, who had also been brought
from Hillsborough.

Well, he couldn't complain if she had introduced
him to a rarefied life-style. After all, that's why he
had married her—because she had real class.

As Eunice talked with Barrett, Justin listened with
pleasure to her soft, cultured voice. However, it was
true that her voice was a bit thick at times, her words
somewhat slurred. He could never understand why
she drank so much. She had everything she wanted.

As his niece sipped her iced tea and nibbled the
dainty sandwiches, she listened attentively to his wife.
Barrett had class, too, he thought with pride. Not
as much as Eunice, perhaps, but with the right clothes
she could hold her own anyplace. Her stepfather was
from the upper crust, too, and had sent her to some
exclusive college in Connecticut. All of the Starrs'
rough edges had been polished and here she was, an
incredibly beautiful jewel. He looked at the pictures
of his carnival forefathers and thought, By God, the
Starrs have come a hell of a long way.

"Lyle's coming here right from the office," Eunice
said. "He's delighted that you're going to be here for
the summer, Barrett. He's staying for dinner, so you
can have a nice visit."

"Wonderful! I haven't seen him for so long."

Justin spoke up. "I ought to go to the office for a
while."

"No, I won't let you!" Eunice put her hand on his
arm. "Darling, I insist that you stay home and rest
this afternoon. You look awfully tired. That office

can get along without you for another day." She turned to Barrett. "Perhaps you're tired, too. I'll show you to your room. After all, you people got up several hours before we did."

Justin chuckled and settled in his recliner. "If Eunice says you gotta rest, you might as well give in and do it. See how she bosses me!" There was affection in his voice, as if he loved her concern. "Unless you'd rather lie around the pool and take a swim."

"Yes, I'd like that. I sat so long on that jet I'd love to really stretch my legs." Barrett stood up. "Then I can sunbathe awhile before I get ready for dinner."

Eunice took Barrett down the hall to one of the guest rooms and showed her the bath and where to find extra towels. She glanced at Barrett's luggage. "If you want one of the maids to help you unpack, just ring this bell."

"No, I won't unpack. After all, I'll be leaving for Lake Tahoe the day after tomorrow. Then I'll settle in. But thank you, anyway."

Eunice turned to the door. "I'll leave you on your own until later. We'll have cocktails downstairs as soon as Lyle gets here. I must go back to your uncle and make sure he rests. It would be just like him to sneak out behind my back and go to the office. He has a heart condition that we must watch."

When Eunice returned to the sitting room, Justin was stretched out in his recliner, asleep. How old and tired he looked. Well, he was home now, and she'd play her role once more, she told herself as she sat down in her armchair. It was her job to flatter Justin and listen to him talk, to placate him, reinforce his ego and cater to his every whim.

She had learned long ago that he wanted them to live up to her life-style—"I want everyone to know we got class," he'd say—and she could never make him feel small, crass, or unworthy of her. He was very sensitive about his crudities and lack of background, although he was always frank and open about them. She had to prove to him over and over, in subtle ways, that she thought he was just as good as anyone else, especially Andrew, her first husband. She had carefully taught the servants, especially the ones she'd brought from Hillsborough, that they must never be supercilious and haughty (as well they might be) but must go out of their way to be respectful of Mr. Starr. She was quick to remind everyone that he was paying their generous salaries.

No wonder Justin had brought Barrett back with him from New York. She was a beautiful girl—charming, too—and he could show her off to all his friends and associates. Eunice could hear the pride in his voice as he would introduce her: "I want you to meet my grandniece, Barrett Starr. Roy, my late brother, was her grandfather." He would make sure they got the message—that Barrett was his blood relative and had not been acquired through his marriage to the former Eunice Bellingham. He would show everybody that the Starrs had class, too.

With her extraordinary looks, youth, and refinement, Barrett could marry money, there was no question about that. But perhaps she wouldn't, Eunice thought enviously; she seemed so self-sufficient and capable. Barrett could take care of herself; she had worked in an advertising agency in New York. She wouldn't be helpless and unable to cope if she were caught in the same way Eunice had been, when she was left penniless and with a sixteen-year-old son to care for and educate. No, Barrett was strong and able to take care of herself. One could sense it. In that way she was much like Justin.

Eunice glanced at him, snoring in his big recliner, his face slack and his dentures loose in his open

mouth. She shuddered and turned away. She longed
to pour herself another glass of wine, but Lyle was
coming tonight and she'd have to be extra careful.
Besides, she was just getting back in shape, having
timed her recovery to Justin's return from New York.

She thought again of Barrett. The girl radiated
self-confidence. How she wished that she herself had
more! Instead, her own sense of self-worth seemed
to need constant reinforcement. She couldn't do anything, really. She wasn't artistic or clever; she couldn't
play the piano very well or paint; nor was she active
in the women's movement or a philanthropist. Her
only accomplishments were that she'd married
Andrew Bellingham, the most eligible bachelor of her
coming-out season, and had had a marvelous son for
him. Eunice leaned her head against the back of the
armchair and closed her eyes, remembering Andrew.

All those years ago, when she was presented by her
widowed mother at the debutante ball in Boston, she
knew that she'd never be the deb of the year. She was
not particularly beautiful, only pretty. She had no
outstanding talents, and her mother had little money.
In spite of her blue blood she was not a prize catch.

But Andrew Bellingham, who was doing graduate
work in anthropology at Harvard, attended the ball,
and the debs were all aflutter. He was tall and handsome, and the Bellinghams were a great San Francisco shipping family. His forefathers had come from
Boston, from where they had sent clipper ships to
every port in the world. The family later moved to
San Francisco and concentrated on the Orient trade.
At first it was sailing ships, then steamships and a
large fleet of freighters and passenger vessels.

For some reason, for which she'd be eternally
grateful, Andrew became interested in her at the
debutante ball. There was a whirlwind courtship, and

they were married just before Pearl Harbor. From then on, Bellingham ships carried men and munitions across the Pacific, and the family fortune increased tenfold. Eunice eventually produced a son, Lyle, who was a constant joy to Andrew and herself. There had never been a more attractive or charming child, the image of his father.

After the war they built a magnificent home in Hillsborough, staffed it with servants and took their proper place in the peninsula society. There was another home in Honolulu, where they spent part of each year, as well as a ski lodge at Lake Tahoe—all maintained with a staff of servants. Andrew sold his shipping lines, and whenever Lyle was out of school, they sailed in their oceangoing yacht with a full crew to the South Pacific islands—Fiji, Tonga, Samoa, Rarotonga, Tahiti, and all the others—where Andrew studied Polynesian cultures and collected artifacts, for he was an anthropologist at heart. He always took Lyle with him.

They also gathered seashells and had one of the finest collections in the world, having learned to snorkel and scuba dive like experts.

It was a glorious life. There was the opera during the season, and concerts, plays, art exhibits, yachting races, parties, and skiing at Tahoe. Then off to Hawaii or the South Pacific. It was their due, for they were Bellinghams.

But one windy March day, while Lyle was attending his private school and Eunice was at a fashion show in San Francisco, Andrew took one of the small sailing boats out on the Bay by himself. The water was choppy, but no worse than Andrew had sailed on a hundred times before. The boat capsized, and his body wasn't recovered for three days.

At first, it seemed to be a tragic accident, but when his estate was settled, there was speculation that it could have been suicide. Andrew, never a real businessman, had made too many bad investments and was close to bankruptcy. Also, they had lived unreasonably far beyond their means; so not only was the great Bellingham fortune gone, but Andrew was deep in debt. It took Eunice six months to learn the truth: she was penniless.

Countless creditors and tax collectors converged upon her. The large yacht was the first thing to be sold, then the home in Honolulu. The estate in Hillsborough and the Tahoe property were put on the market at the same time.

At once, Justin Starr, the gambling czar, always interested in prime lake property, called on her at Hillsborough and made an offer for the Tahoe land and the ski lodge. He felt it had potential as a resort. He mentioned that they had met some years before in Carson City at a reception at the governor's mansion. She remembered the reception, but the guests were just a blur of faces.

Although she referred him to her attorneys, Justin made many excuses to deal directly with her. During the week he spent on the peninsula, he asked her and Lyle to dinner frequently and, in her despair, she accepted. He knew her financial state. The collapse of the house of Bellingham was written up in *Time*, *Newsweek*, and the *Wall Street Journal*. It didn't take him long to size up that she was desperate, emotionally fragile, and unable to cope with her tragic situation.

When they returned to the house after dinner, Lyle would go off to his room, and the conversation would soon turn to her circumstances. Justin Starr offered his sympathy and questioned her tactfully. How could she earn a living? Did she have any skills? She was honest; she didn't. Did she have relatives to whom she could turn for help? No; moreover, she was keeping her invalid mother in an expensive nursing home, as she was crippled with arthritis. Her relatives on the East Coast were in financial straits themselves. Andrew was the last of the Bellinghams, except for Lyle, who was sixteen. What future lay ahead for him? How could he even go to college? Tears gathered in her eyes.

Were there friends who could help her? Not really. Though they had been so kind at first, they were not interested in trying to solve her tangled affairs. They had their own problems. Besides, people soon lost sympathy with her and felt that the Bellinghams should have saved more of their money and come to grips with reality before it became too late. She couldn't blame them. It seemed incredible that so much money had been spent. But she had left their financial affairs up to Andrew, who seemed to be so capable and clever.

Aside from Lyle's future, the thing that seemed to bother her most was losing her closest servants: Wilson, her butler; Jacques, the French chef; and Mary, her personal maid. They were absolute jewels. She had had them for years. They made her life possible. How could she manage without them? Nevertheless, she would have to let them go very soon, her lawyer had told her.

Then, one evening, to return his courtesies to her, she invited Justin Starr to dine with her. The sale of her Tahoe property was complete, and he was ready to return to Reno. As they sat in the drawing room, sipping Cointreau, she told him that she didn't mind losing the home on the peninsula as much as the priceless Bellingham antique furniture. For one hundred and fifty years it had been gathered, piece by piece, from all over the world. It ought to go to Lyle and his children, but now it would all be sold. As she told him this, she broke down and sobbed.

When she got herself under control, she apologized. "Forgive me, but you've been so sympathetic, Mr. Starr. I mustn't take advantage of your kindness."

Justin got out of his chair and moved next to her on the Hepplewhite sofa. "I'm going to level with you, Mrs. Bellingham. I've had this idea in the back of my mind for the last couple months. I want you to marry me."

"Marry you?" She gasped in astonishment. "Why, you don't know me at all! Why would you want——"

"Because you've got class and I don't. I'll be frank. I've made it big. I want a swell home and a wife I can be damn proud of—someone who knows how to entertain right so I can ask anybody I want to my house and know we won't make mistakes: the governor, the president of the university, the VIPs who come to town. I want to know that everything's OK and I won't look like a damn fool."

"But, Mr. Starr, you can hire——"

He shook his head. "No, I don't want that. I want a wife, a real Mrs. Starr, who will be the hostess. A blueblood, a swell." His face was earnest, and he was almost pathetic in his eagerness. "Look, I got the money but no class. You got the class and no money. Why don't we team up and help each other?"

She leaned away from him. What should she say? "Really, Mr. Starr, I'm speechless, too shocked to think."

"Look, I'll be kind to you. I'll treat you right. You'll never have to worry about that. Or about money. You'll have all you want."

"To be frank, it never occurred to me that my background had a market value."

"Of course it has. That's nothing new. In Europe, weren't all those titles bought and sold and married around? The kings and queens and dukes and countesses and all that? They did that for centuries."

"I suppose so," she whispered, her mouth dry. This was unreal. It couldn't be happening. "Tell me about yourself, Mr. Starr."

"All right, Mrs. Bellingham—and I won't hold nothing back. I'm fifty-five, six feet tall and weigh about two hundred pounds. My folks were carnival people. I got my start by opening a little saloon; then I gradually got into gambling in a big way. Well, I've had two wives, and they were both floozies. I met the first one when I opened my first saloon. She was a waitress in a lunchroom next door. But we fought all the time, and she finally ran off with a truck driver. I divorced her, of course. Later I married a showgirl, after I made my first million. But I caught her shacking up with one of my pit bosses and kicked her out on her butt. That's one thing I won't stand for, some broad cheating on me. I got out of that marriage for a measly ten grand."

He looked at her and saw she wasn't laughing at him; so he went on. "I've made millions, and I'm going to make more. I got a lot of years ahead of me. I'll have as much as Bellingham ever had, and I've made every goddamn cent of it myself. I didn't inherit a penny." He thumped his chest. "I made it all on my own. My father ended up with nothing. In fact, I supported him until he died."

In spite of herself, Eunice had to admit that there was something attractive about this big, virile, dynamic man. He was nice enough looking, not coarse or revolting. But still wondering whether she was having a nightmarish dream, she murmured, "That was very admirable of you, Mr. Starr, to accomplish so much and take care of your father like that."

He took her small hand in his. "Maybe you already got someone else in mind for your second husband. A swell like yourself?"

As she fought back the tears, she whispered, "No. I haven't recovered from Andrew's death yet. I. . . ." She looked down at her hand in his and studied the hairs on his fingers. Of course there was no one else to marry her. Who would want to? She was pushing forty, had lost her youthful prettiness and was penniless. The men she knew—there were very few single ones—would want much more than that in exchange for marriage.

On the wall, the ancient birdcage English clock, with its exposed pendulum and weights, struck ten. When it stopped, Justin said, "Mrs. Bellingham, I'm gonna talk turkey. Most of all, I want a son of my own to take over when I'm old. One of the stipulations of our marriage would be that I could adopt Lyle. He's a fine boy, handsome as all get out— smart, too, and he's got class. I like him a lot already. I'd soon learn to love him."

She was panic-stricken. "Adopt Lyle?"

"Yes. I'll send him all through college, to Stanford if he can get in. He can be trained good in business administration. Then, when he's ready, I'll take him into my business so he can take over when I retire. Sure, I can hire executives—I got a lot of 'em already in my corporation—but I want my own son in the driver's seat."

Her heart sank. "Would Lyle have to give up his name?" She could never ask him to do that, never. He was the image of his father. How could she cancel that great heritage?

But Justin said firmly, "That's right, he would. He'd be Lyle Bellingham Starr. But what the hell's so good about the Bellingham name if the dough's gone?" His face darkened. "By God, if he inherits the Starr fortune, he'll damn well carry on my name!"

She looked so distraught that he went on hastily, "I'll tell you what else I'm ready to do. I'll buy all this fancy furniture from the creditors since it means so much to you. We'll build a mansion in Reno for it, and no expense'll be spared. It'll be built to suit you, because you'd know just what it should look like. I want it to have class and not be some cheap-looking joint. I already own the land, right along the Truckee River. Sweetest location you could ever find."

Almost in a trance, Eunice looked at the Aubusson rug, breathtakingly beautiful in its soft yellows, golds, and deep pinks; then across the room at the English Broadwood grand piano; at the wall where a French *millefleurs* tapestry hung; and at a pair of Sheffield candlesticks that were reflected in a Chippendale looking glass. She could keep them all, and the rest of the rare antiques in the house: the Feraghan rug, the Maryland marble-topped side table with its inlaid apron, the porcelain hunting sconces, the Queen Anne walnut chairs. She could build a mansion exactly to her taste, hire architects and decorators from San Francisco.

She looked at Justin's sincere face and kindly eyes. Maybe he was crude, but he was honest and forth-right. He was strong. He'd take charge and solve all her problems. "What about my servants? Could I bring them with me?"

"Hell, yes. Pay 'em whatever you need to."

"That's very kind of you, Mr. Starr."

He pressed his advantage. "Of course, I'll take over your mother's bills, too. If you want, you can have a special room for her in our house and hire nurses to take care of her. Whatever you want is yours if you'll be my wife. Furs, jewels, cars, clothes, money—name it and you can have it. And for Lyle, too."

"How very generous. I just have to think this out. I'm so surprised."

"Take your time. I mean every word I say. And

we'll have our lawyers write up a legal agreement so it'll be all fair and square."

Half-frightened, she looked around the room. What would Lyle say? Would he agree to go along with these plans for his future? Would it be a wise decision? Would it be fair to him? But how can beggars be choosers? How could she afford to turn him down? How many chances would she have to marry a multimillionaire?

"I'll have to discuss this with Lyle, of course. It concerns him, too."

"Naturally."

Finally she looked at him and smiled. "I'm sure I'll say yes, Mr. Starr. So perhaps you'd better call me Eunice."

He lifted her hand to his mouth and kissed it. Tears swam in his eyes, and he said huskily, "My name is Justin."

CHAPTER

5

As Barrett swam back and forth across the pool to loosen her cramped muscles, the water seemed to caress her body. She reveled in the privacy of the pool; she had never seen anything like it, with the grand cabana alongside, with dressing rooms where guests could shower and change without going into the house. With its recreation room and expensive rattan furniture, polished tile floor for dancing, stereo, kitchenette and wet bar, and every amenity for poolside entertaining, including a huge brick barbeque.

She climbed out of the pool and, as she dried herself, looked at the tennis courts, at the back of the beautiful house, and at the surrounding landscape, luxuriant with scarlet and purple rhododendrons, tree roses displaying bouquets of gorgeous blooms, and espaliered pyracantha heavy with green berries.

No wonder Eunice had married Uncle Justin! For years this kind of abundance had been her taken-for-granted life-style with Andrew Bellingham. How could anyone give up such affluence? As Barrett stretched facedown on a pad and felt the warm sun on her back, she wondered whether Eunice had any regrets.

Well, she herself would live like this someday, not through marriage but because she had made it on her own. She'd rise to the top, and she'd have it all—clothes, a beautiful home with a pool like this, and servants—because she'd earn it through her own efforts. If she wanted to marry for money, she could probably meet plenty of wealthy men through her stepfather, and now through Uncle Justin. But to spend the rest of her life at the mercy, so to speak, of a man she didn't love? She shuddered. No. When and if she married, her husband would have to be a real winner, an entrepreneur like Justin Starr, with his dynamic force. But most of all, they'd have to be deeply in love. She wasn't going to settle for anything else. She didn't have to, because she was going to succeed on her own.

Marriage wasn't all that great. Her own mother had made two rotten ones. First there was her father, who had been a ski instructor at Squaw Valley when she was growing up and was now at Aspen, in Colorado. He had had a chance to get started in Starr Enterprises, but the fool had turned it down. If he had been a different sort, he'd have risen right to the top. If he had only gone in with Uncle Justin twenty years ago, they'd be living like this now, too. He was Justin's nephew, and could have been a son to him years before Lyle came along.

No, her father had been too shiftless and lazy to work for a hard-driving, demanding man like Justin Starr—not when he could give skiing lessons by day and sleep with his snowbunnies at night. Her mother had finally got fed up and divorced him. Barrett didn't care if she ever saw him again.

Where did she get her drive and ambition? Not through her parents, or even her grandparents. She and Justin must have inherited something from a remote common ancestor—perhaps a brave, gutsy pioneer who had helped open the West.

She groaned as she thought of her stepfather, Walter Ellsworth. How she loathed him! He impressed one at first, she had to admit—distinguished, urbane, from a prominent Connecticut family, a banker and moderately well off—but he was a penny-pinching, petty, hypercritical tyrant. Her mother had met him when he came to Reno for a divorce, and she was the secretary for his lawyer. A real beauty, she had caught his eye and they were married before he returned home. Barrett remembered how thrilled her mother was at the time. Barrett was in her first year at the University of Nevada, and when she joined them in Connecticut at the end of the term, she found that already the bloom was off the marriage.

But at least the old skinflint had helped send her to college for her last three years, because her mother begged, cajoled and threatened until he consented. He had wanted her to take a business course in Nevada and get out on her own right away, but finally they compromised: Barrett would take business courses each summer and would help earn her way through college, which she had done. They had kept track of every penny he gave her, and some day, as soon as she was able, she'd repay him. She had already paid some of it back, and the day when she sent him the last check couldn't come soon enough.

Anyway, while she was finishing college, she learned how the affluent lived. Her friends were all from wealthy families and she had visited them in their homes, at such places as New Haven, Stratford, and Waterbury. She had observed and listened, so that she knew how to talk and act like those who were more fortunate than herself. She had learned the "in" places to go, how to dress, and how to be "with it." She could hold her own with the men from Yale and the other Ivy League colleges. She and her mother had made her clothes, and although she was dirt poor, she got by.

Now she was tired of being only on the fringes of wealth, of always compromising, of making do with less than the best. From now on she'd have it all. She had the drive and the executive ability; she knew that. With her job in the advertising agency, she'd been in contact with several big companies and had learned about the business world. What better opportunity could she have than with Starr Enterprises? It was quite an empire. And who would make a better empress than she?

Of course, there was Lyle, but surely there would be room for them both. She sensed that her Uncle Justin was impressed with her. She was a Starr, his very own blood relative. She'd keep a low profile and make sure that Lyle never felt threatened. She'd talk about returning to New York, and ask Lyle and Justin for their advice about opportunities on the East Coast. But somehow she'd become indispensable, so that Justin would ask her to stay.

She showered and dressed in a flowered chiffon after-five dress and joined Justin and Eunice in the drawing room downstairs.

"We're having vodka and tonic while we wait for Lyle," Justin said from behind the bar. "Is that OK for you?"

"Yes, thank you."

Eunice was wearing a pale-green Bill Blass original, deceptively simple but just right for a family dinner party. Barrett complimented her and suggested that they go shopping together so she could benefit from Eunice's excellent taste.

When they had their drinks, Justin said, "Well, here's to a good summer."

Barrett touched her glass to his. "I know it will be wonderful. I can't tell you how I appreciate being able to spend it with you."

Eunice smiled. "It's our pleasure. Our family is so small it's important to be together sometimes."

Barrett glanced around the elm-paneled room, carpeted in deep gold with earth-tone furniture. On one wall was a group of watercolors depicting Nevada scenes. It was a comfortable room for family gatherings and for entertaining Justin's friends.

Eunice rose from a deep armchair and said, "Come with me; I want to show you something while we're waiting." She led Barrett and her husband into the living room, magnificent with parquet floor, silken draperies, Bellingham antique furniture, and luxurious rugs. "Did you know that Justin received an honorary degree from the University of Nevada last year?"

In a place of honor, between two stained-glass panels by Holbein, was the diploma, in a large antique gold frame. There was also a color photograph of Justin, in cap and down, being presented the diploma by the president of the university. Another picture showed him with the other honorees: the governor, a U.S. senator from Nevada, and a world-famous space scientist who had given the commencement address.

Eunice touched the picture and explained, "You know, Justin established the Starr Foundation several years ago, which grants scholarships to the university. By now there are hundreds of young Nevadans who owe their education to him."

Barrett seized his arm. "Oh, Uncle Justin, I'm so proud of you!" She kissed his cheek. "Now you're *Dr. Starr!*"

After the women had moved on to examine a Tiffany lamp on an inlaid table, Justin continued looking at the diploma and pictures, though he came every day to see them and to relive that moment when the president placed the scarlet-lined hood over his neck. Lyle and Eunice had special seats on the stage, and all his friends were in the audience.

An honorary degree from the university! Hell, he didn't even have a high-school diploma. He thought again of the great dinner party Eunice had given him that evening in a special tent on the lawn, with the help of caterers and florists from San Francisco. Of course, she knew all about such affairs and could do them right. They all came: the governor, the space scientist, the senator, the university president, and all brought their wives. There were two hundred other guests as well. That party had real class!

But so did getting the degree. You had to be somebody to get an honorary degree, he told himself; they didn't hand 'em out to just anybody. Each day, when he looked at it, he thought to himself, Andrew Bellingham never got an honorary degree, by God! He had asked Lyle about that first thing—as soon as he received the letter from the president of the university.

Nor had Bellingham established a foundation. Justin had queried Eunice about that. "No, dear," she replied, "but he built an addition to a museum in San Francisco to house his Polynesian artifacts."

"But that's stuff from people who are dead and gone."

Eunice had agreed. "You're right, Justin. What you've done has helped young people who have their whole lives ahead of them. When you think what opportunities you've given them, why, the whole state has benefited. Nothing could be more important than that."

He remembered the night, a week after the ceremony, when he came home from the office and Eunice opened the front door, bubbling with excitement. "I have a surprise! Darling, do come and see!"

She took him to the living room, and there were the diploma and pictures, framed and hanging on the wall. In the very spot where there'd been that painting with all the funny lines by that guy Picasso—the painting that Bellingham had bought and everyone raved about, and he hated. He had turned to her in astonishment.

"You mean you really want those there?"

"Indeed I do. We want everyone who comes to our home to see them. That's all right with you, isn't it?"

"Of course." He had hugged her to him and whispered, "It's just that I thought you'd put them upstairs with the carnival and saloon pictures."

When Lyle arrived, they returned to the drawing room for another drink. Lyle sat on the sofa with Barrett. "It's so good to see you again," he said. "I'm glad that you'll be here all summer. We'll have a great time."

Barrett was again aware of his charm, his tall, lean handsomeness, his well-tailored clothes, his brown hair, so becomingly cut, and his friendly hazel eyes. He gave her his complete attention and, for a moment, the conviction that she was the most important person in the world to him. It was his natural manner, she thought; everyone got the same treatment. Talk about a PR man *par excellence!* He must be invaluable to Starr Enterprises, especially when Justin came on so strong. Lyle could smooth ruffled feathers or suavely handle anyone whom her uncle offended.

"I understand that Lea is going to be one of your headliners," Barrett said. "I'll be so glad to see her again."

"I met her at the airport today," Lyle replied. "What a mob scene! But she's fine, and she sent her love to you. I'm taking you both to Tahoe the day after tomorrow." Lyle freshened his drink and returned to her. "Another friend of yours is going to be here—Judith Davenport. She's driving up from L.A. and called me from a motel on 395. She'll get here tomorrow."

"Judith? Will she be here long enough for me to spend some time with her?"

"Yes, she will." Lyle twirled his glass. "To be honest, she's coming home to get a divorce. We'll all have to give her moral support."

"I'm sorry her marriage didn't work out," Barrett said. "Anyway, Lea, Judith and I will have a real reunion after all these years."

"I've known for a long time the breakup was coming. She's been home several times, and we've seen a lot of each other." Lyle turned to Justin. "Dad, how did things go in New York?"

"On the whole, just fine."

As the two men talked, Barrett watched them. There seemed to be genuine affection and respect between them. There was no question that the heir apparent had everything going for him: superb appearance and background, wonderful personality, and all the aristocracy of his parents. He was intelligent, charming, a male and trained in business. Who could offer more?

Later, as they dined under the Waterford chandelier, Lyle said, "Dad, I'm anxious to talk to you. Yesterday I got a call from a friend in Honolulu. I knew him at Stanford, too. There's a terrific deal coming up—some hotels and apartments on Waikiki. It's an unbelievable chance, and he wanted to know if we'd be interested."

Justin shook his head. "You know I've always

made it a policy to stick close to home—Reno and Tahoe—my own stamping grounds, where I know what's going on."

"Can't you two men discuss this business later?" Eunice said. "We mustn't bore Barrett."

"*Bore* me? Never!" Barrett cried. "You forget I'm a businesswoman through and through."

Justin turned toward her. "Lyle's had these brainstorms about Hawaii property before."

"He's right, though, Uncle Justin. Just think if you'd invested there twenty years ago!" Lyle shot her a grateful glance; so she went on. "You must remember that Hawaii is Lyle's home territory. *His* stamping grounds, you might say. He lived there a great deal as a boy and has returned many times; so he's in touch with the business trends there."

Justin shook his head and smiled. "Maybe I made a mistake bringing you out here for the summer. You two'll gang up on me!"

Lyle saluted her with his wineglass. "Now I know whom to turn to for support. I'll make the most of this summer."

"It's none of my business, Uncle Justin," Barrett said, "but in New York all the companies think in terms of diversification. They don't want all their eggs in one basket."

"But we *are* diversified."

"In your enterprises, but not in your locations. You said you like to stick close to home, but why not take advantage of Lyle's background and knowledge of Hawaii? Think of the contacts he has there." She leaned back. "Forgive me. I'm speaking out of turn. Of course, it's up to you two."

"Dad, she's right. We ought to branch out. Times change, you know. And this deal is terrific. I'm familiar with the property; I know what I'm doing."

Justin threw up his hands in mock horror. "I surrender! I surrender! I'm too old and tired to buck you two young people. So jump on a plane, son, and go over and investigate it. I'll leave it up to you to decide."

"Thanks, Dad." Lyle flushed with pleasure. "There's a hell of a lot of money involved, but don't worry; I won't do anything rash."

Eunice rubbed her fingers against the texture of her linen napkin. How wonderful that Lyle will have a chance to branch out in Hawaii. It will give him excuses for going there, she thought, for it is his favorite place in the world.

They talked for another hour, and then Lyle left for his apartment. As he kissed her good night, Eunice thought, If only Lyle would live here with us. She would love to have him under the same roof, but he'd been adamant about that. As soon as he had finished graduate school, he said, "I want my own pad. I love Dad and all that, but don't forget I have him in my hair all day long. I have to be away from him part of the time."

Before he left, Lyle whispered in Barrett's ear, "Thanks, pal!" and kissed her on the cheek.

The next morning Barrett rode to work with Justin in spite of his protests. "Don't you want to sleep in? You must be tired." But she assured him that she wanted to spend the morning in the casino and wander around the streets of Reno. She could take a cab back to the house.

"Do you ever gamble, Uncle Justin?"

"Of course I do—lots of times—but not at Starr's. Neither Lyle nor I can gamble there; it's against state law for operators to gamble in their own clubs."

"Well, there are plenty of other places to go."

"Of course—Harrah's, Harold's Club, and a

dozen others. We're all friends. I always play when a hunch hits, when I know Lady Luck is looking over my shoulder."

"I can understand that."

He chuckled and went on. "Not long ago I had a hunch and walked across the street to another club. The dice table nearest the door was empty except for the dealer. This I like, when no one else is around. Anyway, the dealer and I agreed to terms. The limit of my losing, if it went that way, would be twenty thousand dollars. I gave the house my marker, or IOU, and took ten grand in chips. The dice felt just right; never better. I can still feel them in my hand. I laid five hundred dollars on the line and rolled, and within an hour I won more than thirty thousand. I gave the dealer a five-hundred-dollar toke, went into the coffee shop for lunch and marked a Keno card while I was waiting. I'll be damned if I didn't win another thousand." He laughed heartily. "Nothing tickles me more than winning from another operator."

"Of course, you lose to them sometimes, too."

"Oh, sure, but they come to Starr's and drop their money; so it about evens up."

The chauffeur pulled into an alley and stopped in front of a private entrance to the high-rise casino. They got out of the car, Justin unlocked the casino door, and they stepped into a small hallway. He pointed to another door.

"It's a special elevator to the office suite. Lyle and I can come and go without being seen, if we want. But let's walk through the lounge." He smiled. "I always take a look-see at the beginning of the morning. Besides, it puts the employees on their toes when they know the boss is around."

As they entered the main lounge, Barrett's blood pounded with excitement. The place was filled with customers, many of whom may have been there all night, for the club never closed its doors. Three shifts of employees kept it in operation around the clock, every day of the year. There was a festive air in the huge, windowless room, whose walls were painted with western murals of cowboys lassoing steers, gathered around a chuckwagon on the range, sitting in front of a campfire and leaning against a bar in a saloon watching can-can girls kicking their ruffled skirts high.

Pit bosses kept watch over their enclosures of crap tables, "21" players, and roulette layouts. Lively music provided a background for the clank of slot machines, the clatter of silver coins hitting metal trays, the shrieks of winners, the soft whish of cards being dealt, the tolling of Keno numbers, and announcements over the PA system: "Security officers come to Section Three" and "Long distance calling Mr. Edward Longsmith." Old women yanked at slot handles. At a roulette wheel, three Chinese men stood with a woman in a sari with jewels in her nose, a bearded hippie, and a khaki-clad soldier. A Paiute Indian at a dice table carefully rolled his cubes and saw a twelve, or "craps," appear, then turned away.

Justin chuckled as Barrett looked at him. "I've been watching the expression on your face. I swear that under that fancy veneer you respond to this atmosphere, don't you? You could be a carnie woman or a gambling operator, like the rest of us Starrs."

"Perhaps you're right, Uncle Justin." She smiled and slipped her hand under his arm. "I guess it's in our blood."

CHAPTER

6

It was the middle of the afternoon when Judith Davenport pulled up in front of the Victorian farmhouse at Sage Creek. She parked the Cadillac in the shade, climbed stiffly from behind the steering wheel and reached in the back for her suitcase. As her stomach muscles tightened with dread, she prayed, Please don't let the folks be here. If she could just be alone to rest for a few days, to put herself together and, mainly, to get her defenses ready for her father.

She opened the gate in the white picket fence that enclosed the yard and walked along the brick path. A huge lilac bush was in full bloom, and she stopped to admire it. One never saw lilac blossoms in Beverly Hills. Or calla lilies. Or apple trees in bloom. As she looked eastward to the distant purple hills, she smelled the pungent sagebrush on the range. Even in her fatigue she rejoiced to be home. It was almost over now, the whole messy business. She was home at last.

Mrs. Evans, their plump, middle-aged housekeeper, an addition to the household after her father went into politics, opened the door. "Well, Judith! This is a surprise."

Judith gave the woman a quick hug and kissed her cheek. "I hope you don't mind my coming without letting you know."

"Of course not, dear. Your room is always ready for you."

"Are the folks home, or are they in Carson City?" Ever since her father became lieutenant governor, the Davenports had kept a large apartment in the capital city. Judith hoped they wouldn't be coming back for days, but Mrs. Evans dashed that hope.

"I expect them here anytime. I'm making an apple pie for dinner, and I've got a big pot roast cooking, too. There's plenty for everybody."

"It smells real good." But she wasn't hungry. As she carried her suitcase up the stairs to her room and placed it on her bed, she wondered if she'd ever feel like eating again. Or having sex. Or if she'd ever be truly happy again. She looked around her room: at the family pictures on the walls, the framed Godey prints, her spool bed with the lovely patchwork quilt in the double-ring pattern that her great-grandmother had made for her own hope chest, the crotcheted afghan on the back of the velvet rocker. Well, at least she'd feel like Judith Davenport again. Perhaps that was all she could hope for—just to belong to herself.

She unpacked her pantsuits, her tops and Levi's, her Dacron dresses, and her flowered cotton voile dinner dress and hung them in her closet, but she decided she'd leave her car trunk packed until she talked to her parents. Maybe when her father found out about the breakup, he'd be so mad he'd order her off the ranch. Should she tell them at once or wait until tomorrow? She might as well get it over with.

Should she just blurt out, "Murray and I've split the blanket"? No, Dad would think that too flippant.

Her father was a Neanderthal man. Or, at least, straight from the Victorian age. Was it a major crime to get out of a no-good marriage? How old-fashioned could he be? Didn't half of all marriages break up sooner or later? His attitude was ridiculous. Yet it was a fact she had to deal with.

She put her underwear in the dresser drawers and made neat piles of pantyhose, bras, and slips. She put her cosmetics in the special side drawer, shut her suitcase and put it in the closet.

Almost shivering with fatigue and the stress she'd been through, she threw back the patchwork quilt, lay on top of her bed and pulled the quilt over her. She tried to sleep, but her mind darted about. If worse came to worst, she could always get an apartment in Reno and perhaps a job. But doing what? She wasn't trained in business, or as a nurse or beauty operator. She could hardly see herself as a dealer in a gambling casino. That would *really* antagonize her father.

Perhaps she should go to business school and learn typing and shorthand. Should she go back to the university this fall? For what purpose? She was not as fortunate as the people who knew what they wanted. She was so adrift, so disoriented.

Perhaps, like her mother, all she wanted was a normal husband, a nice home, and children. She had often thought that her mother should have greater goals in life—do something on her own instead of being merely an appendage to her father. And yet, what had Judith Davenport accomplished? Nothing. She couldn't make a success of her marriage; she didn't even have children, because Murray hadn't wanted them. At least her mother had done that much.

She envied Lea Turner, not for her fame or fortune, but because she had a goal and she accomplished it. And Barrett Starr was getting ahead in the business world. Well, they'd all gone full circle, and the three of them would soon be meeting again after five years. Of the three, she was the only one who was a failure. Depression, like a low-lying black cloud, engulfed her.

If only she had stayed at the university instead of insisting on marrying Murray. Now, knowing what he was, she wondered how she could have become so enamored of him. If she had stayed in Reno, perhaps she and Lyle would have got together. He was a real man, the most attractive, charming man she had ever known. But it was too late now. It was inevitable that he would pick one of the fresh, unsullied lovelies who were always hovering around him.

Still, he was a dear friend and he'd rally around and give her moral support. He had promised her that. Poor Lyle had no easy row to hoe, either, she thought. Trying to please Justin Starr all the time would be hard, and as if that weren't enough, he had a lush for a mother. As her grandmother used to say, "We all have to carry our share of the Cross."

Finally she fell asleep. More than an hour later she awakened to hear her mother quietly opening her door. Judith sat up and called out, "Hi, Mom."

"Darling, what a pleasant surprise!" Her mother leaned over the bed, kissed her, then sat in the rocker. She was a heavyset, rather plain woman in her forties, who talked too much but was kind and dear. Judith loved her mother, but she worshiped her father, just as she knew her mother loved her but idolized her brothers. "We weren't expecting you at all. Did you write us?"

"No, I didn't. I just came. Mom, you might as well

know right now that Murray and I have split. I'm going to get a divorce."

Helen Davenport's face fell, and her eyes clouded. "But your father——"

Judith shrugged. "Well, I'd rather take a licking than tell him, but——"

"Do you want me to tell him?"

"No, I will, because he'd be more disgusted than ever if I didn't. Besides, he'd take his anger out on you, and I don't want that."

Her mother rocked back and forth, then said sadly, "I'm not surprised. I've seen it coming for a long time. It's sad—just a shame."

"I'm sorry, too." Judith swung her legs over the side of the bed and slipped into her shoes. "I'll comb my hair. I may as well go down and face Dad right now."

"Why don't you wait until after dinner? We're just ready to eat, and you know how impossible he is when he's hungry. Besides, he's out talking to one of his men now." She got up and smoothed her dress. "Dad has seen your car. He knows you're here. After dinner we'll sit in the living room and talk this out. We'll wait until Mrs. Evans goes. Even so, it'll be bad enough."

"I know. Don't think I'm not dreading it."

During dinner, Elliott and Judith had little to say, but Helen kept up a nervous stream of chatter about her social activities in Carson City. Finally they adjourned to the living room and watched television until they heard the dishwasher going and the back door close.

Then Elliott strode across the room, snapped off the TV and turned to Judith. "All right, out with it! Your mother's been chattering like a crazed monkey and you're here. So what is it?"

Judith looked back at him. "Just sit down, Dad, and I'll tell you. And Mom, too, because she hasn't heard the details. I want you both to know that I've left Murray, for very good reasons, and I've come here to get a divorce. This is the result of careful consideration. Murray, his parents and I all agree that it's for the best."

Elliott's face flushed with anger, and his mouth closed into a hard, grim line. "You know my feelings."

"I do, Dad, and I respect them. But, in all fairness, you must hear my side of the story."

He didn't answer; so she went on. "I admit that I made a mistake when I married Murray. I should have taken your advice and waited. Perhaps I would have changed my mind, I don't know. But the fact is that I did marry him. At first we were reasonably happy. Then, after about two years, I found out that he was a homosexual."

"My God!" Elliott struck the arm of his chair. "Didn't I tell you that you and your mother should go down there to Beverly Hills and visit his family——"

"Dad, if it took me two years of living with Murray to find out, what could we have learned in a couple of days?"

He grunted, then snapped, "How long has he been this way?"

"Apparently, ever since puberty. However, when he was in college, he must have been very discreet, because there was no gossip that I ever heard."

Her mother shuddered. "How awful!"

"Later, I understood why the Rosenfelds welcomed me with open arms in spite of the fact that I am a Gentile. They knew he was gay, and they thought he'd change and be normal because of me. It was very heartbreaking for them when he went back to his old ways. And you can imagine how *I* felt."

Her mother cried out, "Why didn't you leave him then?"

"I wanted to. I guess it was Dad's influence, because I kept hoping and praying that we could work things out."

Elliott snorted. "You could have if you'd tried hard enough."

She looked at her father, and tears swam in her eyes. His opinion would dog her until her dying day. She was a grown woman now, with five years of marriage behind her; yet his censure could reduce her to a frightened child. "Dad, I swear that I did everything I could think of, but it just got worse. I tried with all my might for three years. It didn't help. In fact, Murray got on drugs."

Her father snapped, "That movie crowd was a bad influence on him. Why didn't you move somewhere else, some wholesome place?"

"I tried to, but I couldn't budge him. Murray had turned against me. I had no influence on him at all. He did exactly as he pleased. He'd go away for days at a time, and I wouldn't know where he was. Sometimes I came here, when I had to get away, too."

Helen's eyes were wide with shock as she asked, "But how could he hold down a job? How did he support you?"

"Murray had money of his own, which he'd inherited from his grandmother. He also worked for his father's studio; they put up with him because he was the boss's son." Judith shuddered. Money was not their problem. They had too much, in fact. They might have been a lot better off if they'd had to struggle to make ends meet.

"This is the damnedest tale I ever heard," Elliott growled, but there was a softness in his voice.

Judith sensed sympathy in her father's expression. If only she didn't have to tell him the worst part. Nervously, she rubbed her hands together. "I'm not through yet. Three weeks ago Murray went to a gay bar and met his lover. He got high on cocaine and took this guy for a ride in his Bugatti. Well, he drove down the freeway about ninety miles an hour, hit an embankment and flipped over. The guy was killed and Murray was badly injured. His spinal cord was severed. He's paralyzed from the waist down."

"*What!*" her father roared. "You ran out on him because he's a cripple! I can't believe it!" Shock and horror distorted his face.

Judith bowed her head. It was even worse than she had imagined. "Dad, I spent every waking moment with him at the hospital. Everything possible was done for him. Everything! The Rosenfelds called in the finest neurosurgeons in southern California. Murray will live, but he'll be a paraplegic. After ten days his parents moved him from the hospital to their home, and they hired nurses to take care of him."

Elliott stepped toward her and shouted, "You could have brought him here. You're his wife. We could have built a special house for you here on the ranch. 'Hired nurses'! That was *your* duty!"

Judith shook her head. "I offered to do that. I even said I'd get a house in Beverly Hills, near his parents, but they didn't want that. They asked me to leave."

She remembered that scene in the Roesnfeld's library when her father-in-law had said bluntly, "Judith, you can help us most if you'll leave. Go home and get a divorce. Make a new life for yourself. You have no future here with us. Murray doesn't want you, and neither do we. You're not one of us."

"But, Dad Rosenfeld——"

He looked at her coldly through his horn-rimmed

glasses. "At first we thought you were the answer to Murray's problem. We thought he'd go straight. But he didn't. He wasn't happy with you; in fact, you made him worse."

"No!"

"We'll pay all your expenses while you get your divorce, and you can have the furniture in your apartment and all your wedding gifts. Put it all in storage until you get settled." He waved his cigar. "And when this marriage is dissolved, we'll make a settlement of fifty thousand dollars on you. That ought to tide you over. But just leave—the sooner the better."

But she insisted on talking with Murray. She went into his room, asked the nurse to step outside and sat on a chair beside his bed. "Murray, I want to take care of you for the rest of your life. Let me buy a house and get everything set up just the way you want."

He shook his head. "This is where I want to be, here with my folks. Besides, I can't get a pad any better than this." He indicated the spacious, luxurious room that led onto the patio next to the pool. His stereo, television and radio were all convenient.

"But, Murray, I'll——"

"We had something going for us for a while, but that's all past history. Now you get on my nerves. The folks and I—we'll get along fine. When I get better, I'm going to be a ham operator, collect stamps, read a lot. To be honest, I wish you'd bug off."

Elliott Davenport glowered and said, "Let me ask you this. If Murray had been injured in a war, would you have walked out on him? Let him rot in some veterans' hospital?"

Her chin quivered. "Dad, of *course* not."

"If you'd had a handicapped child, would you have deserted it?"

Helen Davenport protested. "Elliott, you're not being fair."

He turned to his wife, his eyes blazing. "We've had some rough times ourselves! What about the drought years, when we damned near went into bankruptcy? There've been other bad times, too. You know that. But you didn't walk out on me when the going got tough. Hell, no. You've stuck with me through thick and thin for twenty-five years."

Judith started to cry and Elliott slumped into his chair. He drummed his fingers on the arm. "I can imagine what your brothers will say. They'll feel just like I do."

He looked at his daughter equivocally. If she were one of his boys, he'd take her outside and give her a thrashing. How could one of his own flesh and blood desert her spouse? How could she? Where had he failed her? But she was so lovely, so young and so vulnerable. He loved her more than anyone on earth. What a mess she'd made of things. How unhappy she looked. Damn it! He wanted to sob out loud, but he steeled himself. Helplessly, he looked at his hands. Damn it to hell!

For several minutes no one spoke; then Judith said, "Dad, they don't want me at the Rosenfelds', and I'm not going back. As painful as it is for all of us, I'm going ahead with this divorce."

"I see."

"If you don't want me here, I'll find an apartment in Reno."

"No," he sighed, "you can stay here if you want." He got up and moved across the room like an old, old man. "I'm going to bed."

Judith put her hands to her face, and tears ran

between her fingers. Her mother, commiserating, patted her on the back. "There, there, darling. Things will work out in time."

But it was her father's comfort Judith wanted. She loved him more than anyone, and she'd lost him. Nothing would ever be the same between them again.

CHAPTER

7

Lake Tahoe, which to the Indians means "lake in the sky," lies in a geological bowl east of the main Sierra crest at an elevation of more than six thousand feet. It is twenty-two miles long, twelve miles wide and is famed for its spectacular scenery. The state line runs arrow-straight through the length of the lake, allocating two-thirds of it to California and one-third to Nevada. This sliver of deep-blue lake, mountain peaks, granite outcroppings, and forests of red fir, lodgepole pine, and aspen is the only portion of the Sierra range in Nevada. But the Silver State makes the most of its gorgeous segment.

Along the forested eastern shores of the lake; back from its sandy beaches, wave-washed cliffs, and sheltered coves; near the trout streams and the shrubs of green manzanita, bush chinquapin, and huckleberry oak; and among meadows that are laced with lupine, buttercup, red maids, and cream sacs are colonies of gambling casinos that divert their clientele from disturbing the deer, mountain coyotes, and wolverines. Californians, who jam these gambling houses, wouldn't dream of spoiling their side of the lake with casinos; instead, they expand their lake-shore towns into an urban sprawl and build freeways through the forests.

Lyle drove one of the company's station wagons along the winding highway on the shore of Lake Tahoe and listened to the two girls on the seat beside him exchange news about their mutual friends. Except for her lightened hair, Lea looked strangely demure and plain beside Barrett's radiant beauty. If he didn't know that she was a famous entertainer, Lyle would have guessed that Lea was a librarian or a secretary. She seemed subdued, as if something were bothering her.

Lea *was* subdued. In spite of being with her two old friends, it was an effort to keep her mind on the conversation. Deep inside she felt a foreboding, an uneasiness, as if Otto Schroeder would accost her at every turn. She knew she was being foolish, but her mind went back to Tony Rizzi the day before, when she'd taken him to lunch at the Hotel Mapes.

"I'm scared spitless, Tony. Isn't that ridiculous? What could Otto Schroeder do to me, anyway?"

Tony had twirled his wineglass in his plump fingers. "I'm sorry I sent you that wire, honey. I think it was a false alarm. I don't believe Otto was released from prison after all. At least, he never showed up here. I got a grapevine you wouldn't believe. If he registers in a hotel, motel, or rooming house, I'll know it. No matter what he does, I'll hear about it. If he gambles or goes to a bar, I'll know it, and I'll phone you right away. I've got the numbers of Starr's Tahoe Resort and his house right here in my wallet. Don't you worry. I'll get the word to you, and you can hire a bodyguard. There's lots of security officers at the Tahoe casinos. They'll take care of you. You don't have a thing to worry about, not a thing."

But despite his reassurance, she was worried.

The station wagon followed the road around a cove and up a grade to a lookout area. Lyle pulled off the highway and pointed to a large promontory. At the tip, as if rising from the lake, was a large stone house.

"That's Starpoint, where you girls will stay."

Lea gasped. "Wow! It's spectacular!"

"I imagine we can see the whole lake from there," Barrett said.

"Yes, you can," Lyle told her. "Most of it, anyway."

The architect had skillfully blended the house and its setting. The house was stone, like the boulders that thrust through the ground surrounding it, and its roof and trim matched the green conifers that grew nearby. The house might be new, but it didn't seem alien. It looked as if it belonged exactly there and would welcome the winter blizzards that whipped across the lake and sometimes formed snowpacks twenty feet deep in one of the snowiest regions on earth.

Lyle drove on, and they soon turned off the highway onto a private road. Ahead, the promontory curved inward like a scimitar, to form a sheltered cove, and a sandy beach lay between two rocky cliffs. He pointed to a boathouse at the end of a wharf. "That house is for speedboats for water-skiing and motorboats for fishing and all the paraphernalia," he explained. "The groundskeeper, Chuck Moody, has keys for everything and keeps the boats gassed up and ready for the guests here at Starpoint. There are automobiles at your disposal, as well. Chuck will act as chauffeur if you want. And for you, too, Barrett."

She laughed. "I've never had it so good."

"I'd like to try water-skiing," Lea said.

"Sure—Chuck will run a speedboat for you anytime. Just *don't* break a leg." Lyle grinned at her. "That's all we need, just before your opening."

"I won't, I promise."

"There's a tennis court," Lyle went on, "and an indoor, heated pool for guests all year round."

He stopped in front of Starpoint, helped the girls out of the station wagon and opened the tailgate to get the luggage. "I'll show you around and introduce you to the staff. Then we'll go to the resort."

"How much help do you have here?" Barrett asked as she picked up one of her suitcases.

"Well, there's Chuck, of course. And the housekeeper, Mrs. Skowronek. She does the cooking, too—including some great Polish dishes. And there's a maid, Elaine Smith. The three of them live here on the premises. Mrs. Skowronek brings in day help as she needs it. Depends on who's here. Janitors come from the resort once a month to do the heavy work."

The door opened and a pleasant-looking woman came out. "Good morning."

"Hi! This is Mrs. Skowronek, our excellent housekeeper. This is Miss Barrett Starr, who'll be our hostess for the summer, and this is our about-to-be headliner, Miss Lea Turner," Lyle said.

As Barrett led the way into the house after the introductions, she wondered if the servants would resent her, but Mrs. Skowronek said, "I'm mighty glad to have someone in the family here. Sometimes these entertainers get pretty wild and I'm at a loss to know what to do. We can wait on them and all that, but it's not my place to object to the things they do. They'll think twice with you around, Miss Starr."

"Well, I can try."

"You can suggest that they move over to the

resort," Lyle said. "We've got security officers there, if they get spaced out or something."

Lea laughed. "Well, you won't have any trouble with me. When I'm putting on two shows a night and three over the weekend, I'm too tired to do much partying."

Lyle nodded. "Actually, I don't think it's the entertainers who cause the trouble. It's the entourage they bring with them."

"You're right, Mr. Starr," the housekeeper agreed. "There sure are some weird ones."

Lea clapped her hands in surprise and walked into the living room. "Look at that view!" For the first time, she seemed genuinely animated. "I'd forgotten how beautiful Tahoe is." She stood at the floor-to-ceiling windows and looked across the wide redwood decks and the glass-smooth lake to the mountains on the west side. "It's so lovely."

Lyle opened a glass door, and they stepped out on the deck. "From here you can see the length of Tahoe."

"The sunsets must be beyond description," Lea said. "How will I ever drag myself away from this spot?"

Barrett put an arm around Lea's waist. "I wish we were spending the whole summer together. Well, we'll just enjoy this as long as we can."

After a few minutes Lyle suggested, "Perhaps we'd better let Mrs. Skowronek show you the rooms she wants you to use. The headliner always gets the VIP room, so you'll get this same view, Lea."

"What a break from my usual hotel room!"

The housekeeper took them upstairs and explained, "Miss Turner will have the front bedroom and bath. Since you're going to be here all summer, Miss Starr, I've put you in the side bedroom, which

has its own private bath. It's a nice room, too, only
the view isn't quite as good."

"That will be fine. I can look at the view from
downstairs."

"We have four more bedrooms and two more baths
up here, so there's usually plenty of room. Sometimes
the entertainers bring their children, and we can
accommodate them and their nursemaids on this
floor."

The house was expensively furnished, Barrett
noticed, but there were none of the Bellingham
antiques. Everything could be replaced, which made
sense, since the place was used by outsiders as well
as the family.

Her large, cheerful bedroom looked out on the
rugged shoreline of the promontory and toward the
south end of the lake. The walls were painted a pale
yellow, except for one that was papered in a floral
pattern of burnt orange, yellow, and green, which
was repeated in the draperies, the spreads on the twin
beds, and the upholstery on a platform rocker. A
thick light-green carpet covered the floor. There were
a fruitwood desk, dressing table, and chest of
drawers, as well as ample closets and an adjoining
bath with a stall shower.

As Barrett put her suitcase on the luggage rack,
she determined to be here a long, long time. Never
again would she settle for the mediocre; she was
always going to live in luxury like this. She'd make a
place for herself in the Starr empire and truly come
into her own.

Later, after Barrett and Lea had met the young,
outgoing Chuck and the older maid, Lyle drove them
to the casino. On the way, Barrett asked, "Lyle, is
there a path through the woods, so that I could walk
to the casino from Starpoint if I wanted to?"

"Sure. It's not far. I wouldn't walk at night, though. There are plenty of cars to use."

"I won't prowl around by myself at night."

"I know *I* won't!" Lea said vehemently.

Starr's Tahoe Resort had been built in a meadow on the north edge of Stateline Village, one of the first of the lakeside gambling towns. For thousands of years before the white man came, a small tribe of Washo Indians had spent the summers in the meadow, living in bark-slab huts. While the braves hunted deer with bows and arrows under the supervision of their chief, the squaws fished for rainbow trout and gathered pine nuts, thimbleberries, currants, grasshoppers, grubs, crickets, and worms for food.

The luxurious resort, with its swimming pools, tennis courts, and parking lots, covered the meadow. The central hotel section soared twelve stories high, with exterior glass elevators racing up and down to the revolving cocktail lounge, the Constellation Room, at the top. One-story wings, extending from this tower, formed a five-point star.

The two front wings, like welcoming arms, contained the gaming rooms. Open doors on both sides made them easily accessible to the guests who came from the parking areas and to those who strolled in the center court, with its elegant landscaping, recessed benches, and dancing waters that shot upward in changing formations from a long basin.

Lyle parked the station wagon in his reserved spot and ushered the girls into one of the gaming wings. "You'll notice that everything carries out the astronomy motif. In Reno we have the Wild West theme, but that's been done so often that it hasn't much impact anymore. Here we're making the most of our name. This is the Andromeda wing."

Murals depicted the summer constellation of stars

and the Greek myth they represented, about the Ethiopian King Cepheus and his vain Queen Cassiopeia, who incurred the wrath of Neptune. To save his kingdom from disaster, the king chained his daughter, Andromeda, to a rock upon the seashore. But the hero, Perseus, saved her from being devoured by Cetus, the sea monster. A plaque explained the story to those who took respite from their gambling long enough to study the murals.

But no one in the crowded room was looking at the murals. Instead, they were yanking slot-machine handles, signaling for change girls, throwing dice or betting at the roulette and baccarat games.

Barrett looked around with mounting excitement, unable to imagine a more wonderful place, as piped-in music suffused the impressive room. The crowd seemed more affluent, better dressed and in a gayer holiday mood than patrons of the Reno casinos, perhaps because of the resort atmosphere. She felt as if she were about to embark on a whole new phase of her career. This was where she belonged! She had come into her own! She'd learn everything there was to know about the operation of this multimillion-dollar resort. She could hardly wait to begin.

"Come on," Lyle said, "I want you to meet our resident manager, Clifton McMillan. He's been with us ever since we opened, and he does an outstanding job, absolutely first rate. He graduated from Cornell University's School of Hotel Administration and went to Florida as assistant manager of a big hotel in Miami. So he's had several years' experience."

They walked through the lobby, where lines of people at the cashier counters and registration desks were checking in or out. Rows of luggage were stacked by the bellman's desk. The intercom continuously paged one person after another. People sat on divans, talking and laughing. Except for the adjoining gaming rooms, Starr's Tahoe Resort was a *grand hotel* in the Continental tradition.

Lyle took them down a corridor to a suite of offices behind the registration desks. He opened the door marked RESIDENT MANAGER and nodded at the pretty secretary in the front office. "Cliff in?"

"Yes indeed, Mr. Starr. I'll tell him you're here."

After a moment a tall, deeply tanned man of about thirty, who exuded self-confidence from his sun-streaked, wavy hair to his well-polished hand-made shoes, filled the doorway. "Hi!" He put out his hand. "I was just talking to your dad, Lyle."

Lyle introduced the girls, and Barrett liked Clifton at once. She admired a man who believed in himself, as the resident manager obviously did. He seemed fully capable of handling the multitudinous problems of such an establishment.

Clifton took them into his office, moved chairs up to his desk for them, then turned to Lea. "We are all looking forward to your show, Miss Turner," he said. "Have you seen the Celestial Room yet?"

"No, I haven't, but my agent told me how excellent your facilities are."

"They're first rate," Lyle put in. "We hired a theatrical consultant—at an astronomical sum—to assist the architect."

"Your architect built some of the best casinos in Las Vegas; so he knew what he was doing, too," Clifton said. "And since we've never had any complaints from the headliners, I'd say that they're everything you could want."

"How are the reservations going?" Lyle asked.

"Complete sellout for the entire engagement, except for a few scattered reservations on week-nights. We have a table for ten set aside for you, Miss Turner, on opening night. I thought you'd want to ask some of your old friends."

"I'm very grateful," Lea said, thinking of her mother and her mother's current husband, who would come from Los Angeles, Tony Rizzi and his wife, and others.

"Mr. Starr is bringing quite a party for the opening," Clifton said. "And, of course, there's your table, Lyle."

Lyle turned to Barrett. "I'm going to invite Judith. Why don't you join us?"

"Thank you, I'd love to. Judith and I will give you a big hand, Lea."

"I may need it."

"Oh, no, you won't." Lyle shook his head and smiled. "Everyone's delighted that you're home to perform at last. Say, Cliff, why don't you sit at our table, too? You can be Barrett's escort."

Clifton glanced at her. "Now, that's a pleasure I can't pass up!" He turned to Lyle. "Thanks, old buddy. I'll do you a favor sometime in return."

The color rose in Barrett's cheeks. "Honestly, Lyle—don't put him on such a spot. Perhaps Clifton has a wife or someone else he'd like to bring."

"I'm free as a bird. Besides, we should get better acquainted." He leaned toward her. "Mr. Starr says you're willing to help us out in the office this summer."

"I want all the experience I can get," Barrett said, smiling at him. "I hope I'll earn a letter of recommendation from you, because I'll be job hunting in New York this fall."

Clifton picked up a pencil and rolled it between his hands. "You shouldn't have any trouble. I have a friend in a big cosmetics firm who could find a place for you. You might contact him this fall."

"Thank you. Cosmetics would be a good field for a woman."

"In the meantime we'll put you to work here. Mr.

Starr says you're to be on the payroll, so we'll have you fill out a form tomorrow."

"I didn't expect to be paid."

"I have my instructions from the boss, Miss Starr."

She shrugged. "Well, all right. I can always use the money, of course. Uncle Justin is awfully generous. But call me Barrett, Clifton."

"Thanks, I will."

As they glanced at each other, a current of attraction passed between them. What an interesting summer this will be, Barrett told herself.

Then Clifton turned to Lea. "Would you like to see the setup now, Miss Turner? I think they're through rehearsing in there."

"While you're showing the girls around," Lyle said, "I'll dash up to my office and take care of a couple of things, because I'm flying to Hawaii tomorrow. Bring everybody up there when you're through."

The Celestial Room, the main theater-restaurant for the headliners, was in the center of the star, facing the lake. The huge room held twelve hundred guests at a time, at tables on the main floor and in series of horseshoe-shaped booths that rose tier upon tier so that all the diners could see the stage. A star-filled ceiling with the signs of the zodiac in a muted frieze around the walls carried out the silver, light-blue, and white color scheme. A crew of workmen were vacuuming the thick blue carpet, while waitresses set the tables for the dinner performance that evening.

As they stood at the maître d's desk, Clifton explained, "This room is especially well planned. Some entrances and exits open right onto the parking lots, so we can use them if necessary. Otherwise, we bring the crowds through the casino wings. Of course, that's the whole point, to get the patrons to gamble while they're here. And most of them do."

He took them backstage and showed Lea the elaborate equipment for lighting effects, scenery changes, and the panel for the sound system. "We have a well-trained crew, who'll work with your people; so you don't have to worry about the mechanics of your show."

"It looks first rate," Lea said as she shook her head in amazement. "I seldom have a chance to work in a place that has all the latest equipment." Underlying her enthusiasm was the persistent feeling of uneasiness. She wished she could snap out of this ridiculous mood. It was only a week before her opening. This was to be her triumph. She couldn't let an ancient fear spoil everything for her. Besides, Tony thought it was a false alarm. Otto Schroeder hadn't been seen in Reno, so he must still be in prison.

For half an hour Otto Schroeder had been standing in the long line in the corridor, tired and impatient with the slow progress to the box office. Apparently every joker in the country wanted to go to Lea Turner's show. He'd heard that only a few seats were left, and if he wanted one, he'd have to stand in line to get it. He glanced at his watch; it was nearly noon, and he was getting hungry. At least he had plenty of time, for he usually worked the swing shift from four to twelve-thirty, with a half hour off for dinner. His schedule was crazy as hell, but he didn't mind.

As he'd figured, it had been easy to get hired as a pantry helper at Starr's. Someone had quit the very same day he applied. And he had ninety days on "temporary" before he had to join the union. He'd be gone before that. The work wasn't too bad: scraping and stacking dishes in the stainless-steel dishwashers. No worse than a lot of things he'd done in prison for five years. He always reported on time, worked fast and carefully and kept his mouth shut.

He fingered his employee's badge with the name "Owen Shulman," which entitled him to a discount at the show. As the line moved ahead, he played the slot machines on the way. They didn't miss a trick, he thought: wherever there was a queue, there were also slot machines, ready to grab a person's dough.

When three people emerged from a door near the box office, he recognized the top boss, Clifton McMillan. With him was the most beautiful brunette he'd ever seen. Wow, what a broad! Must be one of the showgirls. The other girl was a blonde, but she couldn't hold a candle to the brunette. Then, with a shock, he recognized Lea Turner. For a moment he froze. She passed within inches of him, and he smelled her perfume. But she didn't see him; her head was turned toward the resident manager.

She was here already! It hit him like a blow to the solar plexis, and as he stared after her, hatred surged inside him. Just wait, Lea Turner! Just wait!

The elevator whisked them to the eleventh floor, and they walked down the corridor to the executive suite. Gold lettering on the door read, STARR ENTERPRISES, INC., and below, in smaller letters, "Justin Starr, President," and "Lyle Starr, Vice-President." Barrett could almost see her own name on the door. When they stepped into an outer office, a middle-aged secretary stopped typing and looked up and smiled. "Mr. Starr said to go right in."

The suite, two private offices, occupied one corner of the eleventh floor, and when they went into Lyle's richly paneled office, Barrett caught her breath. It was a large corner room with huge glass windows on each side. The deep orange-gold carpeting blended with the paneling, the walnut furniture, the brown leather chairs, and the open-weave, wheat-hued draperies.

"What a beautiful office!" Barrett exclaimed. "You must want to spend all of your time here." Except in her dreams, she'd never been in such a sumptuous office.

Lyle nodded. "I much prefer it to the one I have in Reno. Dad insisted that I take this corner office, since I'm here much more than he is. We each have a bedroom and bath as part of the suite, so we can stay here if we want, which is particularly convenient in the winter."

Lea stepped toward the window. "How do you get your work done, with this view of the lake and the mountains?"

"Speaking of views—come out on my eagle's aerie." Lyle opened a sliding glass door in the west wall, and they stepped onto a balcony. "It's the only balcony on the building, because of the heavy snow in the winter, and it's painted to match the wall so it can't be noticed from below."

Barrett didn't hear the others. Trying to contain her sense of exultation, she grasped the railing and looked down the side of the building to the pointed wings, far below, that housed the Celestial Room, the kitchens, the restaurants, and the gaming rooms. Her gaze traveled from the parking lots, where the cars appeared small and the people insignificant, to the deep woods on one side and the village on the other, then westward to the cross-shaped snowbank on the side of Mount Tallac and, finally, over the length and breadth of Lake Tahoe.

CHAPTER

8

The next morning, the rehearsal began promptly at nine. As usual, there was the confusion of the first workout on an unfamiliar stage, where everyone felt ill at ease. The backup singers huddled in one group; the dancers, in another group, lined up near their male lead, who was also the choreographer; the stagehands waited at their stations in bored resignation; musicians, on risers across the back of the stage, tuned their instruments, then blew in the mouthpieces while they flipped through the sheet music the arranger had given them and adjusted their chairs. Lea, dressed like the others, in faded jeans and a tank top, stood beside Vicky at one side of the stage.

"What's the matter with you?" Vicky snapped as she looked her charge up and down. "I expected you to be flying high after seeing all your friends. Why so down in the mouth?"

"I'll tell you later," Lea whispered. "I don't want to talk about it now."

"OK, but don't let your grumps spoil the rehearsal.

Tiger Paws is in a foul mood this morning; he lost a bundle gambling last night." She nodded toward the music director, who crossed the stage and stopped at a mike at front center.

"Attention, please. Let's make the most of our time this morning and not goof off. First, we're going to run through the entire show. It'll be rough, but let's get the feel of the whole production first. I want to get the pace and timing worked out and try out the lighting effects." The Celestial Room, enormous, empty, and dimly lighted, echoed his words. "Vicky, you go to the back of the dining room and listen to the sound. Stand in several spots and make a note of any changes that are needed. The sound panel will be adjusted the way you want it."

Finally, when the rehearsal got under way, Lea pushed her worries aside and threw herself into her performance. For the last four years, Vicky had pounded into her, "You're the headliner, and you set the standard. If you give a half-assed performance, don't expect more from the others, because you won't get it."

The orchestra, stagehands, sound technician and lighting crew, perched in ceiling-high booths at the back of the dining room, were employed by Starr's and worked under the direction of its stage manager, who coordinated their efforts with the performers'. They worked very hard all morning. Still, Lea was grateful that they had a whole week to rehearse. They'd put the show together in San Francisco, but the numbers had been practiced separately, without the props, the lights, and the costumes. Of course, throughout the upcoming week the director would tear his hair and declare that he'd never worked with such clods; the choreographer would make a dozen changes; the wardrobe mistress would burst into tears; Vicky would get more sarcastic; and they'd twist ankles, bump heads and skin elbows. But somehow, as always, they'd smooth and polish until a finished production was ready for opening night.

When the first rehearsal was over, the choreographer took Lea and Vicky backstage and said, "Here's the rocket for the 'Love Sends Me to the Stars' number. It's not attached to the overhead track yet, but we'll get the crew to set it up so you can rehearse with it."

Lea looked the rocket over and said, "It's so much bigger than I expected. It must be six or seven feet long."

"Well, we had to make it big enough so you could dance on it yet small enough that it could be whirled around in the air. It shoots a stream from the tail, so that it looks like a rocket blasting off. The prop people did a great job with it."

Vicky inspected the heavy wires that were attached to the rocket. "Looks like you've got some kind of harness arrangement in there with the other wires."

"That's right." The choreographer, slender and lithe as a girl, stepped on top of the rocket. "When the backup dancers are doing their introduction and the spotlights are on them, you get up here on the rocket, Lea. Then you slip your arms through the wire harness, like this. Then you grasp the two ends of this belt and snap them together, just like a seat belt." He demonstrated the procedure, then said, "Here, you try it." Lea took his place, and he went on, "This harness has a separate attachment to the track overhead; so you'll be perfectly safe."

Vicky laughed. "Well, if the rocket blasts off from underneath you, you can float around like Peter Pan or Mary Poppins."

Lea shook her head. "I sure hope I won't look stupid."

"You'll look great. The harness will be covered with

cloth to match your costume. The audience won't notice it. The wires will be sprayed with black paint, so they can't be seen against the dark background." The choreographer unbuckled the harness and helped her down. "We'll rehearse it a lot, so that it'll be OK."

Vicky glanced at her watch, then took Lea's arm. "Come on. I ordered lunch to be brought to the dressing room about now."

As they ate cheeseburgers and coleslaw in the star's spacious dressing room, Vicky said, "You'll have costume fittings this afternoon. Then you're free to swim or whatever. And now out with it. Tell me what's the matter."

"I'm scared, Vicky, that's what's the matter. I'm just plain scared." Lea told her manager about the telegram from Tony Rizzi and her luncheon conversation with him. "Tony said he'd warn me and all that. I suppose I'm too uptight, but I just can't help worrying."

Vicky pawed through her purse and found a package of cigarettes. "Of course, this all happened before my time with you; so I can't judge how serious this threat is."

Lea sipped her coffee. "At least you're not laughing at me."

"Of course I'm not. I suppose we could hire bodyguards, but that would set off a lot of rumors and give the gossip columnists something to chew over. That's all some spaced-out freak would need to set him off. It'd give him ideas he didn't have before."

"I suppose so."

Vicky exhaled a large cloud of smoke and waved it away from Lea. "Of course, I'll be with you during the day, and I'll watch you like a hawk. A lot of other people will be around, too. At night you'll be at Starpoint with your friend Barrett Starr."

Lea finished her coleslaw and wished she had a big

bowl of chocolate ice cream, but didn't dare ask for it. "There's a young man who takes care of the boats and grounds at Starpoint," she said. "I could get Barrett to ask him to sleep inside the house."

"Why don't you do that, lamb? Tell him that sometimes your fans get too troublesome and you'd like the protection of a man. But don't make a big thing out of it. And for heaven's sake, don't worry anymore."

"I'll try not to." Lea knew, even as she said them, that the words were meaningless, for deep inside her fear lay coiled like a taut spring.

Saturday morning, while Lea was rehearsing, Barrett reported to Clifton's office, where his secretary greeted her enthusiastically. "I'm sure glad to have some help, Miss Starr. I was sick a few days and had to take some time off. Now I'm terribly behind. By the way, my name is Shirley, Shirley Denton."

"And I'm Barrett." She looked around the office and saw only one desk. "Where do you want me to work?"

"Mr. McMillan suggested that you use Mr. Justin Starr's office, since he doesn't come in too often and since you're one of the family. Besides, you'll just be here for the summer. Let's take the work up there and get you started." They rode in the elevator, each loaded down with folders and paper. "I usually work only half a day on Saturday," Shirley said, "but I've got to get caught up, so I'm staying most of the afternoon."

"Between the two of us, we'll soon get everything squared away," Barrett said. "I haven't anything special to do, so I'll stay, too. I expect to be a jack-of-all-trades this summer and fill in wherever I'm needed."

"How great for us!"

When they arrived at the executive suite, the secretary had left, but Shirley had a master key. They found an extra typewriter on a table, pushed it into Justin's office, and in no time Barrett was hard at work.

Around eleven o'clock the telephone rang; it was Clifton. "Sorry I was out of the office when you arrived, but there was a commotion on the eighth floor. One of the guests had a heart attack during the night, and the maid discovered his body this morning."

"How ghastly!" After a moment she said: "Shirley took care of me. I'm plugging away in Uncle Justin's office, trying not to look at the lake."

"I wouldn't blame you if you did. Say, I was wondering if you'd have lunch with me."

"I'd love to."

"They have a great buffet at the Constellation Room at noon. I'll meet you there just before twelve."

"Fine."

As Barrett replaced the phone, she wondered where this would lead. Would it be a mistake to be too friendly with the resident manager? Later, however, as she faced Clifton across a small table at a window in the slowly revolving room, she decided it could be quite interesting to know him better, for he was a charming man with a cultured voice. Although he wasn't really handsome, he was very attractive, with a certain air or presence—as if he were always in command of any situation. He'd have to be, with all the employees at Starr's and its thousands of guests. Not a day would pass without decisions to be made or crises to be faced.

She twirled her cocktail glass, looked out at the lake—as smooth as if it were covered with a sheet of ice—then turned back to Clifton. "How have you enjoyed your year here at Starr's?"

"It's been a great experience. A hotel man doesn't often get a chance to open a resort, especially one like this, and he should have that hectic but wonderful opportunity at least once in his career. Of course, I thought I'd go bananas before we got everything functioning smoothly, but we finally did."

"I'm looking forward to being here this summer. I'm sure I'll learn management practices that will be valuable in whatever position I find this fall."

"I hope you do. Feel free to go into every department. We'll all help you." He studied her with his intelligent brown eyes. "I understand you want to have a business career."

"Yes. In spite of the fact that we women have a lot of strikes against us, I think I can succeed. I have as much executive ability as most men."

"I'm sure you have. As I said yesterday, you'd be great in the cosmetics field, or in women's wear or merchandising. There are some very successful women in the hotel and motel business, too. Of course, there are lots of businesses where your sex would be an asset instead of a handicap."

"Just don't mention modeling or entertainment. I have no talent there, and besides I wouldn't want it."

He laughed. "I don't *dare* mention teaching or being a librarian or a nurse."

"No, it's the business world for me, whether it wants me or not."

"You have a real booster in your uncle. Isn't Justin Starr about the greatest man you've ever met? I admire him for the success he's made of himself. He showed me a picture of the little saloon where he started with nothing. He barely could pay his bills at first. No training, no backing, but now look at him. It's an incredible story."

"I know. He's a man after my own heart. He has so much on the ball, and he built his fortune through his own efforts. I wish my father had had a little of

his drive and ability. Twenty years ago he was offered
a chance to go in with Uncle Justin, and he turned it
down."

Clifton shook his head. "You're kidding! That was
before Lyle's time, too. Well, Mr. Starr has ended up
with a fine son in him."

They watched the scenic panorama slowly change
as the room turned from the lake to the village, then
to the mountains in the back, to the cove and Starpoint, and finally to the lake again. They helped
themselves at the buffet, and when they were finished
eating, Clifton said, "We'll have to do this often, Barrett. I hope we see a lot of each other this summer."

She smiled at him. "I'm sure we will, especially
since I was foisted on you by my relatives. Anyway,
thank you for this lovely lunch."

He reached across the table and took her hand. "I
mean *after* work hours, Barrett." Admiration for her
shone in his eyes. Her heart lurched a little, and her
cheeks flushed. She was all too aware of his touch.

After she returned to Justin's office and had settled
down to work again, she thought about Clifton. He
had a dynamic, virile appeal—no question about that.
Before she could develop the thought, however, the
telephone rang.

"Barrett? This is Judith Davenport."

"Judith! How wonderful to hear your voice. I've
been planning to get in touch with you. How are you?"

"OK, I guess. Lyle told me you were coming to
Tahoe—and Lea, too."

"Lea sure looks great. She's been rehearsing for her
opening. Say, we ought to have a reunion. Could you
possibly come up here? We ought to get together before she opens."

"I can come anytime—the sooner the better."

"Jump in your car and come up this afternoon.

Plan to stay with us at Starpoint. There's loads of room."

"Could I? God, things are tight around here! I'd love to get away—especially this weekend while my folks are here at Sage Creek."

"Well, come right along. I'll see you soon. It'll be marvelous to have a real visit again."

As she replaced the receiver, Barrett felt a wave of sympathy for Judith. How hard it must be to go through a divorce. It confirmed Barrett's vow not to rush into marriage. She telephoned Starpoint and told Mrs. Skowronek about Judith's visit and then phoned Lea's dressing room. "I hope it's OK with you. I thought Judith needed to be with old friends for the weekend."

"I can hardly wait to see her!" Then Lea lowered her voice. "She's not the only one, however, who needs her friends."

As Barrett put down the phone, she wondered about Lea and the desperation in her voice. What was wrong? She wasn't acting like a radiant superstar who had come home to a triumphant welcome. Was she heartsick over some broken romance? Or disappointed in her career? How could she be? She was on the top now. Perhaps they'd have a group therapy session. If Lea and Judith could let their hair down with anyone, it would be when the three of them got together.

Late in the afternoon, Barrett replaced the cover over the typewriter, put her work in an empty drawer and, after locking the office, went to Lea's dressing room. Lea was standing on a low stool while a Chinese woman pinned a costume together.

"Hi, Barrett! This is Opal Fong, our wardrobe mistress—my friend Barrett Starr. Poor Opal nearly blows her mind before every opening."

"And during a show, too. Lea's hard on her

costumes. And so are the others. The costumes get torn or ripped or dirty." Opal laughed. "If this girl wasn't so sweet, I'd refuse to go on tour with her and her company."

"I don't blame you for getting uptight with us, Opal. But this is enough for today. I've *had* it. We can finish Monday."

"All right, all right! Now, stand still, you wiggly girl, so the pins won't scratch you."

Opal carefully pulled the costume over Lea's head, leaving her slender body naked except for bikini briefs. Lea pulled on her tank top and faded jeans and brushed at her hair. "I'm a mess, and I'm dog tired, too. I hope we can cut out of here without being stopped by some fans or reporters."

Barrett opened the dressing-room door and pointed to an emergency exit. "I'll go get the car and pull up right outside. You come dashing out. Give me just a couple minutes."

When they arrived at Starpoint, Judith's car was parked in front and Judith was waiting for them at the door. "Hi!" she said. "I just got here." The girls greeted each other jubilantly.

"Let's go to my room," Lea suggested. "I've got to take a shower and get into something else. These are my working clothes."

On the way upstairs, Barrett asked, "What do you gals want to do tonight? Go to a show? Stay here and talk? What?"

"Stay here!" both girls cried in unison. "We've got *five years* to catch up on," Lea said. "I can think of nothing I'd rather do than just sit on the deck and talk."

"I'm sure Mrs. Skowronek will serve drinks and dinner out on the deck, but I'll ask her." Barrett started back down the stairs.

Lea called after her. "Find out if she has some chocolate ice cream. That's what I want for dessert. My manager isn't here, so I can celebrate."

Later, the three girls stretched out on chaises in a sheltered area of the deck with tall, ice-filled glasses of vodka and tonic. Lea, fresh and lovely after her shower, wore a white caftan trimmed in gold and sandals with metallic thongs. Barrett had changed to an apricot jersey jumpsuit that brought out her natural skin tones. Of the three, Barrett was the true beauty, but Judith was breathtakingly attractive when she wasn't depressed.

"Of course," she said frankly, "you know from Lyle that I couldn't hack it with Murray any longer. What you don't know is that he's a homosexual—has been for years. I never suspected it when he was at the university and we were all running around together. Did either of you?"

Both shook their heads in surprise, and Judith told them about her final weeks with Murray. Then she sighed. "The hard part is that although Murray and I are satisfied that it's all for the best and we've agreed to the terms of the divorce, my father is livid about the whole thing. He can't forgive me for leaving Murray now that he's a paraplegic. He says it's my 'sacred duty' to stay with him. It's caused a terrible rift between us." Her chin trembled and tears flooded her eyes.

"But how could you stay, when the Rosenfelds and Murray himself asked you to get lost?" Barrett asked.

They discussed Judith's situation and decided that she'd done the right thing, in spite of Murray's disability and her father's views.

"I'm going to stay at Sage Creek for the next six weeks, while I establish my Nevada residency again. I'm terribly mixed up. I want to be there; yet I don't

want to be there. When I'm divorced, I don't know what I'll do. Get a job? Go back to school? I've got to get some direction in my life."

Barrett looked at her friend with compassion. "Judith, you're just going through a tough period of adjustment and upheaval right now. You'll soon get it all together and know what you want to do. Remember, you can always dash up here to Tahoe and stay with me when your folks are home. As the official hostess here for the summer, I'm running Starpoint, and you have a standing invitation to come anytime."

"Thanks, Barrett. I'll do that. Don't think I won't."

They watched the sun sink behind a mountain peak on the other side of the lake as the sky turned pink and lavender.

Then Lea sighed and spoke up. "All God's chilluns got problems. Since we're baring our souls—but let this die with you—I'm scared stiff." She told them about Otto's threats after Kirt's death and the rumor that he was out of prison. "I keep expecting him to leap out from the bushes and shoot me."

Judith shook her head. "I remember Otto well. If he's out of prison and is really after you, he won't try to shoot you. He's too smart for that. He'll think up some very clever plan, where no one will suspect him."

CHAPTER

9

Monday morning, Justin Starr sat at the massive desk in his Reno office, reading a preliminary report of corporate earnings. He started to ring for Lyle, then remembered he was still in Hawaii. In a way, he regretted that they were leaving their home corral and branching out in Hawaii. It seemed so alien and strange, with all those hula dancers and palm trees. Right here was his world—actually, this city block, bounded by Virginia Street, East Second, Center, and Commercial Row. Of course, now there were casinos all over, but this was his bailiwick, right here. This and Tahoe.

Still, he couldn't alienate Lyle. The boy was so eager to take on this Hawaiian project. He'd been itching to go in that direction for a long time. Better to give the lad a little rope than lose him altogether. Damn it, Lyle was his son legally, but he'd always be a Bellingham. He was not, and never would be, a real gambling man. Justin had never seen an expression on Lyle's face like the one on Barrett's face the other morning. The Starr blood flowed in *her* veins, all right.

He drummed his blunt, heavy fingers on his desk. What would happen when he died? he wondered. What would Lyle do? Would he sell this casino and the Tahoe resort—sell the life's work into which Justin had poured all his strength and dreams, his very guts? His heart sank. He was willing to bet the million dollars or so they always kept in the vault downstairs that that's exactly what Lyle would do. He would sell off everything to some huge conglomerate and invest the whole Starr fortune in California and Hawaii. The very thought of it made Justin feel sick.

And Eunice wouldn't waste any time clearing out, either. She'd sell the house and buy a big apartment in one of those high-rise condominiums in San Francisco, as some of her upper-crust friends from the peninsula had done. She'd move her servants and her fancy furniture there and probably take back her old name and be Eunice Bellingham again. He shook his head sadly. Things never worked out the way he wanted.

His secretary spoke over the intercom. "A Mr. James Nichols to see you, Mr. Starr. He has an appointment."

Oh, yes—that writer fellow who wanted to interview him. He put the report away, glad to be interrupted. Maybe he'd shake off his blues.

James Nichols was a big, well-built man who peered through his horn-rimmed glasses with the knowing, almost cynical eyes of a newspaperman. "I appreciate this interview, Mr. Starr, for the article I'm doing on gambling in Nevada. It wouldn't be complete without a statement from you. Do you mind if I use a tape recorder?"

"Not at all. Sit down, Mr. Nichols. Make yourself comfortable. I suppose you've already been in Las Vegas."

"Yes, I spent a couple weeks there, gathering material."

Justin opened his desk and took out a folder. "I had my publicity department prepare some information for you, and here are some pictures for you to look over. Use any of them you want."

The writer glanced at the prepared material. "I'll keep all of them for now and return what I can't use. I'll want to take some of my own pictures, too. Now, shall we begin?"

He had the insatiable curiosity of the true journalist and asked pointed, searching questions. When the interview was completed, Justin turned the tables. He took a sheet from the folder and studied it. "This is quite a resumé on you, Mr. Nichols, that my publicity department prepared. You sure have a lot of credits. You were a reporter for several years, I see."

"I was with the *Chicago Tribune* for a while, and then I went to Washington as White House correspondent for the *New York Times*. I wrote a biography of Lyndon Johnson that was very successful. In fact, it hit the best-seller list. I've been free-lancing ever since, doing articles and nonfiction books."

Justin studied the sheet. "So I see. You've had articles in *Reader's Digest, Playboy, Saturday Evening Post, Holiday, Atlantic Monthly*—all the big magazines. And you've written a lot of books."

"Yes, I've had six books published. Actually, I prefer writing books to articles, especially biographies. In fact, as I was driving up here from Las Vegas, I was thinking what a fantastic subject you'd be for a biography. You're a real legend, a regular Horatio Alger."

Surprised, Justin sat back in his chair. "You mean people would actually want to read about me? About what I've done?"

"Of course they would. You're one of the most colorful characters in the West. It could be more than just a biography, too—sort of a history of gambling in Reno and Tahoe. You've been part of it right from the start—you, Raymond and Harold Smith, and Bill Harrah." The journalist leaned forward, his face alive with enthusiasm. "I can see a chapter on how you compare gambling here with gambling in Las Vegas. It's different somehow."

"Well, of course, Vegas gets most of its crowd from around Los Angeles. Our customers come from northern California, and they're a different breed."

"One could go into the difference in real depth," Nichols said. "You know, I was thinking how great it would be to paraphrase Mark Twain's *Connecticut Yankee in King Arthur's Court*. If you went to Europe and looked over Monte Carlo, it'd be "The Nevada Gambler in Prince Rainier's Court" sort of thing. You could also visit the casinos along the Adriatic coast in Yugoslavia and put in your reactions to the gambling there and how it differs from Reno."

"That's quite an idea." Justin chuckled. "If you don't look out, you'll be talking yourself into another book."

"I'm afraid I already have—if you're willing, of course. I wouldn't want to do it without your full cooperation, Mr. Starr. I never do anything halfway."

"You're really serious about this, Mr. Nichols?"

"I sure am. That is, if you're willing to work with me—let me interview you and all that."

"You'd have to stay here in Reno awhile. Where do you live?"

"In New York usually, but I have no ties. I'm divorced, and my kids are grown. I can live anywhere. In fact, I sublet my apartment to a friend and came out to the West Coast for six months or a year to do some writing. I can stay however long it takes to get a good book out. I know my publisher'll go for it. How about it?"

"Well, I guess it's all right with me." Inwardly Justin was pleased and flattered. "Of course, I'd reserve the right to approve the manuscript. I don't want to look like a damn fool."

"Of course not. But it would have to be an honest, probing biography, done in depth. Or it could be an autobiography—one of those 'as told to' books. You could use a tape recorder and tell everything you can recall, and I'd write it up. I would interview you and plan the book from your memories."

"I like that idea. I'd have more control over what went in. Again, I don't want to look foolish."

"Fine. Both of our names could appear on the cover as authors. That way we'd also have the advantage of my reputation and readership."

"Of course. You're the well-known writer. I couldn't write a book if my life depended on it."

"Nor could I build a gambling empire, Mr. Starr." Nichols smiled. "Perhaps you'll want your legal department to draw up a contract between us—a working agreement so we both have our interests protected and avoid misunderstandings."

"That would be wise." Justin nodded. His name on the cover of a book! As a coauthor, too. Wouldn't that be something!

"Well, I won't take any more of your time, Mr. Starr. I'm going to look for an apartment and settle in for a while. I've got to find a place to write. Sometimes, if I'm really going good, I sit up all night and bang the typewriter. You can't do that in a motel."

Justin leaned forward eagerly. "Hell, if you need a place to write, we could give you a room here. We're in business twenty-four hours a day, you know; we never close. The restaurants and bars are open day and night; so you could always get something to eat and drink. Your typing wouldn't disturb a soul. Our walls are so soundproof you can't hear a thing from another room."

The writer's expression showed surprise and gratitude. "Say, that would be great! And I'd be right here when we get started on the book. Any cubbyhole will do. It doesn't have to be anything fancy."

"I know just the place for you. Come on, I'll show you."

They took the elevator to the third floor and stepped into a corridor with closed doors along its length. "Here's where we have private gaming rooms for our high rollers and celebrities." Justin opened a door to a room across from the elevator, in which there were a roulette wheel, a 21 table and a crap table. "I'll have this stuff moved out and a desk, chairs, and filing cabinet brought in for you. We'll get a phone installed, too."

Astonished, Nichols looked around the large room, with its thick burnt-orange carpeting, vertical blinds at the windows, and a large painting of a bucking horse and rodeo rider on a wall.

"Oh, Mr. Starr, please don't give up one of your private gaming rooms for me. I don't need anything as plush as this. Christ, I'm an old newspaperman. You ought to see some of the closets I've written in. I don't want to put you out."

"You're not putting me out. I insist that you use this room. It'll be ready for you tomorrow."

"This is terrific, but surely you'll let me pay rent for this room."

"No, that'll be part of the agreement we work out —the use of this room. Just write a good book about me."

"I'm sure I will—*we* will." They shook hands. "I'll find an apartment now and get unpacked."

"Some of the hotels have furnished apartments for the well-heeled divorcées."

"I'll find something and be back tomorrow to get started on my article. When that's finished, we can get going on the book. Meanwhile, let's try to think of a good title—something that'll grab the readers."

As soon as Nichols left, Justin returned to his office, called in his chief custodian and gave orders to have the third-floor room cleared at once and put in readiness for the writer. Then he made a telephone call. "This is Justin Starr. I have a rush order, here at Starr's, and I wonder if you can take care of it right away. I need a name lettered in gold on a door. I'll pay extra if you have someone do it today."

"Of course, Mr. Starr. We're happy to oblige you. I'll be there myself this afternoon."

"Fine. Report to my office when you arrive."

That afternoon, Justin took the sign painter to the door on the third floor, gave him a slip of paper with printed letters and explained just how he wanted the job done. He watched as the man prepared the surface, made his measurements, drew his guidelines and started to work.

All the VIPs stepped off this elevator on their way to gamble, Justin told himself—big entertainers, prominent men and women from all over the world, famous athletes, statesmen, politicians, scientists, great musicians. This door would be the first thing they'd see. Everybody had heard of James Nichols, the famous writer. He was right up there at the top. By God, he'd give the casino some class!

Intense satisfaction rose in Justin Starr as the letters took shape:

JAMES NICHOLS, WRITER IN RESIDENCE

CHAPTER

10

Meanwhile, at Tahoe, Barrett sought out Red O'Donnell, chief of casino security, in his first-floor office. When she introduced herself, the big, redheaded ex-cop put out a freckled hand. "Mr. Starr telephoned me the other day and said you were to have the run of the place while you're here this summer. I'll be glad to show you around."

She smiled. "I'd love to see your 'eye in the sky' security system. Uncle Justin was telling me about it. But first I want to ask a favor of you. Will you keep a special eye on Lea Turner? She's rehearsing here, and she'll be our headliner in the Celestial Room for two weeks, beginning Friday night."

"Of course. But we look after all the entertainers. What's the problem?"

"Nothing special." Barrett remembered Lea's warning to keep her fears of Otto in confidence. "She's my best friend; we went to high school together in Reno. It's just that sometimes her fans get a little obnoxious, especially the males."

The security officer nodded. "You're right. Some of them get a few drinks in them and think they're Don Juans."

"Another thing. Could one of your men drive her to Starpoint each night after the last performance? Or should I arrange for a chauffeur?"

"One of my men'll take care of that." O'Donnell grinned as if it were an assignment he'd like for himself.

"Sometimes I'll be here, or Lyle Starr, or even Uncle Justin, and we'll see to it that she gets home."

"Tell you what I'll do. I'll make a note right now, and we'll check each night before she leaves her dressing room. Then, if she has no transportation, a security man'll run her home."

"Thank you so very much." Barrett gave him her most radiant smile, which made him her slave on the spot. "Now let's see your security system, Mr. O'Donnell."

"Just call me Red; everyone does."

"All right, Red." She did not tell him to call her Barrett.

In the Andromeda Room, O'Donnell pointed to the ceiling. Every few feet, huge black mirrors were embedded in the acoustical material, forming a giant checkerboard. "Customers ask us why we have so many mirrors in the place—on the walls and in the ceiling. We tell them we have a catwalk behind those mirrors, with security men on guard all the time to look out for cheaters. The men can see right through the glass and watch whatever's going on."

"I suppose you have to be alert for con artists especially."

"You'd better believe that we have professional cheaters. 'Crossroaders' we call 'em. We want those guys to know that we have guards on duty up there all the time, watching for them. That helps to discourage them, so they don't try as much stuff on us as they do on smaller places. Come on, we'll go up on the catwalk."

They returned to the lobby, and O'Donnell opened a door that led to a metal ladder.

"Gambling is a billion-dollar legal business in this state, but it's also big business for the crossroaders. They use a lot of sophisticated methods to bilk the casinos out of at least twenty million each year."

They climbed to the overhead, between-floors catwalks. At intervals along the way, observers were stationed over various games, watching their action through the mirrors.

The security chief warmed up to his subject. "We've got over two thousand feet of catwalk across the games, cashier cages, and counting room. We keep an eye on the employees, too, and they know it. Sometimes we have a girl dealer who is 'toke hustling.' She makes sure that a good tipper wins so she'll get a big toke. We get rid of her in a hurry. We watch for anything that's against the rules. For example, some players will 'press bets,' which means that when they have what they think is a sure winning hand, they'll try to slip more money on top of the bet they have on the table. We stop that at once, I can tell you!"

"It never occurred to me that someone could do that." She had a lot to learn, she realized.

"There's lots of ways you can cheat, if you know how. The crossroaders will try anything. We also have to watch the slot machines all the time. They'll use everything, from a coin on a string to an electric drill, to coax the jackpots to line up."

They walked across the catwalks until O'Donnell led her to another area. "We have television cameras trained on all the key areas, especially the counting rooms. We make videotapes so we can recheck the counters' actions. The cameras can zoom in so close we can read the letters and numbers on a bill or take a close look at a check."

They watched while two women in the counting room sorted currency into denominations, counted it and recorded the totals. Then the money went to a third person, who recounted it and confirmed the totals.

"If I'm not boring you, I'll show you how we test our cards and dice."

"You *can't* bore me," Barrett said. "I find all this fascinating, and I'm especially interested because of my uncle and Lyle Starr."

In a few minutes they were in the testing room, which had special equipment for examining cards and dice. "This black light clearly reveals crimps or stains that a player may have put on certain cards," O'Donnell explained. "Also, we inspect the dice to see whether a corner has been dulled. Sometimes we go over them with calipers. All the decks of cards and sets of dice are kept in a vault when they aren't in use, so they can't be tampered with."

"Do you ever have anyone use loaded dice?" Barrett asked.

Red shook his head. "Very seldom, but they'll switch them on us sometimes. We have to be right on top of things all the time."

When they were through, the security chief said warmly, "Look, Miss Starr, I'm at your service anytime. If there's anything I can do to help you, just call on me."

"I will, Red, and thank you." She was glad she'd won such an ally, and she had a hunch that she might very well have to call on him.

As she took the elevator to Justin's office to finish her work for Shirley, she determined to learn about every department in the resort. The best way would be to work in each department, if possible. At times they could all use extra help, she supposed. She would try to be unobtrusive, but she wanted to know the whole operation and all the employees. She'd make herself indispensable.

The week passed quickly. Lea rehearsed every day, stood still for costume fittings and granted interviews. Late each afternoon, Barrett drove her home and they'd spend an hour or so swimming in the lake or sunbathing on the beach. Then they'd shower and dress to go to various casinos for their dinner shows.

"I like to know my competition," Lea declared the first evening. "I worked my tail off getting on top of the heap, and now I have to fight just as hard to stay there. It's not easy."

"I know what you mean—though I've never had any desire to be an entertainer. A good thing—since I have no talent in that direction."

Lea laughed. "You sure have the looks, and if you had what else it takes, you could give me a real run for my money. But it takes a lot more than beauty. It takes talent, complete dedication, and the ability to project your personality. At best, it's a heartbreaking profession, but I wouldn't be happy doing anything else. Sometimes I feel I've got a tiger by the tail."

"Are you nervous about Friday night?"

"Of course. Each time I go onstage to perform, I'm laying myself wide open. Down deep I have a terrible fear of being rejected, and I worry that the audience won't like me. I'm never certain whether I'm good enough. While I'm waiting in the dressing room, I always have butterflies in my stomach. Then, when I get in front of the audience, I just turn on. Somehow, in spite of myself, it all seems to come together."

* * *

Friday, after a dress rehearsal in the morning, Lea returned to Starpoint to rest before a beautician arrived to fix her hair. Barrett stopped work early, too.

In midafternoon, Lyle drove his Ferrari to Starpoint. Judith, sitting beside him, wore a smart yellow pantsuit and was in far better spirits. Lyle was helping Judith from the car, when he saw Barrett coming to meet them. He shouted, "How ya doing?" He, too, was in unusually good spirits.

"Just great! How did things go in Hawaii?"

Lyle rolled his eyes ecstatically and did a hula twist. "Couldn't have gone better. The deal's all sewed up. There are a lot of final steps on such a big venture, but everything's OK."

"Lyle's been telling me about it on the way," Judith said. "He says you really gave him support in convincing his father."

"I'll say you did, cousin dear." Lyle reached in the car for their luggage. "And old Justin Starr is one tough hombre to convince. He can be as stubborn as a mule."

"I'm going to turn you loose on *my* father, Barrett." Judith said. "Talk about being stubborn!"

"No, thank you; I'm not taking on Elliott Davenport. I'll confine my interference strictly to my own family!" Barrett declared, putting her arm around Judith's waist. "I'm sure glad to see you again."

As they moved toward the entrance, Lyle said, "Mom and Dad are going directly to the resort from Reno, and they'll come here afterward. We'll have quite a house party for the weekend."

"I ought to give them my room, but I'm putting you in with me, Judith, so at least the Starrs can have private baths."

"Great, but where's our poor little superstar? She must be having the last-minute shakes."

"No, she's in good shape. A hair stylist is making

her beautiful. They're in her room. Later they'll have a light supper, and then Vicky'll take her to the resort."

Around five-thirty, Clifton arrived, and the four of them had cocktails and hors d'oeuvres on the deck. He looked at Barrett approvingly and murmured, "You look so beautiful in that white dinner dress. I can hardly believe my eyes."

"Thank you. You look very fetching yourself." He *was* attractive, in his white dinner coat, dark pants, and ruffled shirt. And he had such a suave, urbane manner; his years in the hotel world had given him a special polish, Barrett decided. He was one of the most delightful men she'd ever known. How easy it would be to fall in love with him.

At the resort, they were seated at Lyle's table for ten, and his other guests soon arrived. Justin's party was seated at two tables nearby.

It was not her favorite group, Eunice told herself. She was wearing a Halston original, in a dusty-rose chiffon, and an ermine jacket. "You look lovely, as always, my dear," Justin had said earlier, as she put on her diamond pendant and earrings. "I'm sure you'll enjoy this evening. Lea Turner is first rate." But the members of their party were other gambling operators or politicians and their wives, and they didn't feel at ease with her, she knew.

She remembered once before, when they had attended an opening at another theater-restaurant, one of the operator's wives had said after five cocktails, "Eunice, you cramp my style, kid. You're much too la-de-da and upper crust. So damned refined. I can't be my usual vulgar self around you. And I'm not the only one who feels that way." Well, she wasn't comfortable with them, either. She didn't dare drink very much for fear of how she might react. She tried to laugh at their crude, dirty jokes; she struggled to find something in common to talk about. She did her best to make them feel relaxed with her, but she knew her attempts were a dismal failure. There was a gap between them she couldn't bridge, no matter how hard she tried.

Still, entertaining these people at the casino was much easier than in her Reno home. They could watch a show and then gamble or sit in the cocktail lounge, talking, laughing and getting louder and louder, until at last it was time to go home. Over the years, Justin wanted to entertain his friends at the mansion. The cocktail parties weren't so bad, but the dinner parties were painfully strained, until Eunice made it a practice to hire an entertainer from a piano bar to sing and tell double-entendre jokes, which delighted their guests no end. Sometimes she'd have a belly dancer or a magician to get them through the evening after they'd finished eating. She made no provision for after-dinner conversation, because everyone seemed to freeze in her presence. She longed for her peninsula friends, for her life with Andrew. Only her memories sustained her.

During dinner, Barrett watched Clifton, who seemed constantly on the alert, observing how the guests were escorted to the tables, checking on the service and almost tasting their food. "I see that you're always on the job, Clifton."

"I'm afraid I'm ever the resident manager on the lookout for ways to improve. Even when I go to another resort, I'm a hotel man first, last, and always, trying to see if the competition is besting us." He put his arm across the back of her chair and smiled at her. "Here I am with the most beautiful girl in the room, and I'm neglecting you."

"No, you're not. I want to learn all I can, too. I'm

trying to prepare myself for whatever is in store for me this fall."

"Shirley says you've been a tremendous help. She was so far behind in her work after her illness."

"I think she's pretty well on top of things now. So you can assign me to another department, Clifton. I'd like to move all over the resort."

"OK. You can help out in reservations for a while. Also, I'll speak to the chef and see if you can help him in some way. Of course, the kitchen is his domain. I don't even go near it without asking him first. Remember that, Barrett, if you end up in hotel work. The chef is top man in the kitchen, and no one intrudes on him."

"That's the kind of thing I want to learn from you. Who knows—I may be an assistant to a hotel manager in New York."

"Or in Florida. That's where the best hotels are." He pressed her shoulder. "Plan to have lunch with me on Monday."

She nodded. "I'll do that."

It was time for the show at last, and Barrett's pulse quickened. She wondered how Lea was feeling. The curtains parted, and the dance troupe performed a lively, intricate number.

When the applause died away, Lea appeared in a spotlight at the back of the stage, wearing a red sequined evening gown. Despite her big smile, she seemed scared and very young, until she began to sing. The orchestra and her backup singers in the wings supplemented her sound. As she slowly crossed the stage, a transformation took place. She became alluring and sexy—her voice thrilling and true. Then she moved out on the runway to bring her closer to the audience. Suddenly she burst into life with her song and squeezed it out, ground it out, belted it out, wrung it out and flung it out. She was an ear-catching, eye-catching miracle. She captured her listeners and swept them along with her. When she finished, they applauded, shouted and cheered.

"Isn't she *wonderful?* I had no idea she would be so good!" Barrett cried to Judith, who only nodded, too moved to speak.

Blithe, provocative, and thoroughly accomplished, Lea danced with her troupe, then by herself, and then with the male dancers. She sang five more numbers, with several costume changes. When she left the stage, the dancers took over, so that it was a fast-paced, exciting show.

Before the finale, Lea stepped in front of the curtain. "I can't tell you how happy I am to be back home in Nevada. And you're such a wonderful audience! When I was growing up and dreamed of becoming a variety artist, my greatest ambition was to be a headliner at Starr's—and here I am!" Applause broke out again. When it died down, Lea continued, "We've worked out a special finale for our engagement here at Starr's Tahoe. It's called 'Love Sends Me to the Stars,' and I want to dedicate it to Justin Starr. Will you stand up, please, Mr. Starr?"

Justin stood up and waved to the audience and to Lea, who threw him a kiss and disappeared behind the curtain. The dancers, in stylized space suits, did an introductory number; then Lea appeared on top of the red rocket in a glittering silver costume. The rocket blasted off, moving from left to right across the stage, trailing plumes of exhaust. Simulated clouds billowed from the floor around the dancers.

Lea whirled around and around in the air, dancing atop the rocket and then singing. As far as the audience could see, she had no support as she whizzed above the stage, waving her beautiful arms and kicking her slender legs high in the air. She threw the audience a kiss, and the curtain went down as every-

one leaped to their feet and cheered. She made a half-
dozen curtain calls while bellboys brought huge baskets
of flowers up to the stage.

"What a triumphant return for Lea!" Judith said at
last.

At his table, Justin declared proudly, "Best show
anyone's ever had at Tahoe. Come on, Eunice, let's
go backstage and tell her so." He told his guests that
he would meet them in the cocktail lounge, where a
special table was reserved for them.

In the kitchen, even the waiters raved about the
show. Most of them had stood at the back of the room
or in the doorways and watched the performance.

Working unobtrusively, Otto Schroeder listened to
every word and detail.

CHAPTER

11

When Barrett and Judith went downstairs the next morning, Justin and Lyle were already at the table on the deck, eating breakfast and talking about Lea's show-stopping performance. She had put on three shows, and since she didn't get home until after four, she was still sleeping.

"I'd like to visit some of the casinos on the north shore of the lake to see what they're doing," Justin said. "Anyone want to go with me? How about you, Lyle?"

Lyle shook his head. "I'm taking Judith water-skiing. You, too, Barrett, if you want to come."

"No, thanks." She turned to her uncle. "I think I'll go with you, Uncle Justin. I'm here all the time, so I can always ski." She didn't want to intrude on Lyle and Judith, and, besides, she really wanted to be with her uncle.

Justin looked pleased. "I'll rustle up my chauffeur."

"I'll drive the Ford if you want," Barrett said. "I've been using it ever since I got here."

As they headed toward the north end of Tahoe, with Barrett at the wheel, Justin said, "I don't do much driving anymore. I have a little heart condition and find the stress of getting through traffic kind of hard. Sometimes it brings on a pain."

"Well, you can afford a chauffeur, so you shouldn't *have* to drive."

The road followed the shoreline of Tahoe part of the way and then passed through a forest. It was a beautiful drive.

"I'm awfully glad you're going with me," Justin said. "I visit the other casinos up here at the lake every chance I get. Lyle's no hand to do that, but a gambling operator ought to keep on top of what the competition is doing. You can always learn, I tell him."

"I'm sure of that. I brought some money along; maybe you'll teach me how to gamble."

"You just keep your money, my dear; I'll furnish the stakes for us both. The dealers all recognize me, and I'm expected to 'show my money' when I go in another club. One of the primary rules of gambling is never use money you need for something else. Also, if you go to the crap table all tense and worried, the dice'll go against you nearly every time. Prepare your mind to win and expect to win. I warn all my customers, never borrow money or pawn anything to play."

"I suppose you have people who want to put up their watches or diamond rings when they're in your clubs."

"Well, we don't accept them; that's against the state law. They can go to a pawnshop, but I have signs in all my casinos: HAVE A GOOD TIME BUT DON'T GAMBLE MORE THAN YOU CAN AFFORD. We don't want people's rent or food money or what they need to pay doctor bills."

"Of course you don't."

"The bitter truth is that 'needed' money never wins. All gamblers know that. When you play with guilt and worry and fear, you don't woo Lady Luck—you curse her—and you'll lose."

"That sounds like ESP or something."

"Well, it is. Before the summer is out, you'll understand. A real gambler has extrasensory perception— make no mistake about that. He gets hunches—sort of mysterious messages from the back of his mind. He *knows* he's going to win. He has a feeling that a given result is going to occur."

"Is that possible?"

"You bet it is. Remember, Barrett, *always play your hunches!* When you have that gut feeling that Lady Luck is smiling at you, go to the 21 or crap table and play. Do it while your hunch is with you, because it won't last. The longer I'm in this business, the more I believe in the occult and the supernatural."

"That surprises me. I always thought of you as a practical man."

"In most ways I am, but I'm a gambler, too; make no mistake about that. I always play my hunches. And another thing I've learned: to win, you must be in an optimistic, positive frame of mind. You usually won't win a dime if you're grieving about something or if you're blue or discouraged. I never gamble when I'm in the dumps."

They arrived at Crystal Bay and went into the Cal-Neva Club, which was located on the state line and had been in business for many years. As they passed a 21 table, Justin said, "See that dealer there? He's got 'the nuts on me.' That's a gambling expression, and it means that there are certain dealers who'll dominate your play and beat you every time. I've never won with him, and I've lost plenty. I'll never sit at his table."

They approached a cashier's cage, and Justin bought five hundred dollars' worth of chips. He turned to Barrett. "I'm going to give you a hundred dollars' worth. We'll set that as your limit today."

"I hope I win so I can pay you back."

Justin shook his head. "I never saw a girl like you." He took her arm and led her toward a crap table. "Learn to manage your gambling money. Let's say your betting unit is one dollar. This is what you put up and continue to play after every losing bet. Say you lose five bets; that's only five dollars. If you're losing, never increase your bets. Some knuckleheads will do that—the more they lose, the more they increase their bets, trying to get it back. A smart gambler waits until he wins. *Then* he increases his bets, with house money."

"I see."

They stopped at a crap table, and Justin nodded at the pit boss. "Now, you put a dollar chip on the 'line.' That means you're betting with the player who's shooting the dice. If the shooter throws a 7 or 11 on his first roll, all the line players win. If a 2, 3, or 12 appears, they lose. But if he rolls a 4, 5, 6, 8, 9, or 10 and repeats the number before he rolls a 7, all the line players win their bets. If a 7 appears first, they all lose."

At first Barrett lost her dollar chips; then she began to win. When it was her time to throw the dice, Justin said, "Bounce them good." Then he advised her to cover the board with house money, and she won steadily.

They moved to a 21 table, and with his guidance she won more. Her eyes glowed. "Isn't this exciting!" Before the morning was over, she was ahead six hundred dollars. "I can't *believe* it!"

When they stopped playing, they went to the dining room for lunch. Barrett put a hundred-dollar chip on the table in front of her uncle. "I insist on paying back my stake."

He shook his head. "You're the hardest person to do anything for. Most girls I know are out to use me every way they can." But, inwardly pleased, he picked up the chip and dropped it in his pocket. He admired her honesty and independence. "Well, you still have six hundred. Are you going to buy new clothes with it?"

"No, I owe my stepfather some money for my education; so I'm going to put it in my checking account and mail him five hundred dollars. The other hundred I'll put in a special gambling fund. It's not needed money, so it might bring me luck."

"I'm sure it will. You have the makings of a good gambler, my dear. Play your hunches. When you know you're going to win, bet high—all you can. You may get your whole debt to your stepfather paid off that way."

She laughed. "Wouldn't that be something? Perhaps I will, with your help. I'll never forget your lessons today, Uncle Justin."

"We'll have many more. Just remember, play high when you're winning."

"I will."

Justin studied the menu and then looked back at her. "As I told you, Barrett, it's against the law for an operator to gamble in his own casino. So perhaps you'd better not play at our resort. It'd be better if you went to one of the clubs at Stateline. Even though our license is not in your name, you are a Starr."

A wave of excitement ran through her. This was the first indication that he considered her part of the operation, even though temporarily. "OK, Uncle Justin, I won't gamble at the resort. It's true—I *am* a Starr."

Exhilarated with her minor triumph and her winnings, Barrett was radiant all afternoon. Back at Starpoint, she swam with Judith and Lyle, lay on the beach in the sun and then showered and changed to a clinging pale-pink silken jersey dress for dinner. When Clifton joined them on the deck, he couldn't help staring at her exceptional beauty.

She was aware of him, too: his strong, square-jawed face, his disconcerting blue eyes under thick, level eyebrows. She liked the easy way he wore a tan leisure suit, almost the color of his skin, with a chocolate-brown scarf at his throat.

The six of them dined inside the house and then played Monopoly until Justin said he was tired and was going to bed. Eunice rose, also. "Good night," she said, "I've had a wonderful day—so quiet and leisurely, and spent with people I enjoy." She kissed the girls and Lyle and then shook hands with Clifton, who thanked her for the dinner.

Judith watched Eunice climb the stairs with her arm around Justin's ample waist. "I like your mother so much, Lyle. She's one of the most charming women I've ever known, a true lady."

Lyle reached over and took her hand. "She likes you, too, Judith. She told me so."

After talking awhile, Clifton got to his feet. "Guess I'll run along now. I always like to make the rounds of the resort before I turn in."

Judith asked, "You live there, don't you?"

"Yes. I have a great apartment, with a living room and bedroom—even a small kitchen. But I usually eat in one of the hotel dining rooms."

Barrett rose from her chair. "I'll bet you sometimes wish you lived miles away. You must have people running to you with every little crisis."

"It does get hectic, but, well, that's my job." He said good night to Lyle and Judith.

Slipping on a pink sweater, Barrett walked outside with Clifton. She shivered a little in the chill air of the high altitude, and he put an arm around her shoulders.

"Since you're the official hostess here at Starpoint, I want to thank you, too, for the great evening. I agree with Mrs. Starr—it was my kind of evening. I'm with crowds of people so much of the time that it was a relief to be with a quiet, intimate group."

"I enjoyed it, too. In fact, the whole day has been wonderful." Suddenly Barrett broke away and gasped, "Oh, Clifton, just look at the beautiful moon!"

He followed her down a lighted path to a deck that overlooked the cove. Silver moonlight bathed the cliffs, the trees, and the beach and made an iridescent path across the water. Pale stars pinpricked the sky. A gentle breeze stirred the pine trees. An owl hooted softly, ruffled its feathers and settled back on its tree limb.

Moved by the incredible beauty of the view, they stood close together, wordlessly, for long moments. Then Clifton turned and took her in his arms. He kissed her eyelids, her cheeks, her lips. His voice was a hoarse whisper. "Oh, Barrett, Barrett." No other words were necessary. She felt his caressing hands on her back as he kissed her again.

CHAPTER

12

Tuesday evening, no one in the Celestial Room watched Lea Turner's midnight show with more absorption than Otto Schroeder. He sat jammed into a booth with a group of strangers, clutching his highball glass, but he was lucky to get any kind of seat, and he knew it. No one noticed him in his new tan shirt and brown leisure suit, purchased especially for this evening, for he blended in with the others. He wanted anonymity. He applauded at all the right times, too. Don't call attention to yourself, he thought.

Lea was good; he had to admit it. No wonder these jokers were banging their hands together as if to knock them off. "Isn't she terrific?" "She's tremendous!" "Just great!" That's right, he thought, clap! Yell! Stamp your feet! The bigger she is, the sweeter his revenge. Now she was on top. She had fame, money, talent, glamour, acclaim—everything. Well, it would all come to an end damn soon.

She was to perform here nine more nights. He'd have to come up with a plan and act within that time.

Nine days didn't give him too much time. It would have to be a clever idea that would in no way involve him. That ruled out shooting, because at the time of her death he wanted to be someplace else, with witnesses. At some bar, for instance, or gambling in another casino. He'd have to find an excuse to show his identification, so that later, if there was an investigation of the employees at Starr's, he'd never be suspected.

What could he do? Plant a bomb in her dressing room? He'd never made a bomb, but he probably could if he had to; he was clever with his hands. But a bomb would mean buying dynamite and other material that could be traced to him, and he didn't want to do that. He'd think of something. Some idea would come to him.

When the finale came and the dancers leaped around in their space suits, he had a feeling that something good was in the works. Then, when the spotlight hit Lea and showed her on a rocket, excitement coursed through him. Damned if she didn't blast off and go whirling around in the air! She looked as if she were balancing herself on top of the rocket while she danced and sang "Love Sends Me to the Stars." How could she do that? Why didn't she fall off? She must be attached to the rocket in some way.

Suddenly he knew how he'd get his revenge. He'd see to it that the bitch *did* fall off—right in front of the audience. Even if she was not killed, the fall would have to cripple her for life—maybe break her shapely legs and make it impossible for her to dance again or disfigure her beautiful face so she couldn't perform.

A terrific idea! Everyone would think it was an accident. They'd blame the jerks who made the rocket. Even if the fuzz got suspicious, they couldn't blame him. He'd be far away when it happened. Around the north shore. He'd be gambling in the

Nevada Club, or at Cal-Neva, and he'd be able to prove it. He wouldn't leave a thing to chance. He wouldn't get caught like he did five years ago and go back to prison. No way!

When he returned to his room and went to bed, it was hard to get to sleep, he was so revved up. He kept thinking about Lea Turner—kept seeing her taking curtain calls and bowing and throwing kisses to the audience. His hatred for her kept boiling and churning in his guts. She was the one who had tipped off Elliott Davenport. It was her fault that Kirt was killed, he muttered to himself as, at last, he drifted off to sleep.

He had his nightmare again, the same one that had haunted him while he was in prison. Kirt was alive in his dream—handsome, young and vital, his whole life ahead of him, his flesh warm, his blood pulsing in his veins.

But Kirt was pleading, begging, "You've got to let me off this time! You've got to let me off this time!" Then he'd walk a step or two away and turn and ask, "Can't you get somebody else this time? Give him my cut."

In the dream, Otto would shake his head and yell, *"No! No!"*

"Go by yourself this time and keep all the dough. I don't want any of it."

"No! No!"

"I've never wanted to be part of this racket, and you know it! Right from the start I've wanted out. Let me out, Otto."

Then he'd grab Kirt and throw him to the ground, and Kirt would crawl toward him on his knees. "I'm afraid! It's too dangerous. I don't want anything more to do with smuggling dope."

"Coward!"

Then the scene blurred and changed. Otto would

yell, "Get the truck started!" He would snatch his gun and shoot in all directions. Did one of *his* bullets hit Kirt? Oh, God, did it?

Then he'd cradle the fallen Kirt in his arms and sob over his dead body while the sheriff sneered, "Blame yourself, wise guy. If you hadn't resisted arrest, your brother'd still be alive."

As always, he was sobbing and cursing as he awakened. The nightmare, so real and so terrifying, never changed. Sweat broke out on his forehead and ran down his face. Would it plague him all his life? He rolled out of bed, shaking, shivering, nauseated with remorse. He poured whiskey into a glass and drank it straight. Then he grabbed a towel, wiped his face and muttered aloud, "It was Lea's fault. She tipped 'em off. I'll get her." It had to be Lea's fault. It *had* to be.

The next night, while he was working at the dishwasher, he made plans. He had to get backstage and look that rocket over. There had to be some way she was attached to it. Impatiently he watched the clock, until the hands reached twelve-thirty and his shift was over.

He punched the time clock, left the kitchen and went into the hall. Instead of turning toward the men's locker room to change into his street clothes, he headed for the stage-door entrance, still in his kitchen whites. If a security guard stopped him, he'd say he was going to the performers' kitchen, next to the stage.

No one stopped him at the stage door, and he gave a sigh of relief. With more self-assurance, he walked along a corridor, following the sound of Lea's beautiful voice, the orchestra, and the dancers. No one would pay any attention to him now, he was sure of that.

Backstage, he looked around. It was dark except

for strips of blue lights near the floor. The area was illuminated just enough so that the performers could move around without stumbling; yet it was not visible from the Celestial Room. Where could he hide?

Music thundered around him as Lea and the others performed onstage. He'd have to hide himself fast. A big plywood crate was off to one side, against a wall. He pulled it forward far enough so there was room to hide behind it. Nobody could see him now, but had one of the stagehands noticed him? His heart throbbed against the wall of his chest, but no one came. He was safe. He squatted on his heels and peered around the edge of the crate so he could watch the action on the stage.

Long after the show was over and the stage crew and the performers had gone, he remained in his hiding place. He wanted to make sure that he was alone. Sometimes he stood; sometimes he sat on the floor to rest his legs. When he was certain no one would come, he stepped from behind the crate. Everything was dark except the night-lights for the watchman's rounds. Still, he could see reasonably well, now that his eyes were adjusted to the gloom. As stealthily as a cat, he moved to the rocket.

As he expected, it was worked by wires from aloft. So as not to leave fingerprints, he removed his kitchen jacket, pulled his T-shirt over his head and wrapped it around his right hand. So this was it: a harness arrangement, covered with cloth and sequins.

The part that went around the waist was just like a seat belt. He felt the back, where the harness was attached to its lead wire, and to the track above, by a metal plate. Heavy-duty nuts and bolts attached the plate to the harness. Despite himself, he let out a soft whistle of satisfaction. Nuts and bolts could be loosened.

Later, while he changed his clothes in the locker room, he tried to decide when the best time would be to loosen the bolts. On a week night such as this, after the last performance? But Lea might rehearse with the rocket the next morning and have the harness repaired. Should he loosen the bolts between the dinner and the midnight shows? There were too many people around then, and the security guards were more alert.

What about Friday night, when there were three performances? The dinner show, the show that started before midnight, and the one at two-fifteen. Probably the stagehands and the performers took a break between shows. They'd go someplace for coffee. Once he got by the stage door, he'd have a few minutes alone backstage. He could slip in after the midnight show, while the crew was on its break.

Since the stagehands wore Levi's, he would wear them, too, under his kitchen clothes. Then, when he got backstage, he'd slip off his whites and look like the others. Even if someone saw him at the rocket in the dim light, he'd only look like a stagehand making adjustments.

Still, it would be dangerous. He'd better not forget that for a moment. He'd have to have all the breaks, avoid the security guards, work on the rocket at just the right time, when the stagehands were gone. He'd also have to do it right—loosen *all* the nuts and bolts.

On Friday he drove to a hardware store on the California side to buy a wrench, pliers, and a screwdriver. He chose them carefully and balanced them in his hand, trying to get their feel. Would they do the job? He'd have just one chance, and he had to make the most of it. He made his selection and then purchased a pair of black gloves.

After he returned to his room, he put on the gloves, closed his eyes and practiced using the tools in the dark. A flashlight would be too dangerous, so he'd have to learn to work fast and sure in semidarkness.

What a surprise you'll get tonight, Lea Turner!

Think of Kirt when you're on that rocket, whirling back and forth—poor Kirt, rotting in the ground. But Lea would soon join him—Miss High and Mighty, the canary who sang to the fuzz.

Before he went to work in the kitchen, Otto put his new suit and shirt in the trunk of his car. He'd change when he got to the north shore. He didn't want to go into a casino in his work clothes. It would be better to look like he was out for a good time—all dressed up so he could pick up some girl at a bar. There were always hookers hanging around the casinos.

Some were amateurs, housewives, secretaries, store clerks, and others, who drove to Tahoe from Reno, Carson, or California in secondhand vans, on the make for a few extra bucks. But some were pros, who considered the north shore their beat. He'd find a pro, so he could look her up again if it was necessary. He'd pick out one who was just right and flash his paycheck, which he'd receive when he reported to work. He'd make a big thing about showing his identification badge and getting his paycheck cashed. He'd buy her drinks, stake her to some gambling money and then go back to her room with her. She'd remember him, all right, and be able to say that Owen Shulman was with her when Lea Turner was killed. It might not be necessary, but it paid to have an alibi.

When it was time to go to Starr's, he put on his oldest, most faded pair of Levi's, which he would wear under his kitchen pants. He put his tools in a strong paper bag and stuck them in his hip pocket. They felt good, pressing against his body—strong, tempered tools, ready to do a job.

Friday evening, Clifton took Barrett to a dinner show on the north shore. Afterward they drove to a supper club on the California side that had an orchestra for dancing. Clifton was an excellent dancer, and Barrett enjoyed herself immensely. As they drove back to Starpoint, around one-thirty, Clifton said, "The show was very good, but it doesn't hold a candle to Lea's."

"No, not at all. You know, I'd like to see Lea's show again."

"She puts on three shows tonight. We can just catch the last one. The maître d' will put some chairs against the wall for us. I'll run you home afterward. Lea, too, for that matter."

Barrett leaned her head against Clifton's shoulder and said sleepily, "When we get to Starr's, I'll go to Lea's dressing room and tell her we'll take her home. Her midnight show is about over now."

"OK. While you're doing that, I'll make my nightly rounds. I'll meet you before the last show starts, at the maître d's desk."

Content, she closed her eyes and dozed. What could be more wonderful than to be at Tahoe and falling in love with a man as exciting and attractive as Clifton?

From his hiding place behind the crate, Otto watched the performers leave the stage: Lea, the dancers and singers, the musical director, the members of the orchestra, the sound technician and his assistant, the eight stagehands. He counted them carefully. Finally, the lighting technician left the switch panel, and it was deserted backstage.

Otto stepped from behind the crate and moved cautiously to the rocket. The blue lights cast a dim, eerie glow, but he could see well enough. Absorbed in the task, he wasn't aware of Barrett until she had passed by him, not ten feet away. His heart leaped to his throat. Christ! Had she seen him? She didn't look at him as she walked rapidly toward the dressing rooms, but had she *seen* him?

He stared after her. It was that good-looking broad

he'd seen with Lea. Who was she, anyway? Would she give an alarm? He'd have to cut out of here damned fast. His hands shook as he felt each nut and bolt. He forced himself to check each one to make sure they were all loose, yet tight enough that they would hold for a while. Then he snatched up his tools and slipped away in the darkness.

As Barrett watched Lea's third show of the night, she wondered how anyone could continue to put such enthusiasm into a performance. Lea looked as fresh as on opening night. How could she do the same numbers, night after night, and make each appearance as exciting as the one before? Where did she get the strength to dance and sing with such vigor—to say nothing of giving interviews, traveling from one engagement to the next, rehearsing, standing hours on end for costume fittings and then performing over and over? It took a special kind of person to be a headliner, Barrett thought with admiration, and Lea was tops, no doubt about that. The girl had a rare and wonderful talent.

She gave her speech about being happy to be home again, about dreaming of becoming a headliner at Starr's, and again she dedicated "Love Sends Me to the Stars" to Justin Starr, whom she had long admired. Then she was on the rocket, whirling round and round, singing, dancing, kicking her legs high in the air on top of the rocket.

Around and around the rocket whirled, higher and higher, until Lea was twenty-five feet above the stage. Clouds swirled under her. Around and around the rocket turned, faster and faster. Then it tipped forward. Suddenly Lea flew into space, screaming with terror as she fell through the special-effects clouds and crashed upon the stage.

CHAPTER

13

The doctor came out of the emergency room of Tahoe Memorial Hospital shaking his head. "She's dead," he said to Barrett, Vicky, and Clifton, who were waiting in the corridor. "She was dead on arrival; there was nothing we could do. I'm very sorry."

For days afterward the two words, "She's dead," echoed through Barrett's mind as she tried to convince herself that what she had seen actually happened. Somehow, she had to come to grips with her grief, her shock and horror. It didn't seem possible that Lea, so vitally alive one moment, could be dead—in a crumpled heap on the stage—the next.

The fact that there was so much to do helped get her through the worst of it. Vicky was too stricken to function well; so it was up to Barrett to notify Lea's mother, to meet her at the plane and help make the funeral arrangements. Barrett was also the spokesperson at the press conference that was held after the tragedy, and she helped Vicky dismiss the company and arrange for the singers and dancers to return to San Francisco.

On Tuesday afternoon an overflow crowd packed the large chapel in the mortuary. Barrett sat with Judith, Lyle, and Clifton; Vicky sat in the family alcove with Lea's mother and stepfather. Lea's manager looked ashen and bereft. Barrett listened to the organ music and to the minister's service, but she felt no comfort. Her dear friend, so talented and lovely, was dead.

The next day, Barrett took Vicky to the airport to catch the plane for New York. On the way, the older woman said, "My little Lea was so anxious to come home to Nevada. She's here to stay now, poor baby. I'll never get over this, never."

"It's so sad. It's tragic that anyone as talented as Lea had to die in such an accident." Barrett's chin quivered.

"I keep wondering if it *was* an accident. You know how worried and frightened she was about Otto Schroeder."

Barrett gasped. "Do you think she was murdered?"

"I just don't know. I called the sheriff and told him about Lea's fears. He said he'd check into it." Vicky's thin, pinched face crumpled in grief. She wiped her eyes.

"I know the sheriff's been at the resort. The insurance investigators are looking into it, too." Barrett shook her head. "But I doubt that Otto Schroeder had anything to do with it. No one has seen him around."

"I can't stop thinking about Lea when she told me how scared she was. Be sure to let me know if the investigation turns up anything."

"Of course. I have your address in New York. Will you be staying there now?"

"For a while," Vicky said sadly. "I'm executor for

Lea's estate. I have to settle her affairs." Tears ran down her pale cheeks. "I feel like I've lost a child. Lea was all I had. Her career was my life, and now I'm nobody."

"Vicky, I'm so sorry. I've often thought that, of all of us, you'll miss her the most, even more than her mother." Barrett turned into the airport entrance. "Lea dearly loved you, I know that. She told me many times that she couldn't get along without you."

"Of course, there were times when she cheerfully could have wrung my neck." Vicky smiled faintly. "But she was devoted to me, too. She left me a hundred thousand dollars in her will, if you can imagine that. I guess that's proof that she cared for me."

"I'm glad, Vicky. You deserve to be remembered."

"The rest of the estate goes to her mother. There'll be plenty for her, too. Lea made big money, and it was carefully invested."

Barrett pulled up in front of the passenger loading zone and stopped the car. A porter took Vicky's luggage, and they said good-bye.

Before returning to Tahoe, Barrett drove to Starr's and took the elevator to Justin's office. When she entered, Justin rose to his feet and said, "I'm so glad you stopped by, my dear. Sit down."

"I just put Vicky Goldring on the plane," Barrett said, seating herself near his desk. "She's returning to New York. I feel so sorry for her; she's just devastated over Lea's death."

"It must have been hard on you, too, because you and Lea were such good friends. And to have witnessed the accident. . . ."

"It was awful. I can't get it out of my mind. But now that Vicky's gone, I think I'll be able to pull myself together. Just seeing that grief-stricken look on her face got to me."

Justin leaned back in his chair. "Well, I've been

waiting for a chance to tell you what a wonderful job you've done during this crisis."

"Thank you, Uncle Justin."

"I swear I don't know how Lyle and I would've managed without you. You represented Starr's with flying colors."

"You're sweet to say so."

"Well, I mean it, girl. You sure took a burden off our shoulders. The fact that you are a member of the family, as well as Lea's close friend, made it particularly fitting for you to act as our representative."

"I'm glad I could help."

"I particularly appreciate the way you handled the news media. You made it clear that the harness that broke loose was part of Lea's props—something she brought to Tahoe. In other words, Starr's was in no way responsible for the accident."

"Well, that's the truth. I felt it was important to emphasize that point so that future entertainers won't be afraid of the equipment. Nor do we want any ghouls in the audience—waiting for another accident."

"Fortunately, we have an ice-skating show appearing next in the Celestial Room. They open Friday, and they're entirely different from Lea's show, which will be a good thing. Then, after the ice show, a comedian. By that time we'll be back to normal."

"You've taken quite a loss this week, while the Celestial Room's been closed."

"I know, but it couldn't be helped. I didn't think it would be in good taste to bring in a substitute and keep the headliner room open."

"You're right. I'm glad you didn't do that."

Justin leaned forward. "Say, there's someone I want you to meet—James Nichols, the famous writer. Did you know we're doing a book together?"

"Lyle was telling me about it. That's marvelous! I

know that everyone will be interested in reading about you and your career."

"Say, I'll have my secretary send for him, if he's in his office."

A few minutes later, when Nichols joined them, Justin said, "I want you to meet my grandniece, Barrett Starr—my brother's granddaughter. This is James Nichols." He waved the writer to a chair.

After they had acknowledged the introductions, Justin went on, "I'm mighty proud of this girl. She's hostess at Starpoint and has been helping out at the resort for the summer. I've just been telling her what a first-rate job she did during this Turner tragedy."

They talked about Lea's death a few moments, then Justin asked, "Don't I have a fine family?"

"You certainly have, Mr. Starr." The writer looked at Eunice's picture on the desk. "She was Mrs. Bellingham, wasn't she? And Lyle is her son?"

Justin winced and then snapped in annoyance, "They've been Starrs for fifteen years."

Barrett changed the subject tactfully. "Uncle Justin tells me that you two are writing a book about his life."

Nichols nodded. "That's right. Have you any suggestions for a good title? So far I've thought of *It's My Deal* and *I Placed My Bet*."

Barrett laughed. "How about *I Hit the Jackpot*? You really did hit it, Uncle Justin; you've been so successful."

Justin chuckled. "Well, put that on the list of titles for consideration, Nichols."

"I will. Did you know that Mr. Starr and I are flying to Europe the day after tomorrow to visit the casinos along the Adriatic coast and in Monte Carlo?"

"How exciting!" She turned to her uncle. "Is Eunice going, too?"

"Not this time. I wish she were, but she hates flying

with a passion, has a real phobia about it. We're only going to be gone about ten days to two weeks, so she'll stay here. But she'll go anywhere on a boat, so I promised her that we'd take a cruise this fall."

After James Nichols had returned to his office, Barrett said, "Uncle Justin, I really came to see you about something Vicky mentioned. I think you ought to know about it." She told him about Lea's fears of Otto Schroeder and the telegram that Tony Rizzi had sent.

Justin shook his head. "I don't think there's much to that threat. I'd have been dead long ago if every man who said he'd get even with me went through with it. But I'll tell you what I'll do. I'll get in touch with Tony Rizzi and hear the story straight from him. Lyle and I will decide what should be done. Don't you worry your pretty head over this."

Barrett sighed with relief. "I feel a lot better discussing it with you." She rose and said, "Well, I'll be on my way. I just wanted to talk to you. And have a wonderful trip." She kissed him good-bye.

Long after she left, Justin thought about her. She was a winner—not only stunning, but capable. She took right over during the Turner tragedy. He had seen her on the newscast, being interviewed, and she had handled the reporters like a pro, fielded their questions with real expertise. She looked out for Starr's, too, so no one could blame the resort in any way for the accident. The whole crisis proved that she could hold up under stress. When Vicky and Lea's mother went to pieces, Barrett kept going and got things done. He was glad to have her on the spot during the insurance investigation, too, especially now that he would be gone and Lyle was needed in Reno. How fortunate that he'd brought her here for the summer. By God, she was some girl. A real Starr, all right!

That afternoon, before he went home, Justin walked across the street to the Mardi Gras Club. Tony Rizzi came out of his office and held out his hand. "Justin, you honor me. Welcome! Did you come over to do a little gambling and win all my money?"

Justin chuckled. "Not today, Tony, but next time we need some capital to keep Starr's going, I'll be over. There's something I want to talk to you about."

"Come into my office."

Tony poured two glasses of wine, and when they were seated, Justin asked, "What's this business about Otto Schroeder threatening Lea Turner? You don't suppose he's responsible for her death, do you?"

Tony told Justin all he knew, and then said, "The minute I heard about the accident, I thought about Otto. Of course, I wondered if he'd been up there, trying to kill her. I've sent word through the grapevine that I'm to be told if he shows up anyplace, but no one has seen him. Frankly, I don't think he ever got out of prison. I must have got the wrong dope on that. I'm sure sorry I sent that telegram to Lea. It really frightened the poor kid."

"I imagine her death was an awful blow to you."

Tony shook his head sadly. "You'll never know. She got her start here, and she never forgot it. She kept in touch with me all these years. I was the first friend she came to see when she got back to Reno."

"The whole thing's a damn shame. I'm going to be out of town the next couple of weeks; so if you hear anything about Otto Schroeder, get in touch with my son, will you?"

"I sure will, Justin."

After he arrived home and had stretched out in his recliner with a can of beer, Justin told Eunice about Otto Schroeder. "I sure hope he wasn't behind that poor girl's death. It's bad enough to have an accident at a resort, but a murder is far worse."

"Justin, you mustn't worry. You have over a million people a year at Starr's Tahoe. With that many people on your premises, anything could happen, including accidents and even murder. Such a mass of people brings problems."

"I suppose so."

"Just go on your trip and enjoy yourself, darling. Let Lyle and Barrett cope with the casinos."

"I'm glad Barrett is at Tahoe. She's a capable girl, and I can trust her, just like I do Lyle."

"I'm glad she's there, too. Poor Lyle can't be everywhere. But you go on your trip and forget your responsibilities." She patted his arm.

"Dear, speaking of my trip, will you see that my white-tie evening clothes are packed? My full-dress outfit?"

Eunice stared at him in astonishment. "Your full dress? For heaven's sake, why? You won't need formal clothes on that trip."

But Justin's jaw was set stubbornly. "I want them. See that the maid packs them."

"But, darling, I thought you were going to travel light, with just one suitcase. This means that you'll be overexerting yourself, and you know what the doctor says."

She got out of her chair, picked up his empty beer can, put it in a wastebasket, and got another can for him from the refrigerator. "Justin, it's ridiculous to drag those formal clothes around Europe. You'll never wear them."

"But I want them. I'm known all over the world. Some duke or earl might ask me to dinner, and I'll need those clothes. There's Princess Grace and Prince Rainier in Monaco; it's a sure bet they'll ask me to the palace."

CHAPTER

14

By the time Barrett had returned to Starpoint, the reaction to the turmoil of the past five days had set in, and she realized how tired she was. After the housekeeper served her a late lunch of soup and a sandwich, she changed into her bathing suit and walked to the beach in the sheltered cove. She oiled her skin, stretched out on the sand, her head resting on a rubber pillow, and fell asleep. Later, much refreshed, she swam in the cold lake and went back to the house to shower and dress before walking through the woods to the resort.

Clifton rose to greet her when she entered his office, late in the afternoon. "Hi! I suppose you got Vicky off on her plane this morning."

"Yes, she's gone." Barrett sat in a chair by his desk. "I thought I'd check in and find out where I'm to report tomorrow. It's high time I got back on the job. I don't want to get fired."

Clifton smiled and sat down. "No danger of that.

You haven't stopped to catch your breath since the accident. You must be dead tired."

"I am tired, but I took a nap this afternoon and had a swim in the lake, so I feel much better. Now I'm anxious to get back to work. I think after you go through such a terrible experience, you need to do something normal and routine again."

"How would you like to work in the chef's office for a couple of weeks, beginning tomorrow? I talked to Chef Bordeaux, and he was delighted. He said that if you could fill in, he'd let his secretary take her vacation as of Monday. She's been anxious to get away."

"Fine. She'll still be there tomorrow and the next day, won't she, to show me the ropes?"

"Yes. I'll give him a call, and if he's free, I'll take you to meet him. He's probably not too busy right now, since the Celestial Room is closed."

Chef Bordeaux, a heavyset man with a florid face, proudly showed them around his domain. "I designed this kitchen wing myself. While I was chef at Starr's in Reno, Mr. Starr came to me and said, 'Mr. Bordeaux, you're to be the chef in charge at Tahoe. I want you to work closely with the architects and get that kitchen wing designed just right. What you say goes.' For once, I have everything just the way I want it."

The kitchen wing, gleaming with stainless-steel equipment, stoves, and tables and counters, was presided over by white-garbed assistant chefs and their helpers. Everything was immaculately clean and orderly. Appetizing odors came from the many kettles on the ranges.

Chef Bordeaux took them to the adjoining section, where pastry chefs did the baking and prepared desserts. Another area was devoted to salad preparation. "A movable belt brings the supplies from the receiving platform into the storage rooms, which are next to the walk-in refrigerators," the chef boasted. "We handle all our supplies with minimum help."

"I'm always impressed by how smoothly this department operates," Clifton said. "When I was assistant manager in Florida, the kitchen was our biggest headache. But not here, thanks to you."

The chef acknowledged the compliment with a large smile. "We cook for the three main restaurants here—the Celestial Room, the North Star, and the Southern Cross. The coffee shops and snack bars are leased out, so I don't have anything to do with them."

Then he showed them through the section where the dishes were washed and stored, where a bearded worker was unloading the dishwashers and stacking the clean dishes.

Good God, Otto thought, it's the good-looking broad who crossed the stage when I was loosening the bolts on the rocket! Cold sweat trickled down his back. Who was she? Had she seen him that night? What was she doing in the kitchen with Mr. McMillan and Chef Bordeaux? He heard the resident manager say, "You'll find it very interesting in this department, Barrett."

"Now, Miss Starr, come and meet my secretary," Chef Bordeaux said. "She's so glad you can relieve her while she goes on vacation."

Barrett Starr. That was her name. Was she one of *the* Starrs? Related to Justin Starr himself? Why was she going to work here? What should he do? Quit and get out right now? It would be dangerous to stay here, but his job wasn't finished. He still had to even things with Elliott Davenport.

"Stay and have dinner with me, Barrett," Clifton said. "Roast lamb is on the menu tonight, and it's always good."

"I will if you'll drive me home afterward. I walked over."

"Of course. I have some work to do now, but I'll meet you in the cocktail lounge in half an hour."

Barrett walked into the Andromeda Room to watch the play. As always, a sense of excitement came over her as she mingled with the crowd. She loved the festive air, the lively music, the eager men and women at the slot machines and shoulder to shoulder around the crap layouts and the 21 tables, the young and attractive change girls and woman dealers. The room was so full of customers she could hardly maneuver through. She was caught up in the atmosphere, and for the first time in days she forgot about Lea's dreadful accident.

When she met Clifton in the cocktail lounge, they found a secluded table, and he ordered drinks for them. "Here's to us." He toasted. "Say, you're looking better already. There's more color in your cheeks."

"I don't feel tired now. I've been in the Andromeda Room, watching the gambling, and it gave me a tremendous lift. I guess I'm like my uncle, a gambler at heart."

"After dinner let's walk over to Harrah's. I never gamble here; it's a personal policy of mine. I think it puts the dealer on the spot when I join a table."

"I'm sure it does. Uncle Justin asked me not to gamble here, either, but I'd love to go to Harrah's. I have about twenty-five dollars with me that I can afford to risk. Uncle Justin said never to gamble with needed money, because worry and guilt make you lose. The trouble with me is that most of my money is needed." She laughed.

Clifton put his hand on hers. "You're so beautiful when you laugh."

She twined her fingers in his. "It's good to be with

you again, Cliff. The last few days have been so traumatic that I've just been out of it. I feel we've been miles apart."

"We'll have to put the sadness behind us and go on from here. I want to make the most of every minute while you're here this summer."

She lifted her glass again. "Let's make the weeks ahead unforgettable."

He touched her glass with his. "You can count on that."

After dinner, sitting at a 21 table at Harrah's, Barrett tried to recall what her uncle had taught her about the game. She knew, of course, that the object is to make 21 points and that she could call for as many cards as she wanted.

"Twenty-one is a game of judgment as well as luck," Justin had said. "The dealer turns her first card face up. You must guess what her hidden, or 'hole,' card may be and whether you can beat her. You must decide whether to call for one or more cards, and take the risk of going over twenty-one, or whether she'll have to 'hit' herself with a card and maybe go broke."

He had also explained that, in Reno and Tahoe casinos, if the first two cards add up to 11, a player could turn them face up and double his initial bet. One card would be dealt to him face down. "Some players don't like to 'double down' if a dealer has a ten or a face card showing. But I double down on every eleven, regardless of what the dealer shows."

When she won ten dollars, she could almost hear him say, "Now you've got house money, so increase your bets." Soon she was dealt a pair of sixes, and she knew he'd say, "That's a 'stiff' hand, because any ten or face card will break it. So split your pair of sixes and bet on each one. Call for more cards. You might get a five or a four. Then, with a ten or a face card, you'd have a good hand." She remembered him saying, "I always split a pair of twos, threes, sixes or sevens. Never fives, fours, tens or face cards."

She played carefully but skillfully, recalling her uncle's lessons. Like him, she had an instinct for gambling, a true feeling for cards. When Clifton was ready to leave, she cashed in her chips and was ahead nearly two hundred dollars.

"This is wonderful!" she said as they walked down the highway toward Starr's. She told Clifton about her debt to her stepfather. "Nothing would give me more satisfaction than paying back that penny-pinching, stiff-necked, Puritan New Englander with gambling winnings!"

Clifton laughed. "Right on!"

"With my Uncle Justin's expertise and guidance, I'm going to do it, too."

"You played like a pro tonight. You won much more than I did. I'm ahead only twenty dollars. I thought you'd been gambling for years."

"No, I wasn't old enough to gamble when I lived here before. We played the slot machines when we could get by with it, but that was all. The other day Uncle Justin taught me some of the fine points of shooting craps and playing twenty-one. Of course, it'll be a long time before I'm in his league."

"You'll get there. Have him teach you about roulette and baccarat, too. You seem to have gambling in your blood."

"I'm a Starr, that's why. I want to learn *all* the games."

When they saw the marquee at the resort, advertising the coming ice show, Barrett said sadly, "Remember when it said, LEA TURNER RETURNS TO NEVADA? Just a few days ago. Every so often it hits me like a blow to the stomach."

"I know. I try not to think about it. It was awful."

They were silent, and he put his arm around her. "Come to my apartment. We'll have a drink to celebrate your winnings before I take you home."

When they entered his living room, she exclaimed, "Cliff, how charming! You collect modern paintings!" The walls were covered with groupings of contemporary art.

"I feel that as long as I'm getting my board and room provided, I can afford to indulge myself. I have a friend who has a gallery, and he keeps me in touch with up and coming artists." He headed for the kitchen. "There are more in my bedroom, too. Go look at them while I fix that drink."

His room seemed very masculine, containing a king-size bed that was covered with a handsome hand-woven spread. His clothes hung in neat, orderly rows in a large, walk-in closet. The excellent paintings on the wall expunged the sterile appearance of a hotel suite. All in all, the room reflected Clifton's aggressive, dominating personality and sense of organization, as well as his refinement and good taste.

When Barrett returned to the living room, the drinks were on the coffee table, the stereo was on, and the lights were turned low. He patted a spot on the sofa beside him, handed her a glass and said, "I've been wanting you to see my apartment."

"I love it. Your paintings make it look so lived-in and individual."

"I think I have a good setup. This apartment and all my meals are provided as part of my compensation for being the resident manager. It's true that I'm always at the mercy of the help, but it's no different from being captain of a ship or president of a university."

"I guess it isn't. I hadn't thought of that comparison."

They talked awhile, and he freshened their drinks.

Gradually, Barrett leaned back in the curve of his arm. What an attractive man he is, she thought as she studied the bold structure of his face and the shape of his head. The drinks soon made her feel as if she were floating through space. "I'm really beginning to unwind," she said lazily. "For the first time in days I feel relaxed."

"So do I. This room needs a beautiful girl like you to make it complete." He cradled her in his arms and kissed her until she felt her heart throb in her throat and desire for him swept over her.

"I've fallen in love with you, Barrett. I think I did the first moment I saw you. You're the most beautiful, alluring girl I've ever known. I want you to marry me."

She disengaged herself from his arms and sat up. "Oh, Cliff, don't say that! Please don't."

"Why not?" He sounded hurt.

"Because you're such a wonderful guy, and I love being with you. I don't want anything spoiled for us."

"Is marrying me so terrible to contemplate?"

She could tell from the expression on his face that he was wounded. For once, he didn't seem so self-assured.

"Darling, not *you*, but marrying—period. I've got a hang-up about it, I guess, because my mother has had two rotten marriages. I've told you what a loser my father is—shiftless, selfish, and no good—and tonight I told you about my stepfather. Right now, just the idea of a lifetime commitment to anyone, even to a man as outstanding as you, just turns me off. I'm not ready for marriage yet. I want a career first, and self-realization."

He seemed to take hope from that. "Then, you don't necessarily rule it out for the future?"

"No, of course not."

"At least I still have a chance. Here, I'll mix us another drink."

He carried the tray to the kitchen while Barrett stretched out on the sofa and said sleepily, "It's getting late. I should go home."

"We'll make it a short one."

He brought their drinks back, and she pulled her legs up so he could sit beside her. "So you're one of those modern, liberated girls."

"Yes, I am. I want to achieve something in my own right. I'm not going to be trapped in the suburbs with a lot of kids to raise. I want to be just *me* for a while—my own person. I'm sorry, Cliff, but that's the way I feel."

He took her in his arms again. "I'm disappointed, because I'd hoped you'd marry me soon, but I see your point. I wouldn't want anything to interfere with *my* career in the hotel business, nor with my interest in paintings. Perhaps we men are too quick to assume that women want only the traditional role of being a housewife and mother."

Barrett kissed him. "You're a lamb to understand. Let's enjoy the summer and get to know one another. There's so much to learn. I don't know anything about your family, for instance. Or what music you prefer. Or if you like sports. Or what you were like when you were a little boy. There are a thousand things I don't know about you."

"I don't know anything about you, either, except that you're the most desirable, most beautiful girl I've ever known. I just hope that before the summer is over, you'll feel differently about marriage. I don't want you to return to the East Coast."

She smiled to herself and thought, I have no intention of returning, or of getting married, either, for a long time. I'm going to belong to myself for a while yet, and I'm going to become an important member of Starr Enterprises.

Clifton pushed her hair back from her face and kissed her. His arms tightened around her.

"I want to make love to you," he whispered. "Would that compromise your plans?"

Barrett released a breathy little chuckle and said, "I'm willing to take that gamble."

CHAPTER

15

The next few days fell into a pattern for Barrett. She walked to the resort each morning through the shafts of sunlight that pierced the towering, cathedrallike Jeffrey and sugar pine and red fir. Ferns grew beside the path—sword, brake, and maidenhair. She observed the chipmunks and squirrels and birds—the Sierra chickaree, the sapsucker, and green-tailed towhee. Fragrance from the conifers and from the rich, spongy humus permeated the air. It was glorious to be alive and part of Tahoe.

As she walked, she had a chance to be alone and to think about herself and Clifton. How easy it would be to fall deeply in love with him, for he was an expert, tender lover. He wanted to marry her, but did she want to marry him? Was she ready for such a commitment? Was his attraction in himself alone or because he was part of her life at Tahoe? What if he were offered an even better position with a worldwide hotel chain—one that he couldn't afford to turn down? Would she be willing to follow him back to the East Coast or to

Florida or to Europe or Asia—wherever he was assigned? She didn't know. But she certainly wasn't ready to leave Tahoe, not now.

Her step always quickened as she approached the casino. She could hardly wait to enter the gaming rooms and be caught up again in the excitement that was such a basic part of the atmosphere.

She now was recognized by the employees. The pit bosses stood straighter and became more alert, as they supervised their games, when she was around. The girl dealers, in their blue-and-white uniforms with silver stars on the collars, smiled at her and were especially courteous to their customers as she passed. The change girls returned her greeting and moved more quickly through the throng. The cashiers lost their bored expressions and almost snapped to attention as she neared. She was a Starr. She represented the empire, just as Justin and Lyle did, and she loved the feeling of power it gave her.

Only Chef Bordeaux ignored her relationship to Justin and cared not at all whom or what she represented. She was simply a substitute secretary, who was to be endured until his regular girl returned. His department prepared thousands of meals a day, and he was an impatient, quick-tempered man who never hesitated to express his disapproval, whether to a lowly kitchen helper or one of his assistant chefs or her. Everyone got a tongue-lashing if Chef Bordeaux felt they deserved it. He especially resented the time Barrett took from her job to assist the insurance investigators, and he told her so.

At the end of the day, she walked back to Starpoint feeling worthless and deflated after working with the chef. But she was learning about the food services of the resort, and she felt the time was coming when she'd need to know about every department. She learned not only how efficiently the kitchens were run but how the employees could pilfer supplies and how an employer had to keep constant vigilance to make a restaurant pay. Of course, the fine food and reasonable prices attracted the gamblers, but it was the gaming rooms and the bars that made the most profit for the resort. Still, the restaurants had to hold their own. It was hard dealing with the chef, but she was rounding out her knowledge of resort management and all its complexities.

When she got back to her room, she got into a bikini, swam in the clear, cold lake and then lay in the sun to rest before showering and changing for dinner. Sometimes Clifton would come to Starpoint to eat, but usually he'd call for her and they'd dine at the resort or in another casino. As Clifton discussed the problems of the resort with her, she listened with complete absorption, as if she couldn't learn too much.

One afternoon, Barrett was much later than usual as she walked back through the woods. She heard voices ahead of her, and as she came around a curve in the path, she saw a group of people in a small clearing. Three girls were sitting on a log, and four men were standing nearby. They looked familiar, and she realized that they were employees at the resort.

As she approached, their voices died down, but a tall, dark-haired man in his forties called out, "Hello, Miss Starr." It was Carl Rhodes, the floor boss on the night shift. A guitar was slung over his shoulder, and his fingers strummed a chord as she acknowledged his greeting. The others spoke to her, too.

"We're having a beach party at Pirates' Cove," he said. "We're waiting for the others to show up."

"You're welcome to use the beach at Starpoint," Barrett said. "There's no one there, because the ice-skating troupe is staying at the resort."

Rhodes shook his head. "Thanks a lot, but we told everyone Pirates' Cove. Some of the folks might come late and wouldn't know where to find us."

"I see what you mean." Barrett started to walk ahead, but Rhodes partially blocked her way.

"Would you like to come, too?" He nodded toward an ice chest. "We've got plenty of beer and eats. And you can bring Mr. McMillan." Two of the girls, she noticed, exchanged a knowing look.

"Thank you, but we have other plans." She felt the color rise in her cheeks. Apparently her affair with Clifton, so newly begun, was common knowledge among the employees. She felt as if her privacy had been intruded upon, and she resented it. She continued toward Starpoint, kicking at stones in the path. That was the trouble with an intimate relationship: one gave up part of oneself. She was no longer truly her own person. She felt no guilt, exactly, but rather a lack of wholeness, which she hated. She didn't want to share herself with anyone, nor did she want to be gossiped about. If she were truly in love with Clifton, would she mind it so much?

She changed into her swimsuit, put on a terry-cloth beach robe and stood idly at the south window, still rankling from her encounter in the woods. Leaning forward and turning her head, she saw the coves in the rugged shoreline to the east. She could even see the group at Pirates' Cove—five couples and an extra man. What were they going to do? *They* had invaded her privacy, she thought resentfully; now she'd invade theirs. She picked up the house phone and asked Mrs. Skowronek to bring a pair of binoculars. "I want to watch some birds," she explained.

She watched the beach party through the powerful glasses, but they weren't drinking or singing or building a fire. Nor were they smoking grass or using drugs. Instead, they were holding a meeting, seated in a semicircle around Carl Rhodes, who seemed to be in charge. At least, he was doing the talking and apparently giving instructions to the others. In half an hour they left. The ice chest had not been opened; no one had played the guitar.

Puzzled, Barrett put the glasses down and went to the private beach for her swim. Later, when Clifton came to take her to dinner, she started to tell him about the group and then decided against it. He might feel as embarrassed as she did to learn that their names were linked together by the employees.

Late the next day she waited by the window with her binoculars, but no one came. She shrugged it off and decided that she had let her imagination get the better of her.

But the following day, the same group gathered on the secluded beach, with the ice chest and the guitar, and this time, too, they seemed to be having a meeting instead of a party. Was the so-called party a coverup or ruse of some kind? Were they merely ready to stage a party if an outsider happened by? Somehow, she had sensed something phony about Rhodes's invitation to join them.

On the surface, the gathering seemed innocent enough. In fact, the employees were encouraged to use the coves and beaches, which were part of the resort property, when they were off duty during the summer. She supposed it was the same with the ski facilities in winter. But what were these people doing? What was the purpose of their meeting? Of course, they might be rehearsing a skit for an employees' party or something like that. Perhaps she'd been watching too many cops-and-robbers shows.

However, she studied each person carefully through the glasses and tried to remember the eleven faces so she would recognize them at the resort. She was sure that Rhodes and the others had no idea she was observing them. Trees blocked the view of the shoreline from the east windows. It was the peculiar angle of her south window that made it possible for her to see them.

As soon as possible, she'd make it her business to spend some time in Starr's after midnight, when the night crew was on duty; they might all be members of the night shift under Carl Rhodes. When Uncle Justin returned from Europe, she would discuss it with him; he'd know what to make of it. When there were no more meetings during the rest of the week, she thought perhaps she was completely off base and pushed her suspicions to the back of her mind.

The following weekend was a long one, since the Fourth of July fell on Monday. Judith and Lyle arrived Friday afternoon.

"I'm glad to be here," Judith exclaimed as she unpacked her clothes and hung them in the closet in the guest room that was usually reserved for the headliner. "My folks are going to be in Sage Creek for the weekend, so I want to be gone."

"Is your father still uptight over your divorce?" Barrett asked.

"I'm sure he is, but, actually, I haven't seen him since that first weekend when I came home. Whenever the folks come to the ranch, I make it my business to be up here with you or in Reno. Fortunately, Dad's been awfully busy with state business, which has kept him in Carson City more than usual."

"Well, that helps."

"I talk to Mother nearly every day on the telephone, but Dad doesn't call me." She shrugged and placed a pile of undergarments in the dresser drawer. "Anyway, I'm going ahead with my divorce. The case is set for July 25th. I told my attorney that there's no great rush, so he waited until he could get the judge he wants."

"I'm sure you'll be relieved when it's all behind you."

"Will I! But then I'll have to decide what I want to do with my life. Get a job? Go back to school? What?" She slammed her suitcase shut. "I'm at such loose ends, so completely disoriented—and I loathe this feeling."

"Just give yourself a little time, Judith. Things will work out for you."

"I hope so." Her eyes filled with tears. "It's especially heartbreaking to live with this rift with Dad. If it weren't for Lyle, I don't know what I'd do. He's been so supportive."

That night, Clifton joined them for cocktails on the deck, and then they drove to the North Shore Club for dinner and gambling. While they were eating, Clifton turned to Lyle and said, "I heard about a deal today that I'd give my eyeteeth to be in on. A parcel of lakefront property is coming up for sale at a real bargain. The owner is pressed for cash in a hurry. If you're interested, Lyle, and could act fast, then hold on to it for a few months, you could turn it over and make some real money."

"I don't know," Lyle said. "I've just been involved in an expensive deal in Hawaii. But tell me about it, anyway."

As the two men talked, Barrett listened avidly. If only she were a partner in Starr Enterprises, she could take advantage of such an opportunity. She'd be consulted, along with Lyle and Justin, and that's what she wanted—to have power, to have authority to act. How true—it takes money to make money, as well as being in the position to make decisions.

Judith began to talk to her, but Barrett only half-listened. It was the business deal she was interested in; if she could just be a party to it. The two men decided to investigate the property the next morning but said nothing about including her. Someday, she vowed to herself, they'd *have* to turn to her. She'd be part of the action instead of a bystander.

Later, they returned to Starr's for the midnight ice-skating show. When it was over and they were headed for the bar, Barrett suggested, "Clifton, let's make the rounds of the resort. I'd like to see what you do." She didn't tell him that she particularly wanted to check on the night crew.

"All right," he said, and then, to Lyle and Judith, "We'll meet you later in the bar."

They walked through the Andromeda Room, and Barrett looked closely at each woman who worked there. Somehow, the dealer, cashiers, and change girls seemed different from the people she'd seen in the woods and on the beach. Maybe it was the uniforms they wore. Still, a girl who was working at one of the 21 tables seemed familiar. And in the Orion Room, Barrett saw a young woman with long, bleached hair, in charge of a baccarat game, who might have been in the woods. But she wasn't positive.

They entered the counting room, where three girls were separating the bills into denominations, adding them and putting wrappers around the piles. The silver was washed in a special machine and fed into cardboard rolls, to be counted and recorded. As Barrett watched the women work, she was almost certain she'd seen them through the binoculars, as they seemed very familiar. Yet she could have noticed them in one of the employees' lounges instead.

They returned to the corridor and climbed the ladder to the catwalk, then talked to the security guards who were watching the action below. She was *almost* sure they'd been on the beach.

As Clifton helped her down the steel stairs, she asked, "You don't have as many security men on the catwalk for the night shift, do you?"

"No. Our biggest crowd is during the evening. On the night shift those guards move from station to station, and the dealers and the players never know when they're under observation. Those three men seem to be handling the work all right. Besides, things slack off toward morning, and several tables are closed."

They made the rounds of the entertainment lounges and snack bars and took the elevator to the second floor, to the private gaming rooms. They walked up and down the corridors of the hotel, then outside to the parking lot. In a small black book Clifton made notes of spots on the rugs, room-service tables that were left too long in the hallways, the condition of ashtrays, the cleanliness of employees' uniforms, the service in the restaurants and parking area, and the general attitude of the staff.

Barrett smiled at him. "You're like a housewife: your work is never done."

"That's right. Those who are in charge of the various crews get a report from me each day. I want Starr's to be right at the top, and it takes constant supervision to stay there."

As they walked to the bar to rejoin Lyle and Judith, Barrett felt slightly foolish. In spite of twice observing the group on the beach through binoculars, she wasn't sure that she could identify them as being on the night shift, except Carl Rhodes, the floor boss. Even if she could, what had they done? Simply sat in a semicircle and listened to Rhodes. What harm was there in that? They could have been planning a surprise party or compiling grievances for their union representative. She'd better forget the whole thing and not discuss it with Uncle Justin.

"How about a nightcap?" Clifton suggested as he slid into the booth where Judith and Lyle were seated.

"All right," Barrett said, "But then I want to go home. It's late."

They weren't the only ones having a nightcap. Otto Schroeder, who had been gambling away his paycheck at a crap table, came into the bar and sat on a stool in the semidarkness. He ordered a scotch on the rocks and, as he sipped it, watched the party in the booth.

He recognized the boss, Mr. McMillan, and Barrett Starr, who seemed to be at the resort most of the time. Whenever he saw her, he felt a spasm of fear. Had she seen him at the rocket the night of Lea Turner's death? Would she, sooner or later, remember him?

Otto looked at the girl who was with Lyle Starr, the big shot, and gasped in surprise. It was Judith Davenport. She looked older, and her hair was fixed differently, but he was certain that it was Judith.

Now, that was a break. Judith Davenport! He hadn't seen her in five years—not since she got married and left Sage Creek. Was she back on a visit or to stay? He could call up the ranch, give a false name and find out.

As the group got up to leave, he turned his head so they wouldn't see him. But as they crossed the lounge, excitement mounted in him. It *was* Judith Davenport, the apple of Elliott Davenport's eye. He still had a score to settle with that fink, and there was no better way than through his daughter.

More than once, since the death of Lea Turner, he'd been tempted to quit his job and leave the state, but that would have been foolish. He might have called attention to himself. Besides, his revenge was only half-satisfied.

He was too excited to sleep that night, and at nine o'clock the next morning he stopped at a pay phone and called Sage Creek.

"Is Judith Davenport there?"

"No, she isn't. She's at Lake Tahoe for the weekend. Who is calling, please? I'll give her your message."

It was a voice that Otto hadn't heard before. "My name is Leo Duncan. I knew her at the university. This isn't Mrs. Davenport, is it?"

"No, I'm the housekeeper."

"I'm going to be in Nevada a great deal this summer. Tell me, is Judith living there at Sage Creek?"

"Yes, she is."

"Then, I'll call her again. Just tell her Leo phoned."

He felt very pleased with himself. So Judith was back at Sage Creek. Her marriage was probably on the rocks. That explained why she was with Lyle Starr. Well, well. She'd probably be coming to Tahoe often. She'd be hanging around the casino and would be a sitting duck. But he'd have to make some plans. Whatever he did, he'd want to pull it off with the same finesse he'd used on Lea. He couldn't wait too long, either, because there was no way of knowing how long she'd stay in Nevada. Besides, he wanted to go someplace else and make a fresh start.

He thought with satisfaction of his money in Carson City. He thought of Lea Turner, too, but without remorse. Revenge was sweet, and she got what was coming to her. Now there was Elliott Davenport to take care of, and he deserved everything that *he'd* get, too. Davenport had called in the narcs, and so he, too, was to blame for Kirt's death—he and Lea. Well, Lea was out of the picture, and that left the high and mighty lieutenant governor, who had a precious daughter named Judith.

CHAPTER

16

Justin Starr eased his head back on the airliner pillow and closed his eyes. Thank God, he'd soon be home. He could no longer ignore the pains in his chest, which warned of an impending attack of angina pectoris, and he reached in his pocket for his nitroglycerin tablets and put one under his tongue. Even after the pain subsided, however, nausea persisted. At least they'd been able to get first-class accommodations clear through to Reno, when they had changed their reservations in Paris, so he had plenty of legroom and could stretch out.

He had made it off the 747 from Paris to Chicago, gone through customs and boarded this plane without collapsing. James Nichols wanted them to lay over in an airport hotel at O'Hare in Chicago, but Justin insisted on going home. He had just so much strength, he felt—just enough to get home to his own bed. Once there, he would take it easy a few days before going back to work.

He hadn't felt well on the entire trip. There had

been too much flying, too much hurry, too many people to see. And all the time Nichols kept asking him questions, probing for his reactions to every situation. What did he think of this? What did he think of that? The pains in his chest, just twinges at first, had grown progressively worse and were controlled only by the nitroglycerin. By the time they arrived in Paris, on the Fourth of July, Justin decided he had better spend a day or two in bed.

The original itinerary for their return leg had called for three days in Manhattan to discuss the book with Nichols's publisher, but Justin said, "I don't think I'd better try to stop over in New York. My ticker's acting up. I'd be wise to get home as soon as I can."

Nichols, alarmed by Justin's ashen face and waning strength, agreed. "I'll take our tickets to the travel bureau in the hotel and see if we can change our reservations—to skip New York."

"When you get it worked out, send a cable to Mrs. Starr so she'll be expecting us."

"Will do, Mr. Starr. You take it easy, and I'll arrange everything."

Nichols had made the new arrangements, and they'd soon be home. Justin sighed in relief. It would be nearly midnight when they arrived in Reno, but Fred, the chauffeur, would be there to meet them. He'd take care of the luggage and help him into the car. Maybe Eunice would be there, too. He'd sure be glad to see her! He hoped she'd be pleased with the gifts he'd brought her. He tried to ignore the tight feeling and sense of impending disaster that were typical of angina. Finally he dozed, until Nichols touched his arm.

"We're about to land in Reno, Mr. Starr. You're supposed to buckle your seat belt."

The lights of Reno danced in the darkness below. He saw the red glow from the neon lights of the casinos. His own club was among them, somewhere—

his own niche, where he belonged. He didn't care if he never left Nevada again. He supposed Eunice would insist on calling the doctor in the morning, but that was all right; he probably needed one.

They landed, and Nichols helped him into the waiting room. "You watch for your driver, Mr. Starr, while I get our luggage." But there was no chauffeur and no Eunice. Justin sat on a settee, feeling deflated and ill and wondering where they were.

Finally Nichols came with a porter and their luggage. "No one's here to meet you?"

Justin shook his head. "I guess not." Where the hell were they?

The porter spoke up. "If you want a cab, sir, I'd better get one right away. Soon they'll all be taken, and you'll have a long wait for another one."

"Yes, get a cab for us," Nichols said. "This gentleman isn't feeling well, and he should get home at once."

Anger smoldered in Justin. Where was his chauffeur? Where was Eunice? If he had ever needed them, this was the time. "You're sure you sent that cable?" he snapped at Nichols.

"I sent it all right, but apparently they didn't receive it." Nichols's voice reflected his own weariness and irritation, as if he, too, would be glad when the journey was finally over.

As they rode in the cab, Justin took out his wallet, pulled out a bill and stuffed it in Nichols's hand. "You settle with the driver when he gets you home."

When they arrived at the mansion, Justin let himself in with his key, ignored the suitcases the cabdriver had placed in the hall and climbed shakily up the stairs, anger boiling inside of him. Christ, he spent a fortune maintaining a staff of servants and they weren't around when he wanted them. *Someone*

should have met him at the airport. They owed him
at least that much consideration.

Desperately tired, shaking with renewed pain and
feeling his temper rising, he stumbled down the hall
and yanked open the door to the upstairs sitting room,
which was softly lighted by a small lamp on the television. He crossed the room and entered the master
bedroom, a huge room with two queen-size beds.
When he snapped on the light, he saw Eunice in a
stupor on her bed and liquor bottles on the nightstand. An unopened cable was propped against a
lamp.

Blind with rage, he staggered across the room,
leaned over Eunice and shook her by the shoulders.
"You goddamn drunk! You can't do this to me!" He
shook her until a massive pain suddenly squeezed his
chest like a vise. Perspiration burst out on his forehead
and purplish-red face. He fell unconscious against the
nightstand, knocking the lamp and bottles over with a
thunderous crash.

Mary, the lady's maid, appeared in the doorway in
her bathrobe. "Mrs. Starr, are you all right?" Then
she saw Justin crumpled on the floor in the midst of
broken glass, with the cable in his hand. "*Oh, my
God!*" She rushed to the telephone.

For days, numb with guilt, Eunice sat in the green
armchair in Justin's hospital room while he hovered
between life and death. Small electrodes were taped to
his chest and connected by thin wires to a continuous
electrocardiograph. The pattern of his heartbeats was
displayed on a screen above his head, as well as at
the nurses' station, where it was monitored by special
personnel. Private-duty nurses observed his heart
action on the screen in his room, applied an oxygen
mask when necessary, supervised the intravenous unit
and kept him alive.

The cardiologist, a gray-haired, bearded man, explained the tracings on the cardiogram to Eunice. "Look at the elevation of the S-T segments, followed by these Q waves—deep ones—in all these tracings that reflect the front part of the heart. It shows that Mr. Starr has had a massive myocardial infarction, which is an obstruction in a coronary artery."

"I see." Eunice cringed inwardly as she told herself that this wouldn't have happened if she had met Justin at the airport.

"He's running a temperature, which is a good sign in this instance, for it shows inflammation, or that his body has started the healing process."

"Oh?"

The doctor warmed to his subject. "Already there's been an outpouring of special repair cells, new tissue growth and enzyme activity. Scar tissue will form over the damaged area, and the neighboring tissues will come to the rescue. Their arteries will send out buds that'll grow into the injured zone. When this is finished, a new network of blood vessels will have been created, which is called 'collateral circulation.' It's amazing how the heart will heal itself, given a chance."

Eunice looked at him, her chin trembling. "Be honest with me, Doctor. Could he have another attack? In the next few days, I mean."

The doctor nodded. "Yes, there's always that possibility. But he's right here where he can get immediate help, which is most important."

"Would you say that his condition is very critical?"

"Yes, I would. This coming week will tell the tale. Then we'll be able to make a more accurate prognosis."

"So it can go either way?"

"Yes. Mr. Starr is getting every possible care, but his age is against him. Still, older men than he have pulled through and gone on for several years."

So for the next week Eunice kept constant vigil by

his bedside, flagellating herself with remorse. This is all my fault, she thought over and over. Justin didn't deserve such shabby treatment from her—not after fifteen years of devotion and kindness. Lyle came frequently, which helped her, and Barrett drove down from Tahoe. Justin spoke to them weakly, before he closed his eyes and dozed, but at least he was aware that they had come to see him.

Justin slept a great deal, and there were times when Eunice pushed aside her guilt and, in spite of herself, made plans, wonderful plans. If Justin died and she was free again, what would she do? It became sort of a game, considering all the options. One thing she knew for certain: she'd sell the mansion, for it was community property and not part of the corporation's holdings, and she'd move to San Francisco. Perhaps she'd buy a luxurious apartment in one of the high-rise buildings overlooking the Bay, near several friends from her Bellingham days. It would cost only half of what she'd realize from the sale of the mansion.

Her thoughts raced on. It would be easy to sell the house for double its cost, for there were many wealthy people who wished to establish official residence in Nevada for tax reasons. The sale would net her a large nest egg. Besides, she had saved some money over the years. She'd also have a generous trust fund that would provide her with every luxury for the rest of her life.

She'd take her furniture and most of the servants with her. She would come into her own again, with an established place in San Francisco society, she thought excitedly. She could even resume her Bellingham name, which was one of the great ones in the Bay Area. Even as a widow, she'd have a rich, rewarding life. She could belong to any number of social clubs, as well as to the opera guild and the symphony league, or be a lecturer for an art museum. She could play bridge, have luncheon with her friends and shop at the exclusive stores. She could travel and go on cruises.

She thought of her peninsula friends who now lived in San Francisco. She would enjoy being with them again. She wouldn't have to worry about Justin, whether he was impressing her friends or making a gaffe. She wouldn't have to cringe when her friends exchanged contemptuous or scornful looks after one of his blunders. Nor would she have to listen to their lame excuses for not visiting her, nor try to justify their "regrets" when Justin insisted that they be invited to one of his parties. He could never understand why they didn't come. But they'd be glad to be entertained by the impeccable Eunice Bellingham in her San Francisco home.

What about Lyle? Would he stay in Reno? She doubted it. He would inherit the bulk of the Starr fortune, of course. He was young. Most of his life was ahead of him, and he, too, would be free to do whatever he wanted. He, too, could come into his own.

But by the end of the week it became increasingly apparent that Justin was going to pull through. He suffered no more attacks and grew stronger every day. Now her guilt was compounded. Not only had she contributed to his heart attack, she had anticipated her life without him. She had looked forward to it—longed for it, in fact. To compensate, she doubled her efforts to demonstrate her concern.

"Darling, I have some good news," she greeted him one morning. "I've just been talking with the doctor, and you're so much better that you're going to be moved out of the coronary unit to a regular wing of the hospital."

"I wish I was going home," he said grumpily. "I haven't slept in my own bed for over three weeks."

She kissed him and patted his arm. "It won't be

long. You're doing so well, we'll have you home before you know it."

That afternoon he was moved to a private room in the west wing, where he could look out his window at the Sierra range. His night nurse was dismissed. He was permitted to sit up part of the time and even to walk, with a nurse holding one arm while Eunice held the other.

At the end of the second week in the hospital, he had made exceptional improvement and was even more impatient about going home. "All these nurses get on my nerves," he complained when they were alone. "I'm damned sick of having them hover around me all the time."

"But it's been their wonderful care that pulled you through."

"I know that," he snapped irritably, "but they're driving me nuts."

When the doctor came on his daily rounds, Justin said, "I'm tired of being cooped up here. I want to go home."

The doctor smiled. "Now you sound like a man who's on the mend for sure. If I thought I could trust you, I'd let you go home tomorrow, but it means complete rest for a good month—no work, just taking it easy. I could work out a regime with your nurse, if you'd live up to it."

At the word *nurse*, Justin scowled; so Eunice spoke up. "Couldn't *I* take care of him? I'm sure I could make him behave. I'd see to it that he keeps quiet."

"Well, I don't know," the doctor said hesitantly. "You're so petite, Mrs. Starr, I wonder if you're strong enough to manage it. For example, I want someone in the bathroom with him when he takes a shower, in case he feels faint and needs help. Our patient is a big man."

"I'm sure I can work something out. For instance, if Justin and I are confined to the house, our chauffeur won't be doing anything. Fred is devoted to Mr. Starr. I know he'd help me."

Justin looked at the doctor eagerly. "Let me go home. Mrs. Starr may be small but, by God, she can be a regular hard-nosed sergeant when necessary. She'll make me toe the mark. Hell, I got a houseful of servants who can shake their tails a little for a change."

The doctor fingered his beard. Did he dare trust Mrs. Starr to carry out his orders? He knew of her drinking problem; their family doctor had filled him in on that point. Would she stay sober and remember to give Justin his medicine? Would she carefully limit his visitors, who would tax his strength? Would she supervise his diet properly and carry out the regime he needed? Or would she crawl into a bottle and undo all that had been accomplished these last two weeks?

Eunice sensed his uncertainty. "I'll be most conscientious—scrupulous—about everything, Doctor. I know how important it is to follow your orders to the letter. But we'll do it, won't we, Justin?"

"You bet we will. My wife has me buffaloed. She's the boss around the house, and I'll do just what she says. Just let me get the hell out of here."

Eunice touched the doctor's arm. "Please let us try it for a while and see how we manage. I know Justin would be more content if I took care of him, with the servants to help me. He's so used to all of us. You could drop by the house and check up on us."

"That's true."

"And another point. We have an elevator in the house, so we can get Mr. Starr up and down without his climbing the stairs. I had it installed when we built the house, for just such a contingency."

The doctor tried to decide. It was important that the old boy be content. Also, Mrs. Starr seemed so eager to try, in spite of the fact that Justin would be a restive and difficult patient. She'd have her hands full. If he could just believe that she'd stay sober. He shrugged; that was a chance he'd have to take. "Well, all right, we'll try it. I'll dismiss you tomorrow in your wife's care. But it's with the understanding that if it becomes advisable, I can bring in a nurse. Otherwise, back you come to the hospital, Mr. Starr."

Justin smiled. "OK, I agree to that."

"Remember, you're to take it very easy this next month. I'll bring the instruction sheet tomorrow—and a diet list." He was already regretting his decision. Would Justin Starr survive another attack? He doubted it. "You're to have *no* alcoholic beverages while you're convalescing. No beer, no wine, nothing."

He looked at Justin sternly, then at Eunice. Could he trust her?

CHAPTER

17

The following Friday, Judith and Lyle arrived at Starpoint late in the afternoon. When Barrett met them at the door, she said, "Judith can bunk with me, but, Lyle, I'm going to ask you to use your room at the resort. The house is full. Would you believe that the headliner brought his wife, four kids, his mother and a nursemaid?"

As they walked up the stairs, Judith said, "Even with that crowd, it's better than being at Sage Creek with my folks this weekend."

Lyle, who followed them, carrying Judith's suitcase, stage-whispered, "You can always come to the resort and share *my* room, Judith."

The girls laughed, then Barrett said, "That might be very sticky, with the divorce trial coming up Monday."

"At least, the divorce ought to go through without a hitch," Lyle said. "No one is contesting anything."

"You're so right. They can't get rid of me fast enough." They entered the bedroom, and Judith opened her suitcase and took out a cotton voile dress. "I *knew* this would be wrinkled. Would it be all right with Mrs. Skowronek if I go downstairs and press it?"

"Of course. Or one of the maids——"

"I'll do it myself. The help must be swamped, with so many guests."

When she had gone, Barrett asked Lyle, "How is Uncle Justin? When I called Tuesday night, Eunice told me she was bringing him home the next day."

"Oh, he's home, all right, and he's impossibly crabby and demanding, if that's a good sign. I think Mother's out of her mind, trying to take care of him herself. He'll run her ragged."

"She said she thought he'd be more content without a lot of nurses around."

"Content or not, she should consider herself." Lyle walked to the window. "The maid told me how Dad found Mother passed out the night he came home from Paris. Mary heard him shouting and carrying on, and that probably brought on his heart attack. I suppose that's why Mother is playing the martyr role. But, hell, who *wouldn't* drink if they had to live with Justin Starr?"

"He must be especially difficult now." Barrett joined Lyle at the window. "You have to remember that he's been desperately ill. He worries about himself and the business, and he takes his frustrations out on you."

"Oh, I know that. I shouldn't be impatient with him, but I'm glad to get away from Reno for the weekend. Dad wants me to brief him on every move I've made for the last month, and he finds fault with every damn thing." Exasperation showed on his face. "Sometimes I'd like to chuck everything and leave. Dad's impossible now!"

"Lyle, his heart attack scared him."

"It didn't stop him from keeping tabs on me. The

only right thing I've done is buy that property at
Tahoe that Clifton told me about. Dad agreed that
I got a real bargain there—did something correct for
once. Other than that, he's been on my back about
everything."

"That's too bad."

"I shouldn't talk like this. I'm actually devoted to
the old boy. Where would I be without him? It's just
that he drives me up the wall sometimes."

"You'll have to get Clifton to find you another
good deal."

"You better believe it! Dad is ranting about the
Hawaii operation, too. He thinks we've tied up too
much money over there, and he doesn't like the idea
of joining a limited partnership to raise venture capital.
He says we should do everything on our own so we
have complete control. He doesn't appreciate the in-
come-tax advantages I've worked out on it. He's so
far behind the times it's pitiful."

Barrett rose to her uncle's defense. "He must have
done *something* right to make all his millions." She
wanted to ask, and who's going to benefit so handsomely from his efforts? But she held her tongue.
Lyle was already too morose.

She had to admit that it must be dreadfully hard
on Lyle to be under Justin's thumb. Her uncle was a
domineering, tactless man who always spoke his
mind. Lyle worked hard and had much ability in
many ways, but she sympathized with Justin, too.
As devoted as he was to his son, she sensed that he
often questioned Lyle's judgment. In spite of Lyle's
sophistication, there were times when he could be
surprisingly naïve and easily moved by flattery. He
hadn't come up the hard way, like Justin, so he lacked
his father's tough, practical experience.

She looked out the window and saw that the night-shift group was at the beach again. To change the subject she said, "Look down there at Pirates' Cove. See those people?" She told him about their meetings and how she'd observed them through binoculars. "They're all from the night shift, and I think I have them pinpointed. Carl Rhodes, the floor boss, seems to be in charge. What do you suppose they're doing?"

"Obviously, nothing very wicked." Lyle laughed. "They're just sitting in a semicircle and listening to Rhodes."

"But why do they meet so often? It's three or four times a week. Why pretend that they're going to have a party, and always bring the ice chest and a guitar?"

"You seem determined to make a mystery out of it, Barrett. Did it ever occur to you that they might be a TM or AA group? Or Gamblers Anonymous? Or a therapy group for divorced people who are trying to help each other adjust? Or something equally innocent?"

Maybe you're right." She felt a little foolish. "It just struck me as strange, and I wanted to talk to you or Uncle Justin about it."

Lyle turned away from the window. "Well, forget it. Don't bother Dad about it. They're not doing anything wrong. They could be holding a prayer meeting, for all you know."

"Could be." Still, it bothered her that Lyle was so brusque about it. When Uncle Justin was better, she'd talk to him about the mysterious gatherings, anyway.

Judith came back with her dress pressed and on a hanger. "Wow! Mrs. Skowronek is really pushed out of shape about those kids. It seems that they're spoiled brats and don't mind anyone—least of all her."

"They don't mind me, either," Barrett declared.

"They're not destructive, but they're impudent and smart-mouthed. I'd like to give each of them a good whack on the bottom."

"Better not," Lyle warned.

Later, when they were having dinner at the resort with Clifton, Barrett said, "Lyle, tell Cliff how pleased Uncle Justin was about the property you purchased."

"According to Dad, it's the only correct move I've made in the last month. If you hear of anything else, please let me know."

Clifton smiled. "I sure will, but I'm a hotel man, not usually in on business transactions. But if I get onto something good, I'll call you. We should keep you in your father's good graces."

"You can say that again. Ever since his heart attack, I've been in the doghouse."

"Move over," Judith said, "I'm in there with you, Lyle. Only I'm in worse shape. Dad and I aren't even communicating. At least you and Justin are doing that, and he approved of your purchasing the property here at the lake."

Clifton leaned forward. "You know, Lyle, it might be a good idea if we see that real-estate man we dealt with. We could see him tomorrow. Something else might have come up that would please Mr. Starr."

"OK. I'll be here at the resort. Whenever you're ready in the morning, we'll buzz over to his place."

After dinner they went to a movie and returned to the resort for dancing. A bearded man in an old Chevy watched them as they parked in Clifton's reserved space, just before one o'clock.

Otto Schroeder gripped the steering wheel as he watched Judith Davenport and Lyle Starr standing in a pool of light. They were waiting for Clifton McMillan to lock his car. Then the resident manager put his arm around Barrett Starr's waist, and they joined the other couple. Otto's lip curled in disdain. What a cozy foursome!

He returned to his room, poured himself a drink and sat in his easy chair. It was time to lay out a course of action. The excitement over Lea Turner's death had died down, and though the insurance adjusters still came and went, they were spinning their wheels. He'd wrap up the deal with the Davenports and split. He wanted it to be unique—drawn out and agonizing. Otto had suffered for five years and, even now, grief over Kirt's death still stabbed at him; so why should Elliott Davenport get off easy? He should have nightmares, too.

He thought of ways he could get revenge: burn Sage Creek to the ground when the Davenports were gone, poison his cattle, or murder Elliott Davenport. But his mind kept coming back to Judith, the lieutenant governor's weak spot. Otto remembered all the time that Elliott had spent with his daughter, as a child and as a teen-ager. How the old man doted on her! If anything happened to Judith, it would hit him right where he lived—he'd never get over it. And he'd still be alive to suffer.

Suppose he did settle on Judith. Then what? What would be most excruciating for Davenport? He considered a half-dozen ideas, but nothing seemed worse than kidnapping. Especially if ransom letters kept coming to the parents, so their hopes were buoyed up, then crushed, time after time.

It was risky, of course, but he grew more excited as he developed the thought. What if he kidnapped Judith, hid her in an abandoned house or cave in the Sierra—tied her up so good that she couldn't escape —and just left her there?

Once he got her hid away, he could head east and mail ransom letters all along the way, with no intention of keeping the rendezvous. He wouldn't try to collect the money; that would be taking too big a chance. A lieutenant governor has a lot of clout, and the FBI and all the fuzz would be on the job. He'd keep mailing the ransom letters to keep Davenport in a stew.

After he left Tahoe, what would be the danger? He wouldn't have Judith with him. He'd be an ordinary drifter, heading east in an old car. Every few days he would swing off the highway, drive through a small town in the back country and stop just long enough to mail a ransom note. The cops wouldn't know what was going on, and he could sit back and enjoy the excitement. He could watch the news on TV and read about it in the papers. He'd get his revenge, all right.

In the meantime, what would happen to Judith? If she starved to death, so what? Davenport would find out for sure what it's like to lose a loved one— someone close, as Kirt had been to him.

He'd have to make careful preparations—not do anything rash or hurried. First, he'd find a place to hide her. Somewhere remote, where he wouldn't be observed and where she wouldn't be found by a fisherman or a hiker. Still, it would have to be near a road, so he could drive there in a car. He'd also have to figure out the right time to do it. She'd have to be here, at Tahoe, and by herself; and she seemed to come here frequently. The important thing was to act when the opportunity presented itself and to leave Nevada as soon as he hid her away.

He finished his drink and banged his glass on the end table. He'd start looking for a hiding place right after breakfast. He could wind everything up within three or four weeks.

Late Monday afternoon, Barrett stood at her window with her binoculars and watched the group from the night crew on the beach at Pirates' Cove. In spite of Lyle she knew they weren't conducting a group-therapy session or a prayer meeting. They looked as if they were getting instructions from Carl Rhodes, and one of the men was making notes in a little book. Impulsively, she stepped to the telephone, called the mansion in Reno and asked to speak to Eunice Starr. "Would Uncle Justin feel up to seeing me if I drove to Reno tonight? There's something I want to discuss with him."

"Yes, I think so; he seems to feel quite well tonight. He's almost ready to have dinner, but he could wait and eat with you."

"No, have him eat now. I had a huge lunch, and I'm not at all hungry. I won't stay too long and tire him. I'll leave right now and should be there in an hour."

Barrett was shown into the upstairs sitting room, where Justin was in his recliner, looking thinner but much improved. Eunice excused herself. "I'll leave you two alone so you can talk. Before you leave, Barrett, come downstairs to the family room. A snack will be waiting for you." She took a timer from a table. "I'm setting this for fifteen minutes. When you hear it ring, it's time to leave." Then she closed the door behind her.

Justin shook his head in mock despair. "She does that with everybody. Sit down, my dear."

Quickly, Barrett told her uncle about the meetings, her surveillance, and Lyle's reaction. "He's probably right, Uncle Justin, and I'm all wrong, but I thought you should know about it."

Justin drummed his fingers on the arm of his recliner. "For the sake of argument, let's assume that you're right, that there *is* something fishy about those meetings. What do you think is going on?"

"I think the casino's getting ripped off." She hitched her chair forward. "I think it's more than a coincidence that three security guards, three girls in the counting room, some dealers, a pit boss and a floor boss meet that often. All from the night shift, too. Is it possible that they could cheat the house in some way?"

"Of course they could!" Justin's face flushed with anger. "They could rip us off in a dozen ways if they worked together as a team. For example, the girls in the counting room could be skimming the receipts. That's the way the underworld operates in the casinos they control. In other words, when the money comes in, a lot of it is stashed away before it's recorded for the house and the tax collectors. Of course, the security guards on the catwalk would have to be in on it."

"And the dealers?"

"Well, I've told you about toke hustling. There are lots of ways a dealer can see to it that a customer wins—if the pit boss isn't doing his job, of course. It would be especially easy on a night shift, early in the morning, when the crowd thins out.

"Suppose certain customers were part of the racket. They could get in a twenty-one game and keep track of the cards. That's called 'counting aces,' and some gamblers are experts at remembering all the cards that have been played. If most of the fifty-two cards in the deck have been played and a sharpie realizes that a fistful of high-value cards are left, which throws the odds against the house, he will increase his bets. He might jump from five to five hundred dollars a hand."

"And that's not against the rules?"

"No, it's perfectly legal, but a dealer is supposed to reshuffle the deck long before most of the cards are used. But let's say she doesn't, and let's suppose that the pit boss lets her get by without reshuffling. You can see how easily the player who's counting aces could win big and how the house could lose big."

Barrett nodded. "And what other ways?"

"A dealer could mark cards with infrared dye, which can only be seen through special contact lenses, which a confederate would wear. They could sure clean up that way."

"I can imagine."

"Another thing. When a dealer pays a winner off, she could hand over one-hundred-dollar chips to a confederate instead of ten-dollar chips. Or actually steal chips. There are a lot of things she could do if the security guards and the pit boss let her get by with it. Of course, that's their job—to prevent that sort of thing."

"I think a lot of things like that are going on, but how do we prove it?"

"First, take several pictures of the group at the beach. There's a camera with a telescopic lens around here someplace. Ask Eunice for it. Lyle bought it to take pictures of animals and birds, but he's over that kick now. You could go to a camera shop at Tahoe and learn how to use it." Justin swore softly as the timer signaled, but he went on, quickly, "Get yourself assigned to the personnel department as soon as possible and find out all you can about the group. When you have some information, come see me again."

"I will, Uncle Justin."

"In the meantime, don't tell anyone about this— and I mean *no one*." He shook his finger at her. "And be damned careful, my girl. This could be a tie-up with organized crime. So watch yourself. They play rough."

As Barrett rose to her feet, an ominous foreboding

came over her. "I'll be careful. I could be all wrong about this, Uncle Justin. You'll forgive me if I am, won't you? It's just that I have this funny feeling."

"Play your hunches, my dear. You're a true Starr. If you have a gut feeling that something's wrong, look into it. Always play your hunches. I do."

She kissed him good-bye and joined Eunice in the family room downstairs, where a carafe of coffee and a plate of sandwiches and cupcakes were ready for her.

"How nice of you, Eunice. Thank you." She poured herself a cup of coffee and another cup for Eunice. "Uncle Justin is looking so much better." He might be difficult, she thought, but she admired him and was very fond of him.

Eunice sat across from Barrett. "Justin is improving, but we still have several weeks of convalescing. He gets terribly impatient sometimes."

Her aunt looked tired, Barrett thought. Still, she was more clear-eyed than before. Her face had lost its puffiness, showing her patrician bone structure to advantage. It was obvious that she wasn't drinking.

"Uncle Justin was in a good mood this evening."

Eunice nodded. "Of course, he was delighted to see you. And Lyle was here this afternoon about more property at Tahoe. It's a particularly good buy, so Justin was happy about that. Sometimes the two of them are at loggerheads, which naturally upsets me." Eunice sighed, sipped her coffee and then looked up with a smile. "I asked Lyle how he happened to find two great bargains at about the same time. You know how expensive that lakefront property usually is."

Barrett refrained from giving the credit to Clifton. Instead she said, "Well, Lyle is a fine businessman. No doubt people tell him about property that comes on the market, since they know he is able to make investments."

When she'd finished eating, Barrett asked Eunice for the loan of the camera, and while her aunt went to find it, she telephoned Judith to learn about the divorce.

Judith sounded relieved. "Actually, it was just a matter of going through the motions. This morning I took Mrs. Evans, our housekeeper, to verify my Nevada residence, and it was all over very fast. The Rosenfelds paid all the costs and their attorney handed me a check for fifty thousand dollars. So I'm flush at the moment."

"What are you going to do with the money?"

"I've put it in a savings account until I decide what to do. I was thinking that I might buy a boutique or a gift shop. I think I'd like that better than working in an office or going back to school."

"Judith, let an old businesswoman give you some advice. Don't rush into anything. Work in a boutique or a gift shop for a while and get some experience before you invest a cent."

"That's a good idea, if I can find a job. I haven't had any working experience."

"Would you like me to speak to the manager of the gift shop at the resort? Even if you helped out on a voluntary basis, it would give you some training and be worthwhile."

"Yes, please do that, Barrett. You know, for the first time since I left Murray, I feel good about myself and want to start a new life."

"Wonderful! And congratulations on your divorce. You have your whole life ahead of you, and it'll be a good one, Judith. Just don't buy a shop until you know what you're doing."

"I promise to ask your advice first."

"I suppose you've talked to your mother today."

"Yes, and she's glad it's all over."

"Now that your divorce is behind you, why don't you go to Carson City and see your father? Maybe he feels differently by now, and you could have a reconciliation."

There was a long silence, and when Judith replied, her voice broke. "Mom told me he hasn't changed. He never will, I know that. I think he could accept the divorce but not my leaving Murray in his condition. I'm afraid our break is permanent."

"I'm so sorry, Judith. Forgive me for bringing it up when you were in such good spirits. Anyway, I'm glad the trial is behind you. Well, I'd better hang up and drive back to Tahoe."

"Say hi to Clifton."

"I'll drop by the resort tonight and tell him the news about your divorce and the settlement."

All the way back to Tahoe, Barrett worried about the casino. She'd suspected from the first that there was an organized racket to rip off the gaming receipts, but she had thought it was a local plot, involving only a few employees. Justin's warning that it could be connected with organized crime sounded much more ominous. How could she handle the situation? Justin was still too ill to do much. Would Lyle give her any support?

She parked in the employees' lot at the resort, locked the camera in the trunk and went directly to Clifton's office. He was ready to go on his nightly inspection tour, so she went with him. She loved every foot of the place and felt a proprietary interest in each entry in his notebook, as she, too, wanted everything in perfect condition. The thought that the underworld could have a foothold in this luxurious resort, now such a part of her, was abhorrent. If only she had an official position in Starr Enterprises. If only she had the authority to act on her own, instead of through Lyle. She had never felt so helpless and frustrated.

When they were finished, they went to Clifton's apartment. She longed to discuss the situation with him so as to get his help and take advantage of his expertise, but she remembered her promise to Justin and said nothing.

Clifton fixed them a drink and sat next to her on the sofa. He took her in his arms and kissed her. "I want you to marry me, darling. I'm not satisfied with this arrangement."

"Oh, Cliff."

"I want us to make a home together and have children. I want you with me all the time."

"But, Cliff, we're together *most* of the time." He was so appealing. She loved being with him. But marriage. . . . "Just give me a while longer."

"It's been almost two months now. Surely you could have made up your mind by now."

"I've said from the first that I'm not interested in marriage—not now. I've never deceived you about that. I'm still not ready for such a commitment. What's wrong with the way things are?"

He took her hand and kissed the palm. "I want to have a feeling of permanence. I'm nearly thirty-one, and I want to get married. I want to know that if I should ever leave here, you'd be with me."

Leave Tahoe? It was unthinkable, she told herself. This is where she belonged, Clifton or no Clifton. The resort was too important to her; she could never leave it.

She pulled him close. "Please, let's not talk about marriage now." And they didn't mention it again during the entire night.

The next morning Barrett went to the gift shop and spoke to the manager about Judith. "You wouldn't have to pay her, you understand—unless you have an opening. She's mainly interested in learning the business. Job training, you might say."

The manager, a middle-aged woman, nodded. "I can't afford to hire more help. It's not just the salary; it's all the fringe benefits I have to pay, too. But I'd be glad to let her work without salary and to give her some training."

"When could she start?"

The manager thought a moment. "I'm taking some time off for minor surgery, so I'd rather she came after I got back. Let's say the tenth of August."

Barrett called Judith and told her about the arrangements. "You could stay with me at Starpoint."

"No, I don't want to freeload on you all the time. Perhaps I can rent one of the cheaper rooms at the resort. I have some money, other than my settlement, that will keep me going."

Barrett laughed. "I've never worried about your finances. You've never been really poor, like me."

"Anyway, it'll be great to be near you and Cliff and to have some direction in my life, for a change. I took a long horseback ride this morning and was thinking how wonderful it is to be Judith Davenport again."

"I told you to be patient and that things would work out."

At noon, Barrett drove to the California side of the lake to a camera shop, bought several rolls of film and learned to use the telescopic lens. However, at the end of the day, when she went back to Starpoint to shower and change, before Clifton picked her up for dinner, she saw no one at Pirates' Cove.

The next afternoon, the group appeared on the beach again, with Carl Rhodes in charge. To use the telescopic lens, she had to lean out the window. Hoping she had made the proper adjustments, she snapped several pictures of the group in the semi-circle. Then she waited until the meeting was over and took individual pictures as everyone turned from the beach and filed into the woods.

At the next meeting, she snapped pictures of the members as they stood on the beach and sat in the sand, listening to the floor boss. Her arms ached from holding the camera in such an awkward position, but she finished the roll of film.

As she withdrew from the open window, she glanced down and saw Chuck Moody, the grounds-keeper, standing behind a shrub, with pruning shears in his hand, staring at her intently. There was no trace of his affable manner; instead, he seemed distinctly hostile and alarmed.

How long had he been watching her? What was he thinking? As Barrett stared back at him, icy fingers of fear crept up her spine.

CHAPTER

18

Eunice worked out a routine for Justin. He rose each morning at eight and, still wearing his pajamas and bathrobe, ate breakfast in his recliner and watched television. At nine, the chauffeur came to help him shave, take a shower and dress. After Justin rested, it was time for his exercise. With Eunice on one side of him and Fred on the other, they took the elevator down to the first floor.

Jacques, the chef, always stepped out of the kitchen to greet him with a smile. "Good morning, Mr. Starr. You look fine. That makes me very happy." He would clasp his hands to his chest and beam. Then the butler would appear and hold the door open. "Good morning, sir. How much better you look today." If a maid was nearby, she, too, would add her good wishes. Justin, basking in all this attention, would usually answer, "Guess there's life in the old boy yet."

Outside, they walked slowly along the paths, stopped to talk to the gardeners, watched the birds and the squirrels, sat in chairs by the pool, then walked again until Justin began to tire. Back in the upstairs sitting room, he would stretch out in his recliner and doze until lunch was served.

Eunice carefully supervised his diet, gave him his medicine, and spent all her time by his side, ready to wait on him. Only when visitors came did she leave, and then only for a few minutes. She always set the timer to limit the visits but would invite the callers for refreshments in the family room before they left.

To sustain her through Justin's mercurial moods and the endless television programs, she worked on needlepoint as she sat near him and thought about her life with Andrew or what she could be doing in San Francisco if she were there. Mentally, she would visit a different area of the city each day—Union Square, St. Francis Woods, Chinatown, North Beach, the museums in Golden Gate Park—or she would visualize the shops and imagine that she was lunching or dining in one of the famed restaurants.

As Justin improved, he became increasingly restless, impatient, and difficult. Eunice wondered how much longer she could stand it. If she could only have a drink, just one. She often thought of the bottles of liquor in the downstairs family-room bar, but she steeled herself against her impulse. Even one would be too many. She'd see this through until the doctor dismissed him. It was all her fault; so the least she could do was help him recover. Also, she was fully aware that the doctor had reservations about her and knew of her drinking problem. When he came to the house, she felt she was as much his patient as Justin. She was determined to show the doctor she could take care of her husband.

Sometimes Justin talked about his trip with James Nichols to Monaco and Yugoslavia. On the whole, it had been interesting and would add a good chapter to the book, he felt.

Once, as Eunice watered the plants with a long-spouted can, she asked, "Tell me, darling, did you ever use your formal evening clothes? Did Princess Grace ask you to dinner? Or some duke or earl?"

An embarrassed flush darkened his face. "No, they didn't. You were right. I should have left the damn monkey suit home."

She had turned her back so he wouldn't see her smile. When she could talk without laughing, she said, "I'm sure they must have been on vacation; that's why you weren't invited. After all, it was the end of June and early July that you were there."

"Maybe so," he grumped and buried his head in a newspaper.

That same afternoon, James Nichols dropped by with a tape recorder. "Now that you're feeling better, Mr. Starr, could you talk into this and get your reminiscences on tape?"

"That's a wonderful idea," Eunice said. "You can do it at your convenience, when you feel able to."

"Well, I don't know."

"Just say anything that comes into your mind," Nichols urged. "It doesn't have to be in chronological order. Talk about the things that impressed you the most. It doesn't matter what they are. As I listen to the tapes, I'll weed them out and decide what should go in the book."

Justin growled. "I'm not sure I can talk into the damned thing."

"Of course you can," Eunice told him. "Oh, you'll feel self-conscious and awkward at first—everyone does—but just talk, and after a while you'll find it's very easy."

At Eunice's insistence, he finally gave in. It was easier to listen to the low droning of his voice than to the television, she decided. When he started talking, she would slip into reveries of her own, with her head bent over her needlework. But after the first few hours, when he grew more at ease, she found herself listening to him instead of daydreaming. Finally she put down her needlepoint.

"There was just my brother, Roy, and me; we were the only kids my folks had. It was lucky we were boys, because a carnival is no place to raise a girl. Too many rough characters around.

"Now, Roy liked the carnival better than I did, and he got along with Pa better, too. Of course, Roy was four years older than I was—maybe that made a difference—and he just drifted along with things. He never had something inside of him like I did that kept driving me all the time and making me want things to be better than they were. He just floated along with the current instead of fighting upstream.

"Roy was the one with the looks, too. He was real handsome as a kid. Later on his son was that same way—just like a movie star. Barrett kind of reminds me of Roy's appearance. Of course, he was her grandfather. Funny thing, too, because Barrett's got more push and gumption in her little finger than he ever had.

"Anyway, Roy was Dad's favorite; at least, I always thought so. He was old enough to be of some use to Pa, and he knew how to wheedle around the old man and get what he wanted. I've always been too outspoken and blunt. I'd blurt out just what was on my mind, but Roy played it smart and changed things and twisted facts until they came out better, so Pa wouldn't get so mad over something.

"We had sort of a gypsy trailer hitched to a wagon that we lived in as we traveled along with the carnival. A team of horses pulled the wagon from town to town. Pa had a concession in the carnie where you'd throw darts to pop balloons and win a prize. He carried all the prizes, the boxes of balloons, the darts and the boards in the wagon. Usually Roy stayed in the back with the stuff, sitting on a box. Sometimes I rode with him, but I'd usually get sick, so I'd much rather sit in the seat between my parents. I always slid over closer to my mother, though, because I was kind of scared of Pa. He was hot-tempered and mean, especially when he'd been drinking, and if I'd blurt out something he didn't like, he'd haul off and give me a whack that shut me up in a hurry.

"I was my mother's boy. She'd put her arm around me and hold me close to her when we were traveling. She had a little rocking chair, too. At night, when Pa and Roy'd be working, she'd hold me in her lap and rock back and forth and sing to me. I thought she was an angel, and I just about worshiped her. Secretly, I was convinced that I was her favorite, just as I knew Pa preferred Roy. Mom and I were a lot alike in that we both ached to be settled and living in one town all the time. She grew awfully tired of traveling with the carnival, and I never did like it. Sometimes she'd nag at Dad about quitting and settling down like regular folks, and I'd chime in with my two cents' worth, until we'd both get a crack from his hand; so we'd shut up.

"When I was about nine years old, there was a dancer named Trudy who joined the can-can troupe that traveled with the carnival. She had dyed red hair, false eyelashes and plenty of curves. For some reason she took a real shine to Pa, and when she wasn't working, she'd hang around his concession, giving him the eye. It wasn't long until he fell for her, too. Then my mother'd be mad, and Pa would get too much liquor in him, and they'd have a real fight.

It usually ended with him beating her up and going off with Trudy. How I hated that Trudy!

"One May, things came to a head when we arrived at a small town in Colorado. It was the first time the carnival had been so far west. The town was called Riverton, because it was along the banks of a little river in a green valley. In the background were the Rockies, with snow still on the peaks, looking a lot like the Sierra. There were wildflowers everywhere and birds singing. I thought it was about the prettiest town I ever saw.

"One morning real early, when Pa was sleeping off a drunk and Roy was at the river fishing, Mom and I walked into Riverton. The houses were made of brick, one after another along the street, and looked solid and settled. There were white picket fences around the yards and apple trees and flowers and grass. It looked like heaven to me. How I wanted to live in one of those brick houses and play baseball with the kids in a vacant lot and go to school all the time instead of just in the winter when the carnival was off the road.

"As we walked along, I saw a boy riding a bicycle delivering papers. I watched him stop in front of each house and throw a paper so hard it'd zing through the air, hit the wooden porch and sort of skitter to the front door. I was so filled with envy I could almost taste it. I never owned a bike in my life. Every time Roy or I'd ask Pa for one, he'd growl and shake his head. 'We've got too much stuff now in the wagon. You got plenty to do helping me and your ma, without riding around the country on a bike.'

"As we strolled along the sidewalk in front of the stores, Mama said, 'I sure do like this town.' There was a grocery store, a drugstore and ice-cream parlor and a lodge hall where they showed movies on Friday and Saturday nights, with a kids' matinee in the afternoon. There were posters advertising Tom Mix, Dorothy Gish, and Mary Pickford.

"We looked in all the windows of a dry-goods shop. I took her hand. 'Mama, could we live here all the time? I don't want to be in the carnival anymore.'

" 'I know how you feel, hon. I don't, either.' She squeezed my fingers. 'I hate it, as a matter of fact. I might just settle here in Riverton. I've been looking for a nice little town like this for a long time.'

" 'Yeah, let's stay here.' I could hardly believe my good fortune.

" 'I could get some kind of job,' Mama went on, 'working for the telephone company or in a store or being a waitress. I could do something to support you boys and myself.'

" 'And Pa? What would he do?'

" 'Oh, he wouldn't leave the carnival.'

"I visualized how Pa would travel with the carnival, then come to Riverton to spend the winters with us. That was all right, too, just so I got to stay here all the time, I told myself. As we walked back toward the carnival lot, I tried to pick out which house I wanted to live in. I could see a school with the kids playing out in the yard. I'd soon be with them, I told myself.

"That night, when the concession was closed and all the townfolk had left the carnival grounds, I woke up and heard my folks arguing again. Mama was determined to stay in Riverton, and Pa was just as set on traveling on with the carnival. I heard Ma accusing him of sleeping with Trudy, and he didn't deny it.

"Finally she screamed, 'I'm leaving you for good. I'm pulling out of here tomorrow, and I'm taking the boys.'

" 'Oh, no, you're not!' Pa yelled back. 'You can

take one or the other, but not both. Take your choice.' He climbed out of the trailer then and went to find Trudy, I suppose.

"I listened to Mama getting ready for bed and then crying in her pillow. I could hear Roy breathing next to me. He'd sort of shudder and half-sob, as if he'd heard Pa, too. I felt so sorry for him. Mom would choose me, of course, and poor Roy would have to put up with Trudy and the heat and the dust.

"The rest of the night I lay awake worrying about Roy. He wouldn't be living in Riverton in a brick house with a white picket fence around it. He wouldn't have dogs and cats and rabbits to care for. He wouldn't have apple trees to climb or a swing, or the chance to play baseball with the other kids, or a bike and a paper route. Nor would he have Mama.

"The next morning I couldn't talk to Roy. I wanted to go someplace and hide while Mom told him what was going to happen. Poor Roy. All the time he was eating his mush, I kept stealing glances his way, wondering how he'd feel when Mama told him. The suspense was awful. I kept looking at her and wondering when she was going to do it. I didn't want to leave Roy behind. Sometimes we fought a lot, but just the same he was my brother, and I didn't want him left out.

"How would Mama tell him? I tried to eat my mush and get it past the big lump in my throat. What would Roy do when she told him that she was leaving him here in the trailer while she took me and went to live in Riverton in a brick house? What would he do?

"Finally Roy finished his mush, drank his milk and slid off his seat. He opened the trailer door and reached for his fishing pole.

" 'No, you're not going fishing this morning,' Mama said. 'Come here. I've got something to tell you. You're to pack your things, Roy, because you and I are getting out of here. We're going to live in Riverton.' "

Justin turned off the tape recorder, leaned back in his recliner and closed his eyes. Scarcely breathing, Eunice put her needlework on the table and hurried into the bedroom. Trembling all over, she dabbed at her eyes and slumped into a chair. How could his mother have done such a thing? How *could* she? He was only nine years old. She thought of Lyle at nine —in the fourth grade. Oh, Justin, how could your mother have done that to you?

How could he ever forgive her? But he had. Astonished, Eunice realized that his mother was the same woman she had known—an old lady in her eighties. Justin had been devoted to her. She had had a stroke and was infirm, but her mind was clear. He had provided for her care in the finest hospital in Reno.

They had eventually moved Eunice's mother to the same hospital and had gone to see both of them nearly every day. As long as the two ladies lived, Justin had showered them with flowers and gifts and paid all their bills.

Roy had been taken care of, too, Eunice recalled. Justin had given him a job in the casino, supplied him with gambling chips to keep him happy and paid for his funeral when he died of a heart attack six years ago.

But her mind went back to the nine-year-old Justin. How could his mother have been so unfeeling? Still shaking, Eunice went back to the living room to comfort her husband, but he was asleep.

As the days passed and Justin related his story, Eunice found herself looking forward to each episode. She kept her head bowed over her needlework, however, and made no comments, for she didn't want him to feel inhibited or self-conscious and unable to talk freely.

Justin never told of the years he spent with his father; instead, he skipped over this period and resumed when he was fourteen. He had run away from the carnival, which was in Ohio, and headed west for Riverton. He made friends with a hobo, camped with him and learned to ride the rails on a freight train to Denver. When he reached Riverton, he found that his mother had married a widowed shopkeeper with three children. She lived in a brick house, all right, but his stepfather soon made it clear that Justin had no place in it. Roy was working on a nearby cattle ranch, so Justin got a job there too.

Eunice thought of herself at fourteen, attending an exclusive school and taking ballet lessons. And of Lyle at fourteen, in his private school and vacationing on a yacht in the South Pacific or lolling on a beach in Hawaii, so cherished and protected.

Justin's life story then jumped to his first saloon and cardroom in Reno. He talked about the crossroaders who worked for him and cheated him, and how he learned from them the hard way. And he talked about the sharpies, ever on the lookout for the beginning operator. In spite of all his years in the carnival, Justin had been a greenhorn in the gambling world. Sooner or later, all the crooks in Nevada came to his club to play at his poker tables and in his dice games. Con artists crimped his cards, switched dice and palmed his chips. His establishment, started on a shoestring, barely survived.

Also during the first year, the mob sent a goon squad to wreck his club and beat him up in the alley. They tried to put him out of business, but he fought back and kept going. At the end of five years he was on his way to real success.

One day he told about his feelings after Pearl

Harbor. He was thirty-five, but he couldn't see himself running a gambling house when the country was at war. He didn't feel right about it. So he leased his club to another operator and enlisted in the army. He talked about his fears during the fighting in Italy and the horrors of battle. As he squatted in a foxhole, waiting for the command to advance and trying to screw up his courage, he dreamed about the brick house he'd have someday and the family he would raise in it. He longed for a home—something he'd never had.

Another time he talked about his previous marriages, his initial high hopes and the bitter disappointments that followed.

As Eunice listened to him day after day, she realized that although she had lived with Justin Starr for fifteen years, she had never really known him.

CHAPTER

19

Barrett, working in the personnel department, told herself that she'd have to be very careful. She didn't want to arouse anyone's suspicions about her motives for being there. She kept thinking of Justin's warning: "This could be a tie-up with organized crime. So watch yourself." If there *was* a connection, the underworld would surely have a key person in this office.

She picked an empty desk in a secluded spot in a back office. "This is the make of typewriter I prefer," she explained to the personnel manager, who was showing her around.

The manager, an attractive woman in her forties, had been with an insurance company in San Francisco until she came to Starr's Tahoe, when it opened. Barrett couldn't imagine that she'd have underworld connections; still, that was one of their skills—choosing impressive "front" people.

"We've been wanting to get all our records up to date," the manager told her. "You see, I brought in a new system when I came, which I think is very efficient. All our new employees are written up on the new forms, but quite a few were transferred from Reno, and their records are different. We've been too busy to search the files and change them over; so that will be your task, Miss Starr. We really appreciate your help."

Barrett smiled. "I appreciate the opportunity to gain this experience."

The manager showed her what to do, then left, and Barrett settled down to work, aware that the other employees were watching her, as if they didn't know how to peg her. She was a Starr, related to the big shots, and was often seen with the resident manager. Still, she was here just for the summer. Was she important or not?

As in all the departments where she had worked, Barrett was called Miss Starr. The instant-intimacy, first-name-basis didn't seem to apply to her, and she never encouraged it. Someday her name would be on the door of the executive suite, right under Lyle's— BARRETT STARR, VICE-PRESIDENT—and the sooner the better. Therefore, let the employees start out on the right foot.

A good typist, she worked fast. She had found that the faster she settled in, the less attention she attracted; and as soon as the others took her for granted, she could be less cautious. She could arrange the pictures in the center drawer of her desk, study them covertly and eventually identify the eleven suspects and check their records.

The pictures had turned out surprisingly well but, in themselves, weren't evidence of wrongdoing. Fortunately, her task of typing the new records gave her access to the files, where the employees' folders were stored in alphabetical order according to their last names. Without opening each folder and inspecting it, there was no way of knowing which records were on the new form and which were on the old. Since a photo was attached to each application, she could look them over carefully and pull out the folders for those she suspected, along with the forms she had to retype.

After a few days, she had matched the eleven beach-group members with their records. Many of them were married and had children, but otherwise, aside from their common employment, there seemed to be no correlation between them. Barrett was sure, however, that their meetings on the beach were to settle their accounts and get their share of the take before it was turned over to the higher-ups in the mob. Did some of Justin Starr's revenue finally go to underworld leaders in Las Vegas after it passed through Reno? Then to Chicago or New York? How far-reaching was this rip-off?

As she worked with the records, Barrett kept thinking that this was her big chance to prove her worth to Justin and Lyle, to make herself indispensable to the Starr corporation. So far, all she was going on was intuition. The agents from the State Gaming Control Board and the federal government would demand evidence of wrongdoing before they would act. How could she convince them that some members of the night crew needed investigating? She couldn't confide in Clifton, although his help would be invaluable; she had promised Justin that she would talk to no one.

As she typed the information from the old forms onto the new ones, she considered ways to proceed. What did the five women and the six men on the night shift have in common? Rhodes had come from Las Vegas, highly recommended by his former employer. The stated reason for his change in employment was to be near his aging parents, who lived on a chicken ranch in the Sierra foothills in California. Did the others have connections with Vegas? Perhaps they'd been sent to Tahoe from an underworld mob. But, she remembered, the pit boss had transferred from Starr's in Reno. The dealers, the security guards and the counting-room girls had worked at various jobs in Reno and Carson City before they were employed by Starr's, and all had been trained right here at the Tahoe resort. None of them had a criminal record, for they had been fingerprinted and cleared.

Every line of thought ran into a dead end. It was frustrating to be so close and yet be unable to get any leads. If she didn't come up with something soon, Justin would lose interest, and Lyle would say, "I told you so!" There had to be something to indicate that the eleven employees were ripping off the casino, something that would at least justify an investigation.

One afternoon, right after lunch, the personnel manager came to Barrett's desk. "Would you stop what you're doing, Miss Starr, and type these lists? These are the schedules for the relief force that takes over for the floor personnel on their days off. Those on relief move from one shift to another."

The words *days off* struck a spark. Did all of those who met on the beach have the same day off? Wouldn't that be necessary? *Of course*—if they were working as a team, they'd all have to be on the job at the same time. No employee could act alone and get by with it for very long. They'd all have to be in on the racket. She typed the lists with flying fingers in her eagerness to check the schedules.

As soon as she had an opportunity, she went to the files and inspected a folder—after ascertaining that no one was watching her. She checked the eleven names, then shut the drawer in triumph. Sure enough, all eleven members were off on Monday and Tuesday! For the first time she felt she had a real lead.

She returned to her desk, picked up the folders she had finished and refiled them. As she worked, she asked herself, So they have the same day off; what does that mean? If she were right and they were all on the job Wednesday through Sunday, skimming the revenue, wouldn't the receipts for Monday and Tuesday show an increase in revenue?

In the middle of the afternoon, she took her fifteen-minute break and went to the employees' lounge as usual. On her return, she stopped in the accounting department and talked to a girl she knew. "Could you get me printouts from the computer showing the gross receipts from the gaming rooms for each day for last month? Also from the restaurants?"

"Of course, Miss Starr, if you can wait just a minute."

As she waited, she glanced around nervously. Would anyone be curious and wonder why she was in the accounting department? Would a spy report her to Carl Rhodes? She mustn't get paranoid, she scolded herself. Still, she asked for a folder for the printouts after her friend explained how to read them. She didn't want to be seen carrying them through the offices.

She returned to her desk, went back to work and stayed after the others left at the end of the day. When she was alone, she studied the printouts. Sure enough, the restaurant receipts were lower on Monday and Tuesday nights, which proved that the crowds were smaller. But the gaming receipts did not show a drop. She was onto something at last.

She phoned Clifton, made an excuse not to meet him that evening and began to prepare a report. It would not be only for Justin and Lyle but for the authorities as well. She worked out a graph that showed the daily receipts according to the days of the week. The gaming receipts were written with a red pen and the restaurant revenues in black. Without question, there was a great disparity between the two sets of figures. She Xeroxed the schedule of days off for the beach group and made copies of their employment records. She mounted their pictures on the records, with identifying captions. Finally, she wrote a careful report about the meetings at Pirates' Cove.

The next evening, when she showed the report to Justin, she said, "As you can see, the restaurant receipts show a consistent drop on Monday and Tuesday nights. Surely that means there were smaller crowds on those nights: it would be an outlandish coincidence for a certain number of our customers to *always* eat at Harrah's or Harvey's Wagon Wheel or some other club on Monday and Tuesday nights. Yet the gaming receipts do *not* show a proportionate drop." She took a pocket calculator and worked out the percentages.

Justin let out a low whistle. "I'll be damned!"

"Now, look at this schedule. It shows that the suspects are always off on Monday and Tuesday nights. Naturally, they'd choose the slowest nights to be off."

"And they're back with their hands in the till on Wednesday, Thursday, Friday, Saturday, and Sunday nights."

"That's how it looks."

"I'll be damned," Justin said again. He studied the report. "Lyle's coming over pretty soon. I want him to see this. Girl, you've done a bang-up job."

"Of course, I realize that it's not enough to prove anything, but it could interest the authorities, couldn't it? Enough to start an investigation?"

Justin snorted. "You bet! Not only is a racket like this illegal but, don't forget, no taxes are collected on the amount that's stolen. You can be sure that a lot of agencies will be *more* than interested—the State Gaming Control Board, Internal Revenue, the FBI, a lot of 'em."

"To say nothing of Starr Enterprises." Barrett pointed to the graph. "It's mind-boggling to think how much of your money has gone down the drain. That's what I regret." She hoped she was scoring points. This was her big chance. She hoped mightily that Justin was impressed.

"I hate to think of that, too." He shook his head in disgust. "Probably been going on ever since we opened. Funny that no one else got wise to it. It took a slip of a girl like you to uncover all this."

"It was those meetings on the beach that made me suspicious."

"Lyle just brushed them off, did he? It took someone with perception to get wise."

"But Lyle has a lot of other responsibilities. He's had so many things on his mind these last few weeks, with you out of the picture."

"Sure, sure, but it just proves that we need someone at Tahoe who really has our interests at heart." He paused and looked her up and down. "I've been thinking, Barrett—can I persuade you to stay at Tahoe permanently? Would you be willing to do that, instead of going back to New York?"

Her heart leaped with excitement. This was it—the big chance! "Of course I would! I'd love to! I'd rather be at the resort than anyplace in the world. I'm like you, Uncle Justin; we're both gamblers. I *love* it there!"

"Good! We need someone there we can trust." He slapped the report. "You can't have a business and leave everything to the hired help. I've told that to Lyle all along."

"I'm sure you've never been ripped off like this in Reno, not with you and Lyle there all the time."

"You're right. By God, I want you to be a real part of Starr Enterprises, a vice-president in charge of the Tahoe end. We've got a lot of property up there besides the resort, you know."

Barrett could hardly contain her joy. She threw her arms around Justin and kissed him. "I'll do my best, Uncle Justin. You'll see that I have as much ability as any man."

"This report proves it, my dear. You've done a first-rate job." Justin tapped the folder. "You leave this with me. I know just the agent I'm going to talk to tomorrow. He'll be after the big fish, I'm thinking, so he'll work under cover for a while. This is part of a widespread operation, I'm willing to bet."

"That seems likely."

"They're like some big octopus with long tentacles, reaching out in all directions—into gambling, drugs, horse racing, prostitution. We're fighting them all the time. One tentacle gets cut off and they grow another one somewhere else. We need someone like you on guard at Tahoe."

Lyle arrived, and Justin began at once: "You ought to see this report that Barrett's prepared. Beats me how she got wise to what's going on. You explain, Barrett."

Barrett went over the graph and showed Lyle the pictures and the material from the personnel reports, but he was not impressed. "Let's not go off the deep end. It's all right for someone to scrutinize things at the resort, but we need a lot more proof than this to get up in arms."

Barrett sensed his annoyance. Was he merely cautious, or did he feel she'd shown him up and made him look foolish?

Justin sputtered, "Hell, there's plenty of proof here! *Plenty* to get up in arms about! The restaurant receipts go way down on Mondays and Tuesdays, don't they? But not the gaming revenue. How come? Because the bastards aren't there on Mondays and Tuesdays, skimming off the top, *that's* why."

"Well, perhaps. At least you can look into it."

"You bet I'm going to look into it! I don't want Starr's to be ripped off. I know just the man to turn this report over to. He'll be mighty interested. So will a hell of a lot of government agencies."

"That's true if we are *really* being ripped off, but that remains to be seen."

"As I was telling Barrett, we need her at Tahoe all the time to look things over. The sharpies won't pull any more tricks like this if someone in the family is on the job. She's agreed to stay, instead of going back to New York. What do you think of that?"

"That's fine, Dad." But his voice lacked enthusiasm. "In what capacity?"

"I'm going to take her into the corporation."

"What?" Lyle almost shouted, his neck reddening.

He doesn't like it a bit, Barrett told herself. Why didn't her uncle handle the situation with more tact?

Justin plowed ahead. "I'm going to make her vice-president in charge of our Tahoe holdings."

Lyle's voice was tight and his expression was grim as he said, "Vice-president! Don't you think I should have been consulted? What am I—just a flunky? I thought I was running Starr Enterprises, but apparently not, if I'm not even asked about a matter of this importance. Besides, you'll have to bring it up before the board of directors. We do have one, if you recall."

Justin looked surprised. "Hell, I thought you'd *like* the idea. It never occurred to me that you wouldn't. Barrett has done such a fine job at Tahoe."

Furious, Lyle paced the floor. "All right, let's review what Barrett has done. She's only twenty-three. She's worked one year in an advertising agency.

She's done some odd jobs at Tahoe. And that's it. Period! Yet you want to make her a vice-president in charge of multimillion-dollar holdings at Tahoe. It's ridiculous."

Justin thumped his hand on the folder. "What about *this*?" He, too, was angry.

Barrett interposed. "We've talked enough tonight. You shouldn't get too tired, Uncle Justin." She kissed him and started for the door. "Come on, Lyle. We don't have to decide anything tonight."

When they were in the hall, Lyle turned on her, his voice shaking with anger. "I thought you were going back to New York, but you had no intention of doing that, did you? You deliberately deceived us."

She didn't answer.

"You ought to return to the East Coast and get some real business experience before you try to run the Tahoe operation, or you'll be so out of your depth it won't be funny."

"Lyle, I have as much executive ability as anyone—man or woman. All I need is a chance to prove it."

"Well, you won't prove it at my expense. I've enjoyed having you as a friend, Barrett. I can understand why Clifton has fallen so hard for you. But scratch that beautiful exterior of yours and underneath is a ruthless, ambitious, scheming woman who'll do anything to get what she wants."

He turned away and started down the hall, but she grabbed his arm. "Lyle, that's not fair!"

"Look, you've pulled the wool over Dad's eyes, but not mine. All this investigation of the night crew is nothing but nonsense to impress Dad. It's phony as hell, but you sure impressed him. My God, he's ready to make you a vice-president of our company!"

Anger boiled in her, too. "And what's wrong with that? After all, I am related to him. I'm a Starr, too."

Lyle shook her hand away. "I'll tell you what's wrong with that. I've had two years of graduate work in business administration, and I worked like a dog for five years before I was made a vice-president. Also, I put up with a hell of a lot of Justin Starr. I resent this Barrett-come-lately act of yours, flattering the old man, doing a little witch-hunting and falling into a position you haven't earned and aren't capable of filling!" There was no charm or friendliness in Lyle's manner as he bit off his words: "Well, get this straight, Barrett. Don't plan on any big job with Starr's, because you won't get it. You'll become vice-president of my company over my dead body!"

CHAPTER

20

The next morning, as she walked through the woods to the resort, Barrett thought about her confrontation with Lyle. According to him, she'd never get a permanent position in Starr Enterprises, much less become vice-president in charge of the Tahoe holdings. She was utterly wretched, after being so near her goal.

She thought Justin had handled the situation badly, and she knew what she would have done if she had been in his position. First, she'd have prepared Lyle. Then she'd have bolstered his ego and sought his advice. And, finally she'd have presented the idea in such a way that he'd believe it was his own suggestion. Her uncle was too blunt and outspoken, and without finesse. He came on like a sledgehammer. Right from the first, he'd put Lyle's back up.

What would happen now? Fortunately, she'd ended the set-to before Justin and Lyle were irreconcilably at odds. It had more or less been left in the air. Would Justin withdraw his offer in order to placate

Lyle? Who had the real power in the organization, the final word—Lyle or Justin? Regardless of the consequences, would Justin plunge ahead and bring the matter before the board of directors? If so, Lyle would no doubt try to make them turn it down.

Disappointment welled up in her again. She could hardly bear it. She had dreamed of moving ahead and having a real position in the company. She wanted power, influence, money—to be in on the planning sessions, to have real authority to make decisions. It was ridiculous to say she couldn't handle the Tahoe holdings. It was unfair. Justin and Lyle could guide her over the rough spots until she learned. It wasn't as if she'd be completely on her own. There were also the executives in the head office in Reno to turn to. They'd answer any questions and give her advice.

Still, she could understand Lyle's resentment, especially at the way his father had presented his idea—as a *fait accompli*. Lyle had worked terribly hard. He had devoted years to being Justin's right-hand man and no doubt had often been the whipping boy. It was true that she'd been at the resort only a few weeks. She *had* been ingratiating herself with Justin. Perhaps she'd been deceitful in pretending that she would return to New York, but until she'd had an offer, how could she have done otherwise?

The most unfortunate result of the fiasco was that Lyle would now be prejudiced against her. He felt threatened, which she had tried to avoid. Now he wouldn't concede that she had any good points at all, such as showing real promise and ability, though she knew she had. Eventually, she could make an enormous contribution to the organization. In the first place, she had more interest in the casinos than Lyle. She had a genuine love for the gambling world. No doubt Lyle was excellent in the other areas of

Starr Enterprises, but his heart was not in gaming.

A chipmunk startled her as it scurried up a lodge-pole pine, dashed to the end of a limb and chattered at her as if to scold her for intruding on his domain. She looked up at the animal and called, "Oh, knock it off!" Its attitude reminded her of Lyle.

What would Lyle do? Tell her to get lost? Insist that she leave next month, as soon as the vacation season was over and her services were no longer needed? How could she leave Tahoe? She loved it all: the beautiful waxy-leafed manzanita, the incense cedar, the pines and Douglas fir, the dogwood and cascara buckthorn—the lake, the mountains, the desert. Tears welled up in her eyes as she listened to the cry of a hermit warbler, the precise tap of a nuthatch, and the breeze way up in the pine needles. As she inhaled the mountain air, she thought of how the lake changed from cobalt blue to green and gray, of the winters with the snow-mantled peaks and frosted trees. Also, there was the excitement of the Androm-eda and Orion wings, the entertainment in the Celestial Room, the crowds in the lobby. How could she leave all this?

Her jaw tightened. She *wouldn't* leave. She wasn't licked yet.

Suddenly a shot rang out, and a bullet passed over her head and lodged in the trunk of a sugar pine. She started and looked around. Was it a stray bullet, fired by a hunter, or was someone trying to kill her? Her knees trembled and her heart pounded as the sound of the shot reverberated through the forest. She ran toward the resort, her heart thrashing against her throat. Should she call the police? She ran to a phone booth in a corner of the parking lot. First she would call Justin and tell him.

"That was a warning," he said, "to you and to me.

Someone's trying to scare you away, to make you clear out."

"But *why*?"

"Because you've been nosing around too much. They must be getting mighty uneasy about you, Barrett."

She glanced behind her. "Were they trying to kill me?"

"Hell, no. If they wanted to kill you, they'd have done it, make no mistake about that. They want you to stop poking into their business. Did anyone see you take those pictures?"

"Yes, Chuck Moody. Do you think he——"

"Not necessarily. I don't know if he's part of the operation or not, but whoever's responsible had an expert shoot to scare you, without hitting you. They want you to leave, that's all."

"Should I call the sheriff?"

"No, I'll tell the agent I'm turning this report over to. He'll know how to handle it. But be careful. Don't walk through the woods anymore."

"I certainly won't." Her heart still hammered.

"Listen, Barrett, could you come back to Reno soon? There's something I want to tell you—you and Lyle."

"Anytime. Do you mean tonight?"

"No, it's not that urgent."

"I'll come tomorrow night, then, around seven."

"Listen, Barrett, don't tell anyone about this shooting, and don't do anything. Just wait for the agent, who'll be talking to you. Be awfully careful."

Finding a hiding place for Judith Davenport was easier said than done, Otto Schroeder decided that same morning. Ever since he settled on kidnapping, he had explored the lightly traveled roads off the main highway and near the lake. When he found a promising spot, he would park his car on the side of the road and take a fishing pole from the back seat, in case anyone should see him. Then he'd tramp around in the isolated areas, looking for an abandoned cabin or mine or a cave. He found some possibilities, but they were either too hard to reach in the dark or too far from a road or too close to other cabins.

Although he wanted the spot to be remote, it should be close to Stateline. The longer he had to cope with Judith, the more dangerous it would be. Also, he wanted to keep her in Nevada. Wasn't it a more serious crime if you crossed a state line? He didn't really know, and it wasn't the sort of question you could ask anyone. A place off Highway 19, the Kingsbury Grade Road, would be fine, for it was in the state and close to the resort. So he drove along 19, watching for side roads, and found one that he hadn't noticed before. It was a corrugated lane, with a roadbed of aspen trunks and full of bumps and ruts—obviously an old-time logging road—that disappeared into the forest and ended at a deserted sawmill.

He stopped the car and looked at it. It probably hadn't been used for fifty years, not since Tahoe became a tourist attraction and it was important to leave the trees. He climbed out of the car and walked across low-growing squaw carpet to the sagging door, shoved it open and stepped inside. The machinery was covered with rust. He walked through the front room to a small one at the back. It was just what he'd been looking for. He investigated the area carefully and then drove back to the main road. He should make some trial runs, especially after dark, he decided, because he'd be nervous when Judith was with him.

* * *

That afternoon, the personnel manager told Barrett that someone wanted to see her in her uncle's office. She found a gray-haired man sitting at the desk with her report in front of him.

"My name is Al Dixon. I'm an agent with the Gaming Control Board." He showed his identification and closed the office door so the secretary couldn't overhear them. "I had quite a talk with your uncle this morning, and he thinks you're onto something."

"I think so, too." Barrett liked this man. He seemed experienced and knowledgeable, and she was greatly relieved that someone was looking into the matter.

After asking some questions about her report Dixon leaned back in the chair and said, "As far as everyone else is concerned, I'm here on a routine inspection. I'll examine the books, measure and weigh the dice, inspect the roulette wheels and all that. But actually, under cover, I'll be making an extensive investigation. If Mr. Starr is right and this group has underworld connections, I want to find out who's masterminding all this. And it's vitally important that you keep quiet."

"I will, Mr. Dixon. I haven't talked to anyone, except my uncle and Lyle Starr. Uncle Justin cautioned me about that."

"Good." The agent nodded. "I'll be here for some time. Mr. Starr has turned this office over to me and is letting me use his sleeping room. So if you want to reach me, I'll be right here."

"All right."

"Now, tell me about this morning, when you heard the shot."

After she related her experience, she said, "I can show you where it happened, even the bullet in the tree."

"OK, let's go see it."

Barrett soon found the place where she'd been shot at, but when they found the sugar pine, the bullet was gone. There was a deep hole and marks where someone had dug with a knife.

Dixon put his finger in the deep hole. "Now we know for sure it wasn't a hunter after a deer."

The next evening, when Barrett pulled up in front of the Starr mansion, Lyle's Ferrari was in the driveway. She rang the doorbell wondering what was in store.

Lyle greeted her politely, if not with his usual friendliness. Eunice, gracious as always, kept the conversation cordial and then excused herself. "I'm sure you will want to talk business, so I'll take a walk in the garden. It's still light out, and so balmy and lovely."

When she had left, Justin said, "Sorry to bring you back to Reno so soon, Barrett, but I think it's important. I've been telling Lyle about the shooting."

Lyle looked skeptical. "You're sure it wasn't a hunter or your imagination?"

He doesn't believe me, Barrett thought.

"She was on resort property," Justin said. "It's posted against hunting. I doubt if anyone would trespass so close to the resort and Starpoint. No, she was given a warning."

Lyle shrugged. "From whom?"

Justin snapped, "From the gang that's ripping us off, who else?"

Anxious to avoid another argument, Barrett said, "Well, all I know is that a bullet zinged over my head and lodged in a tree. But when the agent, Mr. Dixon, and I went to look for it, it wasn't there."

"Imagine!" Lyle's response was heavy with sarcasm.

Justin whacked the arm of his chair. "That shows that they didn't want the bullet in the hands of the authorities."

Lyle extended his legs and clasped his hands behind his head. "What's on your mind, Dad? I have to go to a meeting soon."

Justin tipped his chair forward and looked at them intently. "I called you together to tell you something I've never told another soul. I didn't intend to tell anyone, either—didn't think it would be necessary. My heart attack, though, made me realize that I could pass out of the picture real quick. This shooting experience of Barrett's sort of brought it to a head."

Lyle also leaned forward. "What is it?"

"Well, I know who's the head of the underworld here in Reno. I'm not going to tell you his real name, because he's a prominent citizen. You know him, too, son. He's active in service clubs, lodges, and his church. But in the underworld he's known as Mr. Hightower. Remember that—Hightower. Don't write it down. Just remember it."

"Hightower," Barrett said.

Justin rubbed his hand along his jaw. "You know that I've always fought organized crime, along with the other legitimate operators, but it's everywhere. At least Hightower keeps the worst elements under control. I guess that's why the authorities go along with him. They probably can't prove anything against him, and they might get someone who's far worse directing criminal activities."

"I suppose they could," Lyle said, looking genuinely interested.

"About eight years ago, when you were still in college, Lyle, an informer offered to sell me some evidence: copies of papers that revealed Hightower's identity and the fact that one of the Reno casinos is owned by the underworld through a union retirement fund. There are front men in front of front men, but it's actually run by organized crime, and I can prove it. A lot of skimming goes on there, I can tell you."

"I can imagine," Barrett interjected.

"I decided I might be smart to buy that evidence as a form of insurance," Justin said. "All my life I've been on the side of the law and run a legal, above-board establishment. I've never had a 'flat store,' a dishonest gambling house. I paid twenty-five thousand dollars for the information because I decided that it might be a good investment. I knew the underworld could never get a hold on me for anything illegal, but they might try to nail me by kidnapping you, son. I wanted to make damn sure they wouldn't try it. The evidence is in my safe-deposit box."

"Did you tell anyone about it?" Lyle asked.

"No, but I have a paper on file in the legal department, so that if anything suspicious happens to me or any member of my family, that envelope is to be turned over to the authorities. Hightower knows I have that information—and that I can reveal his identity, if necessary. So the underworld has left us Starrs alone. That's why that bullet went *over* your head, Barrett. They hoped to scare you but were careful not to kill you."

"Do you think there's a connection with the night-shift group and Mr. Hightower?" Barrett asked.

"I think so. There's a mastermind behind all this. They've been wanting to get a foothold in Starr's for a long time."

Lyle shook his head. "Now, don't jump to a lot of hasty conclusions."

"Son, I've been in the gambling business for a long time. The vast majority of operators are legitimate businessmen like myself, but I'm the first to admit that gaming also attracts the crime element—crooks, the underworld, the syndicate, the Mafia, con men, gangsters, and what have you. I'm a realist, and I know the score. From the time I adopted you, I knew you were a prime target for kidnapping. I just made damn sure it wouldn't happen. Hightower and his henchmen didn't dare try that, because I could have their casino license yanked so fast it would make your head swim. They know it and I know it. Now the two of you are in on the secret. I don't have to tell you never to breathe a word of this; it's just between the three of us."

Lyle looked puzzled. "Why are you telling us? Aren't you making us a party to something illegal— a form of blackmail?"

Justin snorted. "Maybe so, but you're dealing with the underworld. Son, there's nothing I wouldn't do to protect you and your mother—*nothing*, legal or not!" He thumped the arm of his recliner. "I have that information where they can't get their hands on it. It's a case of live and let live."

"I, for one, feel better knowing this," Barrett said.

Justin nodded. "Good. And another thing, which is mainly why I sent for you. If you're ever in a spot with the criminal elements, so bad that you're desperate, just call on Mr. Hightower. Call this number: 987-6050. It's the number his henchmen use when they have to go to the very top boss. Don't write it down, just memorize it: 987-6050. It's easy to remember because the numbers are in order backwards. Just call him up and give him the word, nice and polite, but in a way that shows you mean business."

Lyle whistled. "*I'll* never call that number. It's too dangerous."

"I'd have to be really desperate to call Mr. Hightower," Barrett half-whispered, "but I could if I had to."

"Only call as the very last resort. I've used it just once, to tell Hightower that I have the goods on him." Justin shook his head. "You don't play games with those boys."

Lyle left, and Eunice appeared at the door. "There's coffee for us downstairs, Barrett. We'll let Justin rest now."

Barrett kissed her uncle good-bye and whispered, "Thank you for telling us your secret."

Justin was glad he had told her, because she had steel in her spine. She'd call the number if she had to.

CHAPTER

21

Elliott Davenport settled back in the airplane seat, hooked the heels of his hand-tooled boots over the footrest, and held his big Stetson hat in his hands. He was on his way to a state conference on water resources, to be held at the Hilton Hotel near Los Angeles International Airport.

No doubt he should have worn regular shoes with his new summer suit, but the boots felt good on his feet. That was what he was used to, and he was going to wear them, new suit or not, in spite of Helen's protests.

Ordinarily, he'd be looking forward to the conference. He liked meeting men from other states. It gave him a new perspective to take back to Carson City, for he found out that other states also have problems, and that made Nevada's troubles less worrisome.

But he wasn't anticipating any pleasure this time. Since Judith came home and they had their clash, all the joy had gone out of his life. He hadn't seen her or talked to her since. Of course, Helen kept in touch with her, so he knew she was all right. In spite of his feelings, Judith had gone ahead with her divorce. His heart ached as he thought of her; it was a sorrow that was always present, like a pain that never went away. It was always there, underneath all his thoughts and activities, ready to flare up and make him feel sick in the pit of his stomach.

His own girl. She'd been his main reason for living. He smiled when he thought of when she was born and how he had celebrated all night with the cowboys on his spread. The next day he was so hung over he could hardly drive into Reno to the hospital to see Helen and his brand-new daughter. For her second birthday he had special boots made for her little feet and a tiny wide-brimmed hat. Then he tucked her in front of him on the saddle and, holding her with one arm, rode the range, looking after his cattle. He was surprised at how long she could stay with him without tiring, in spite of the wind in her face and the swirling dust.

The hands all thought she was something special, too. Whitey Lewis made her a doll cradle for Christmas, and Curley Johnson carved her a whole herd of cattle to play with. The carpenter built her a seat high on the corral fence so she could watch when they broke a horse or did some branding. In time, he and his men had taught her to do everything: ride, jump, lasso.

He could still see her pushing her doll buggy round and round the house on the porch. Then, when she went to school, he often met her at the bus stop with her pony. They would race up the lane to the house, and his horse knew better than to win. He thought of how quickly she grew up and was in high school, going to parties and looking pretty as a rose. All too soon she was in college, and then married to Murray.

When the boys were born, he was mighty pleased, also, for they were fine lads, both of them, and would take over when they were ready. The Davenport spreads were getting so big they needed to be divided. It made him feel good to have someone to pass the ranches to, just as he'd got his start from his father. He loved the boys and was proud of them. But Judith had always been special—his firstborn, his little girl, his delight. The word *love* seemed so inadequate for the way he always felt about her. And now they were at odds. It would never be the same.

If anyone had told him six months ago that he'd be torn away from Judith, not even in touch with her, he'd have called him a liar. But here it was, so painfully true and eating away at him. It was as bad as when his folks died and he realized that having them around was irretrievably over. This business with Judith was a kind of death—in some ways worse, because of the shame he felt that his daughter would leave her husband when he was injured and paralyzed. Murray and his folks had merely offered her an easy way out, by pretending they wanted her to go, and she had grabbed at the chance. She just walked out on him, in spite of her wedding vows, "for better or for worse." To think that one of his own would do such a thing. It was incredible. He thought she had more decency, more honor and character. He couldn't understand it.

Three days later, the conference ended with a luncheon speech; it was only one-thirty, and Davenport's plane didn't leave until seven. He supposed he could take a sight-seeing tour, but his heart wasn't in it. He picked up his bag and his hat, walked to the taxi entrance and climbed into a waiting cab. "I'll be needing you most of the afternoon, if that's all right."

The cabdriver smiled. "Certainly, sir. Where would you like to go?"

"Take me to Beverly Hills." He gave the Rosenfelds' address. "I want you to wait for me while I see someone."

As he settled back in the seat, Davenport winced at the likely cost. It'd be cheaper to rent a car, but he wouldn't buck all this Los Angeles traffic for the price of a steer on the hoof. The driver worked his way through the traffic and got on a freeway, while Davenport thought about Murray. Poor guy. It was bad enough to lose the use of your legs, but he even lost his wife. She could have been a great comfort to him these last two months.

When they reached the neighborhood where the Rosenfelds lived, Elliott recognized the area. He had been there before, when the family visited Judith and Murray. It was a plush neighborhood, and the Rosenfelds' house was one of the plushest. They were wealthy people. That was one of their problems—too much money. In spite of the Davenport holdings, his boys had always had to work hard, which was what he believed in. There wasn't time to get into trouble when there were plenty of chores to do.

The taxi stopped in the curved driveway, and the driver got out to open the door. Elliott said, "I don't know how long I'll be, but you just keep your meter running."

"I'll be right here, sir, when you come out."

A maid met him at the elaborately carved door and led the way through to the back of the house. "You'll find Mr. Rosenfeld and his attendant by the swimming pool, sir. Shall I take your hat?"

"No, thank you. I'll just keep it with me." His heels clicked on the cement as he walked toward the huge, free-form pool. Murray, stretched out on a chaise in the sun, with mammoth dark glasses shielding his eyes, looked tanned and fit.

A light-haired young man in white briefs stepped

forward. "I'm Ron Holden, Murray's nurse and therapist. May I help you?"

Elliott introduced himself.

"I've heard of you. You're from Nevada?"

"That's right. Is Murray up to seeing me?"

"I guess so. He's just had a snort and is still floating, but he's OK, I think." He walked to Murray and nudged him. "Get with it, man. Your father-in-law's here to see you—Mr. Davenport. You remember him, don't you?"

Murray giggled and put up a hand. "How you doing, Elliott?" He giggled again. "Get him a chair, Ron."

The attendant pulled a deck chair near Murray and moved a patio umbrella so Elliott could sit in the shade. "It's hot this afternoon. How about a beer?"

"That would be fine." Elliott sat down and stared at Murray, who had a silly grin on his face. What did this Ron mean by "snort and still floating"? Was Murray drunk?

When Ron returned from the cabana with three cans of beer, Elliott put his big hat under his chair. He felt awkward and ill at ease and was grateful to be holding the can of beer and having it to drink. Ron found a chair for himself and sat with them.

Why doesn't he leave us alone? Elliott wondered. It was hard enough to talk to Murray, because there was no eye contact—the black glasses covered most of his face. Also, there seemed to be a peculiar expression behind the glasses, euphoric and foolish. But he sipped his beer and began, "I've been at the airport at a conference on water resources——"

Murray laughed hilariously. "Old Elliott's lieutenant governor of Nevada. The cowboy himself. Imagine that, Ron!"

"Knock it off, Murray. Mr. Davenport's trying to tell you something."

With that, Murray yanked at the arms of his chaise, so that the back rose up. When the pad hit him, he laughed uproariously again. He wiped his eyes and said, "So you want to tell me something?"

"Well, I was in the area, and I thought I'd come to see you."

"That was nice of you, Mr. Davenport," Ron said. "Wasn't it, Murray?"

"Yeah."

"We were all mighty sorry to hear about your accident. Is there anything we can do for you?"

Murray giggled and laughed. *"You?* Do anything for *me?"* He waved his arm toward the house. "I've already got the best. Tell him about our pad, Ron."

"Murray's parents turned the master bedroom suite over to us. Actually, it's like an apartment. Big bedroom, two dressing rooms, a sitting room with a bar. We have a refrigerator and an electric range, if I want to cook something for us."

"That sounds just fine. I was going to suggest that, if you'd like, I'd be willing to build a special house for you at Sage Creek——"

Murray threw his head back and laughed as if he'd never heard anything so funny. "You've got to be putting me on! Why would I want to live in Nevada, when I can live here? Especially out there at Sage Creek—at the end of nowhere!"

Ron gave him a shake. "Murray, shape up. Mr. Davenport's trying to be nice." The attendant turned to Elliott. "That's very generous of you, but Murray's better off right here, with his folks. You can see that he has every luxury. We work out in the pool. Also, I take him to a special hospital in Los Angeles for therapy."

"Yeah. Ron takes care of *all* my needs." He

grinned at the attendant. "We get along all right, don't we, Ron? We make out OK."

Elliott, as he looked from one man to the other, remembered what Judith had told him about Murray's homosexuality, and a shudder of revulsion ran over him. The two men must be lovers. He felt sick to his stomach. He finished his beer, then reached under his chair for his hat. "Well, as I say, we were all sorry to hear about your trouble." His big, gnarled fingers worked around the edge of his hat brim. "If there's any help we can give you. . . ."

Murray turned toward him, and Elliott stared at the opaque glasses. "Now you sound like Judith. You Davenports never give up, do you? Let's get this straight. There's nothing you can do for me—nothing! Thanks to my grandmother, I have plenty of bread. I've got every comfort, and I've got Ron. Now, what could *you* do?" He threw his head against the pad in a paroxysm of mirth.

Elliott's face reddened, and his fingers worked rapidly with his hat. He turned to Ron. "What the hell's the matter with him? Is he drunk?"

The attendant shook his head. "I told you he's just had a snort and he's still floating."

"What do you mean?"

"He sniffed cocaine."

"My God! Does he do that often?"

"Sure. At least once a day." Ron shrugged. "Why not? He can afford it."

Elliott got out of the chair and jammed his hat on his head. "Guess I'll be going. Got a taxi waiting." He shook hands with Ron and stepped over to Murray and put out his hand.

Murray turned the black glasses toward him. "How's my former wife, good old Judith?" He extended a limp hand.

"She's fine. She's out at Sage Creek."

"Lord, I had to tell her a half-dozen times to get lost. It cost me more than fifty grand to get rid of her, but it was the best money I ever spent. Worth every dime of it to have her out of here."

Elliott yanked his hand away, doubled his fist and shook it in Murray's face. "Damn you, don't you dare talk like that about my daughter! If you weren't a cripple, I'd give you the thrashing of your life!"

Shaking with fury, he turned and strode back through the house, out the front door and into the cab. "Take me back to the airport."

That rotten drug addict! That fag! That worthless bum! He wasn't worth a hair on Judith's head. Why should she waste her life with a no-good like him? Davenport made a fist. If only he could have given him the beating of his life! That spoiled, worthless nothing. No wonder Judith left him. He didn't blame her. She was well out of it. He ground his fist in the palm of his other hand. He should have hit the guy and knocked him flying through the air, into the pool!

When they arrived at the airport, he paid the driver, thanked him and gave him a large tip. He picked up his suitcase and entered the terminal. He wanted a double scotch on the rocks. It was only four o'clock, and he still had three hours to kill. After checking in at the airline desk, he'd have a couple of drinks and an early dinner.

As he sipped the scotch he thought of what Murray had said: "I had to tell her a half-dozen times to get lost. It cost me more than fifty grand to get rid of her, but it was the best money I ever spent." The nerve of the bastard, to talk to me, Judith's father, like that! Well, the cab fare to Beverly Hills was the best money *he'd* ever spent. He had to see the situation for himself. Judith was well rid of that rat. Why should she waste her life on anyone like that? She was right to cut her losses.

He sat back in the booth. When Judith tried to tell him, he wouldn't listen to her. Yet he'd had the gall to pass judgment on her. What a stubborn, opinionated old fool he was! She knew what she was doing. She was only twenty-three, with her whole life ahead of her. Why should she throw it away on someone like Murray, even if he was crippled?

As he thought of the heartache he had suffered for the last two months, Elliott swore under his breath. I deserved it, he thought, every minute of it. Why didn't I trust Judith's appraisal of the situation? She knew best. And Judith was probably eating her heart out, too. It was all so unnecessary. If he hadn't been so damned stubborn!

He was tempted to phone Sage Creek and tell her what a fool he'd been and apologize to her. But, no, it would be better to tell her in person. He kept glancing at his watch. The hands didn't seem to move ahead. If he could only be on his way! At five o'clock, he went to a restaurant for dinner. The steak was tough, the peas were canned, and the mashed potatoes tasted like cotton. They ought to come to Nevada, he thought, and get some decent beef. Finally he was on the plane, heading home.

It was dark by the time he got there. When he climbed out of his car, he stood for a moment and let the breeze from the desert hills hit his face to blow away the revulsion of the afternoon. He opened the gate and walked toward his house, where his father had lived and his grandfather before that. He thought of the land that would pass to his sons and their sons, and he thought of the lavish house of the Rosenfelds. No wonder Judith had come back here; it was where she belonged. He opened the front door, turned on the hall light and took his hat off.

Judith, startled, stood in the hallway at the top of

the stairs. "It's you, Dad! I thought I heard someone. Is something wrong?"

He watched her come down the stairs, hesitating, uncertain, somewhat fearful. She was the prettiest sight he'd ever seen, so sweet and lovely—his first-born, his little girl. He turned his hat round and round in his big hands and for a minute couldn't speak.

Finally he said, "I went to see Murray today. I've come to tell you that I was dead wrong. Judith, I apologize."

"Oh, Daddy!"

He held out his arms, and she ran to him.

CHAPTER

22

Early one Friday, when he got off work, Otto Schroeder read the notices on the employees' bulletin board. He was on the night shift, which he didn't like, but he couldn't complain because he needed the job awhile longer. One of the notices caught his attention:

> Visit Starr's Gift Shop in the lobby and get acquainted with our new trainee, Judith Davenport. She will be with us a few weeks and invites all her friends, old and new, to drop in and see her. She will be happy to tell you about selected items that are now on sale.

Judith Davenport? Right here—at the resort? Why would Judith Davenport be working in the gift shop, when her father was the lieutenant governor and a big-shot cattleman? Could it be another girl with the same name?

He decided to stay at the resort until the gift shop opened and see for himself. Besides, it was Friday, and he could pick up his paycheck later that morning.

To pass the time, he went in the Orion Room, got five dollars' worth of dimes and played the slots. When some dimes clattered into the tray, he picked them up and absentmindedly fed them back into the machine. If Judith Davenport was here, he might as well finish the job and cut out. The sooner the better.

The big question was how he could get Judith into his car and out to the sawmill. He couldn't just go up to her, in front of everybody, and force her to go with him. Nor could he wear a mask or anything like that. If he got close to her, she might recognize him, in spite of his heavy beard. And how could he drive and hold a gun on her at the same time? Or should he make her drive? She must have a car; if so, should he use hers? That would give her an advantage, if she had control of the car. There were a lot of problems to solve before he could act. If only he had someone he could trust to help him.

When it was time for the gift shop to open, he walked into the lobby and glanced through the glass wall. Sure enough, there was Judith Davenport, listening to a woman in a green smock explain something. Apparently she really was going to work here. Funny thing, with all the money the Davenports had.

Before he went back to his room, Otto collected his paycheck and cashed it, as he'd be seeing Rita Jordan tonight. He looked forward to it. In fact, being with her was about his only diversion. She was a hooker and kind of dumb, but she was pretty and had a cute figure and blonde hair. She was also a lot of fun, and she laughed at everything he said. He'd pick her up at her apartment about six o'clock, and they'd go to a bar and have some drinks, then eat dinner, take in one of the lounge shows and gamble awhile before he went home with her.

The night Lea Turner was killed and he had needed

an alibi, he'd spotted Rita in a casino on the north shore, and he'd been seeing her two or three times a week ever since. He knew she "entertained" other men after he left her, but so what? She had to earn a living. She'd been raised in foster homes and had no idea if she had a family someplace. For all her troubles, she was a happy-go-lucky girl who shrugged things off by saying, "That's the way the cookie crumbles." He liked being around her. In fact, he was falling for her in a big way.

He slept some, then showered, trimmed his beard and put on a new sport shirt, slacks, and jacket. When he called for Rita, she looked real sharp. Usually she wore pants that stretched tight as wallpaper over her backside, but tonight she wore a pretty pink dress.

"I sure like your dress," he said as they walked to his car. "You really look great."

She hugged his arm and smiled at him. "I bought it special to wear for you because you said you liked pink."

That made him feel good, to think she'd buy a dress especially for him. She must like him a lot, too, or she wouldn't go to that trouble.

They sat in a booth in their favorite bar, listened to rock music and had several drinks.

"I've been thinking that I might cut out of here one of these days."

"Oh, no! Not when we're getting to be real good friends!" She pouted. "You won't go right away, will you?"

"Not for a while. Haven't made up my mind just when."

She leaned against him and whispered. "I'll tell you a secret. I'm saving my money to get out of here, too. I need another two thousand dollars, and then I can leave. I want to go to a cosmetology school and learn to be a beauty operator. Then I'm going to buy a shop of my own."

"Say, that sounds great. But you shouldn't have any trouble picking up that much. . . ."

"Well, it's hard to save anything. I have to pay off so many people. My landlord gets a cut. So do the pit bosses who get me customers. And I have to pay Mr. Big in Reno. You don't do anything without cutting them in."

"That's a shame. The rats."

"That's the way the cookie crumbles."

She finished her drink and put her elbows on the table. "It's getting worse all the time. I can't wait to get away from Nevada. I hate what I'm doing. I'd do most anything to pick up a couple grand and call it quits."

He looked at her and saw that she wasn't laughing. She meant it. He thought he saw desperation in her eyes. Perhaps she *would* do most anything to get enough money to make a fresh start.

What if he offered her two thousand to help him with Judith? She'd be worth it. Could he trust her? He'd have to think it over carefully. Deliberately, he turned the conversation toward guns. Was she afraid of a gun? Could she handle one if necessary? "I want to settle someplace where I can go hunting a lot. I was thinking of Idaho, for example. Did you ever go hunting?"

"No, but I'd like to. I used to go trapshooting. I'm a good shot."

"How about that? So am I. As a matter of fact, I'm an expert, you might say. I can handle any kind of firearm; you name it and I can handle it. But I didn't suppose a girl like you. . . ."

Her voice lowered. "I own a gun. Wouldn't be without it. I can use it, too, if necessary. There's always a lot of cash around my place, and I want protection if some jerk tries something."

They left the bar and went to a casino for dinner and the free entertainment in the cocktail lounge. But all the time he thought about having her help him with Judith. Rita would be great. She'd been around and she wouldn't scare easy. In fact, they could use her gun and he wouldn't have to get one, which would be one less hassle to worry about. The more he thought about Rita, the better he liked the idea.

Then, maybe, when it was all over, she'd go with him. They could settle in Idaho, Wyoming, or Montana, where he could open a garage and she could go to beauty school. They'd put their past behind them. Of course she wanted to "get out"—she was too nice a girl for that. In her pink dress, she didn't look at all hard or tough or brassy like so many others. It would be nice to have a girl like Rita with him. He had plenty of money to get them started.

When they got to her place, he tried to approach the subject without telling her too much. "I've been thinking about what you said, about needing two grand. I'll pay you that much if you'll help me do something. There's a little risk involved."

She unzipped her dress and hung it on a hanger, then faced him in her lace-trimmed slip. "If you're thinking about robbing a bank, forget it."

He laughed. "No, of course not. I wouldn't be loading dishwashers at Starr's if I was willing to rob a bank."

"It's not holding up a service station or a store or something like that?"

He took her in his arms. "What kind of a guy do you think I am!" He kissed her. "It's more of a practical joke. Nobody'll get hurt."

"And you want me to help you?"

"Yeah. And I'll give you two Gs, too."

"Why so much bread if there isn't much to it?"

"Because you're so pretty and you need that much. I've fallen for you hard. When I get this joke pulled off, I want to leave. How about going with me?"

She squeezed him to her. "You mean it?"

He kissed her for a long time. "You bet I mean it. We could find a place we like and start over together."

She put her head in the hollow of his neck. "It sounds too good to be true."

They sat on the edge of her bed. "Let me tell you about this practical joke I want to pull. There's a big shot that did me dirt one time and I want to get even."

She looked skeptical. "How?"

"I've kicked a lot of ideas around, but there's one I like the best. His daughter works at Starr's. I was thinking of hiding her someplace and scaring the hell out of him for a day or two. As soon as we got her hid, we'd leave."

"But you'd finally get in touch with the father and tell him where she was?"

"Sure, something like that." She really seemed interested, so he went on. "I've got it all doped out, except I can't figure out how to get her to come with me. See, I worked for her old man at one time, and she might recognize me. She knows we had a big argument."

"I suppose that's where I come in. But why would she come with me?"

He rubbed his hand along her bare thigh. "You'd have to get her to come to the parking lot some night. She'd be more willing to go outside with another girl than with a man."

"I'd have to have a darned good reason." Rita bit her lip in thought. "Like her father was outside, sick or something."

"But then she'd want to send for a doctor."

She turned to him excitedly. "I've got it! Why not spot her car in the parking lot the night we're going to hide her? Then I could rush into the resort and say I had accidentally backed into it with my car. Naturally, she'd rush out with me to see what damage I'd done."

He hugged her. "Rita, baby, now you're talking! You're something else! I wouldn't of thought of that in a dozen years. Of course, she'd come barreling out of the casino when she heard that. All shook up, too, and she wouldn't be expecting anyone to be waiting for her with a gun."

"A gun? You're going to use a gun?"

"Of course. We want her to keep her mouth shut and not scream or anything. I told you there was some risk, didn't I?"

"Yes, but. . . ."

He could have kicked himself for blurting out about the gun. He didn't want Rita to chicken out now. "Listen, sweetheart, it'll only take a few minutes. I've found the perfect hiding place for her, too —an old sawmill that nobody's used for fifty years, right off the Kingsbury Grade Road about five miles from Starr's. It'll be the easiest two thousand bucks you ever earned."

Rita looked uncertain. "I want my two Gs in advance."

"Now, wait a minute. How do I know——"

"In *advance*. How do I know but what you'll get me to help you and then run out without paying anything?" Her chin was set stubbornly. "That's the way the cookie crumbles sometimes."

He patted her arm and kissed her shoulder. "How about compromising? The minute we get back to the car after we tie her up in the sawmill, I'll settle with you."

"You'll have the cash all ready for me right then?"

"Sure. I'll tell you what else I'll do. Before you go in the resort to get the gal to come out, I'll show you the money and you can count it. I'll have twenty one-hundred-dollar bills."

"Where'll you get that kind of money? You'd have to scrape a lot of dishes——"

"Don't worry, I've got it. You'll see it, too, before you take any risks. You can't ask for a squarer deal than that." He held her close to him. "You'll help me, won't you?"

She nodded. "Yes, if you'll promise me you'll let her father know where she is so he can get her. I don't want her hurt or anything like that."

Otto nodded. "I'll be in touch with her old man. I just want to scare him awhile." Rita need never know what happened to Judith. He doubted if she ever read a newspaper or listened to news reports. She was as cute a broad as he'd ever seen—to make up for her lack of brains. Besides, they'd be long gone before there was any publicity about Judith in Nevada. "Let me see your gun, Rita."

She got off the bed and opened a chest of drawers. When she handed the gun to him, he shook his head. No use getting his fingerprints on it this soon. "It's a good revolver—a Smith and Wesson .38 special. You can put it away, Rita." He wondered where she got it. Probably some customer had given it to her instead of cash. After she put the gun back and closed the drawer, he asked, "Could we use it that night, Rita?"

She shrugged. "I guess so, if you hold the gun on her while I drive the car. How about that?"

"It's a deal. But we've talked about business long enough." He patted the bed.

CHAPTER

23

During her afternoon break, Barrett got two bottles of cola and went to the gift shop to see Judith, who was in the back room unwrapping packages at a work table.

"Thanks," Judith said when Barrett placed the drink beside her. "Unwrapping all this merchandise is like having Christmas every day." She held up a moon-shaped vase. "It's from Portugal and hand-painted. Isn't it beautiful?"

"Yes, it is." Barrett sipped at her cola. "You look great. I assume that everything's all right with you."

Judith turned toward Barrett, her face radiant. "I haven't been this happy in years. I love working here, and I'm learning so much. And now I know why you advised me to get some training and experience before I bought a shop of my own. It's a lot more complicated than I thought."

Barrett smiled and asked, "And is your room comfortable?"

"It's fine, but it could be a tent on the beach, for

all I care. Since Dad and I made up, I feel like a different person. As I've told you, it's like having the weight of the world off my shoulders. He calls me every day, or I call him, or he and Mom drive up here to see me."

"I'm so happy for you. You even look different."

"That's what Lyle says. By the way, he's coming here this afternoon, right after work."

"I've noticed him around a lot lately. I guess you're the big attraction, Judith."

"No—not today, anyway. He's involved in a big deal with some men up here." Judith took a swallow of her cola. "Maybe the four of us could do something together tonight."

"Yes, if Lyle is willing."

"Why shouldn't he be? Is there something wrong between you two? I've noticed a certain coolness."

"Just a little misunderstanding over business. Don't worry about it."

"Well, you can clear it up tonight. I've just come out of a long, dark tunnel, and I don't want anything to spoil my happiness now."

When Lyle arrived that afternoon, he called Barrett at the reservation desk, where she was working, and asked her to come to his office. He was polite when she entered. He offered her a seat, then picked up a ballpoint pen and rolled it between his hands. "Judith and Clifton want the four of us to go out together tonight, and that's fine with me. As I said before, I've enjoyed you a lot as a friend."

She tried to hit a lighter note. "I thought we were more than friends—members of the same family, kissing cousins."

Lyle shrugged. "Friends or relatives—whatever. Just as long as we're not business associates."

"Surely you're not——"

"Firing you? No. Let's just say that we're reverting

to the original agreement. You came here for the summer, and that season ends after the big Labor Day weekend. So does your work here. You have a little over three weeks to make other plans."

"Uncle Justin——"

"I have no intention of discussing this with Dad. He was premature. I'm sure he thinks so, too, now that he's thought about it." He stood up to end the discussion. "Don't forget that I'm in charge, officially, by action of the board of directors when my father had his heart attack."

Barrett had never seen him come on so strong, biting off each word. She got out of her chair and glared at him.

"I have no intention of leaving Tahoe."

Lyle shrugged. "It's your privilege to live where you please, Barrett, but you'll have to get a position somewhere else, or marry Clifton. Do whatever you want, but understand that your job terminates as of Tuesday, September 7th. You're finished here, once and for all."

"We'll see about that!" She turned and walked out of his office, depressed and sick. How could she fight Lyle? He had the authority, and he was using it. As far as he was concerned, there was no room in Starr Enterprises for both of them. He would take no chance having her compete with him.

No doubt about it: Justin had acted impulsively and had ruined her chances. How much better it would have been if she had ascended the ladder more slowly, more gradually. She could have changed her temporary status to a permanent position, then slowly made herself indispensable. Why hadn't she foreseen Lyle's resentment? Naturally he had been against her quick rise, when his own had taken years. If she had been smart, she'd have channeled Justin's enthusiasm and settled for a run-of-the-mill position at Tahoe.

She was as much at fault as Lyle. On the other hand, wasn't it worth the risk—to grab what she could when it was offered? If she had chosen the slower method and her uncle died, she would still be out on her ear.

She had dreaded the evening ahead, with Lyle; he had gotten the best of her. However, it turned out to be surprisingly lighthearted. Judith was animated and vivacious, and when they gambled in a north shore casino after dinner, she couldn't lose. She carried the men along with her *joie de vivre,* and they, too, had winning streaks. Lyle seemed especially ebullient. He spoke of a business transaction he had just concluded, but Barrett wondered if his triumph over her wasn't the main reason for his jubilance.

Only Barrett, depressed and nursing her disappointment, consistently lost. For one thing, she was gambling with needed money. Certainly, she now needed every cent, as she'd sent far too much to her stepfather in her anxiety to lessen her debt to him. With her uncle's backing, she'd been so confident; there was no place to go but up.

But it was more than money she wanted. Wherever they went, Lyle was called by name, welcomed by the security guards, the maître d', the floor bosses, the operators. He was a Starr and now was the head of the great empire. At each casino he had to show his money, because he had to prove that his business was prospering. Barrett wanted that recognition and deference. After all, she was a true Starr, whereas Lyle had not a drop of Starr blood in his veins. She couldn't settle for being just a satellite, a hanger-on. No, she wanted to be one of the important Starrs, too.

Resentfully, she thought of her conversation with Lyle. Why shouldn't she be part of Starr Enterprises? What right did he have to ostracize her? Except for her father, who had bowed out twenty years ago, she was Justin Starr's only blood relative. If her father had just shown some promise, think where they'd be today! She wouldn't be taking a backseat to an adopted son. Oh, no; she'd be the one with the power.

When the evening came to an end, they returned to the resort, and Clifton offered to drive Barrett home. When they were alone, Clifton said, "You've been very quiet all evening. What's the matter?"

"I'm lower than a snake. I'm not often depressed, but I am now."

"Come to my apartment and have a nightcap. You can tell me all about it and maybe I can help."

They sat on the sofa, with the lights low, the music soft, and tall drinks in their hands. She told him about the offer of a vice-presidency from Justin, Lyle's resentment, and the ensuing fiasco. "In all fairness, it was as much my fault as Uncle Justin's. I should have anticipated Lyle's reaction and avoided this showdown."

Clifton twined his fingers with hers. "The answer, of course, is for you to marry me. I'll give you a job as my assistant. Lyle can't object to that. I have the final say on resort personnel."

"No, he wouldn't fight that, not if I were safely bound to you and, hopefully, awaiting the patter of little feet." She twirled her glass. "But if I didn't get pregnant soon, Lyle would use his influence and connections and you would be offered a position far, far away, with an international hotel chain, that you couldn't resist."

"Perhaps. But marry me, darling, anyway."

She shook her head. "You're too fine a person to marry in a rebound. I don't want you as a way out, a solution. You don't deserve that, Clifton. Someday, when I marry you—or whomever—it's going to be because it's the only way to go. It's got to be all or nothing. I'm not going to settle for less."

She stayed with him that night, taking comfort in

his passion, his physical nearness. As he slept, she listened to him breathe. Maybe she should marry Clifton. There was so much she admired about him— his maleness, his urbane charm, his sophistication, his complete self-confidence. He was intelligent and an excellent administrator. Perhaps they could buy a hotel somewhere—a casino-resort at Tahoe, on the north shore. They could run it together. What a challenge that would be! Clifton could handle the hotel end, and she the PR, advertising, promotion, and the gaming. No doubt she could get Justin to back her, with private funds that he could use without Lyle's approval. With his influence, he could help Clifton and her get the necessary licenses and permits.

She snuggled close to him. There was no question that Clifton was deeply in love with her, that he adored her. She was still awake at five o'clock, when the phone rang.

Clifton answered the call and listened for a moment. "All right," he said, and hung up the receiver. "It's an emergency." He dressed hastily in Levi's and jacket and was gone for an hour.

Barrett was shocked at his appearance when he returned. He seemed badly shaken, and she saw fear in his eyes.

"What's the matter?"

"Nothing much." He avoided her and headed for the bathroom. "I'm up, so I might as well shower and get ready for work."

Why was he so evasive? Barrett wondered. So unlike his usual confident self, always in command of a situation? Then, dressed in a handsome summer suit, he leaned over the bed and kissed her good-bye, but his eyes avoided hers. "See you later, darling."

What had happened? Something had hit him hard; there was no doubt about that. Sleep eluded her, so she got out of bed, shivering as the mountain air hit her naked body, and padded into the bathroom. She stood under the shower a long time, enjoying the sensation of hot water flowing over her skin. Then she wrapped herself in a big towel, went back to the bedroom and selected a pantsuit from the closet.

Why the mysterious summons for Clifton at five in the morning? It couldn't have been an emergency call from the night engineer or from a floor boss asking for an OK for an IOU. Nothing like that would shake Clifton; he dealt with such crises every day. Something had frightened him.

Clifton never spoke of the telephone call, and she didn't probe, but a few days later, when she stayed with him again, the telephone again rang at five in the morning. This time when Clifton answered it, she pretended to be asleep. Once more he dressed hastily and slipped out. Barrett jumped out of bed, rushed to the window and saw Clifton cross the highway in front of the resort and disappear into the woods. Quickly, she pulled on her clothes and followed him.

He'd taken the path to Squaw Rock, a favorite walk for guests at the resort. It led to a meadow where a granite outcropping formed a work table for the squaws of long ago, who ground acorns and seeds into meal. Barrett moved as quietly as possible and stayed near the trees for cover. It was barely light, and she shivered with the cold. Why had Clifton been summoned to this place at such an hour? She approached the clearing, hid behind an incense cedar and saw Clifton and a burly, dark-haired man standing in the grass beside Squaw Rock, talking to each other. A brown-and-tan Chrysler was parked in a fire lane that crossed the meadow.

As she watched, the stranger seized Clifton by his jacket and, as if to emphasize what he was saying, shook him like a rag doll. Clifton offered no resistance, which was frightening in itself—so unlike the Cliff she knew. Who was this man? What was going on?

Not wanting to be discovered, she retreated into

the trees, then ran along the path back to the resort, took the elevator to Clifton's apartment and slipped into his bedroom. She undressed, climbed back into bed and pulled the covers over her head. When Clifton returned, she pretended to be sound asleep.

While he showered and shaved, she reviewed the scene in the woods. The stranger seemed so tough and threatening, and obviously had some kind of hold over Clifton. Like someone's henchman from the underworld? He looked the part. But what was the connection with Clifton? As Clifton finished dressing, she yawned and stretched as if she'd just awakened. She opened her eyes and looked at him. "Cliff, you're up so early."

"I couldn't sleep, so I thought I'd get up. I have some extra work I want to get out." As he leaned over to kiss her, his eyes seemed haunted and his face was pale. There was no doubt that the mysterious stranger had intimidated him. She wanted to question him but something about his manner stopped her.

After he left, she lay in bed, puzzled and frightened. What was all this about? Was Clifton being threatened or warned? Maybe blackmailed? Her mind went back to the group on the beach, to the skimming and cheating that she was certain were taking place, to the shot that someone had fired just over her head, to Dixon's investigation. And now this hood who was menacing Clifton.

What did it all mean? Who was behind it? Mr. Hightower ultimately, no doubt, who worked through henchmen, such as the one she had seen at Squaw Rock. But there must be someone at the resort who was under direct orders. Was it Carl Rhodes? She doubted it. He seemed more like a sergeant in charge of a special squad. Someone must be above him in rank—a "lieutenant" or "captain"—someone with authority, who could have hired the night crew in the first place. Was it the personnel manager? Somehow, she didn't fit the role. Finally, when all the pieces fell into place, she could hardly breathe. It had to be Clifton!

The idea was ridiculous. She tried to laugh it off. What connection could there be between suave, cultured Clifton, from the fastidious East Coast, and the Nevada underworld? None, of course. It was disloyal and unfair of her even to consider such an idea. How could she entertain such a crazy notion?

But all morning, as she worked at the reservation desk, the memory of Clifton and the dark-haired man with his threatening manner kept returning. Underneath her guilt at harboring such thoughts about her lover was the nagging fact of the time of the meetings: daybreak at Squaw Rock. Wouldn't a legitimate caller have come to Clifton's office or his apartment at a reasonable hour? Weren't the meetings purposely clandestine—held at a time and place so that no one would see them together? And if the hood came just to intimidate Clifton, why did Clifton meet him the second time? Or was it just one of many meetings? If Hightower wanted to contact someone, he would send a henchman with a message; he'd hardly risk telephoning or coming in person. Moreover, Clifton was badly upset; he acted as if he were at the stranger's mercy. She could stand it no longer; she had to talk to someone. She called the executive suite and told Mr. Dixon she wanted to see him. Then, embarrassed and self-conscious, she faced the agent across Justin's desk, wondering if Mr. Dixon was a square, a straight arrow, and whether he would condemn her.

"To begin with, I'm going to tell it like it is," she finally said. "Clifton McMillan and I are lovers. He's asked me to marry him, and I might accept him. He's a wonderful, beautiful man, and that's why this is so difficult." She faltered, then plunged in and told the agent about the early-morning telephone calls and the meetings. She described the Chrysler she had seen in the fire lane at Squaw Rock. "I'm probably doing Clifton a grave injustice. What possible connection could there be between him and the Nevada underworld?"

Dixon smiled. "That's the misconception that everyone has about the underworld. We expect them to look like Al Capone. Well, I can assure you that the front people are usually the most sophisticated, well-informed, personable men and women imaginable. That's why they're so hard to ferret out.

"We know for a fact that the underworld wants to get a stranglehold on Starr's. Their plans are long-range. They've been waiting for years for Mr. Starr to drop out of the picture. It's not inconceivable that they'd pick some promising young man in the East, send him to college and train him to take over one of the Starr casinos."

"But that doesn't prove that Clifton has anything to do with the underworld."

"Probably not, but if he's innocent, no harm has been done. What you've told me will stay between us and go no further. But if he's guilty, you've made a major contribution to solving the problem. I'll bring in the proper authorities, and we'll go on from there."

"I'm sure he's innocent."

"I hope so, but something's been going on. While I'm here, they're all lying low—no meetings at the beach, no skimming in the counting room, no cheating in the gaming rooms. Everyone is doing his or her job to the letter. Everything's been on the up and up."

"And the receipts are also up, I assume."

"Yes, they are. Of course, this is one of the biggest vacation months. I'm sure they're hoping we'll assume that the upsurge is due to all the tourists here at Tahoe."

"If Clifton is one of their men, is that why he's in trouble—because nothing is flowing into the underworld from here?"

The agent shook his head. "I doubt it. They've no doubt had word from the top to lie low while I'm on deck. They're too smart to risk a year-round racket just for the skimming they could do while I'm here."

"Then, why?"

"You."

Barrett gasped. *"Me?"*

Al Dixon leaned toward her across the desk. "Don't think that your relationship with Clifton McMillan has gone unnoticed, because it hasn't. That is, if he's one of their boys, I mean. They have spies everywhere, and every move you two make is no doubt reported to the top."

Her face flushed. She remembered Carl Rhodes in the woods, inviting her to bring Clifton to the so-called beach party. And the knowing looks between the two women. "I'm afraid you're right."

"Is there any evidence of your visits to Clifton's apartment—something a maid could find?"

She thought of her clothes, the extra towels by the shower, her cosmetics. She nodded.

"It's my guess, then, that he's been told to get himself another girlfriend. They don't like him playing house with Justin Starr's grandniece—especially if she works all over the resort and takes pictures of their meetings." He laughed. "I bet you've driven them crazy!"

Embarrassed and shaken, Barrett picked up her bag. "Well, that's about it."

Dixon walked with her to the door of the office. "Wish I could take you to lunch as a reward for your information, but it might complicate things if we were seen being chummy."

She felt almost ill with remorse. What had she done to Clifton? He was one of the most wonderful guys she'd ever known. He truly loved her and had asked her to marry him. For over two months he'd been kindness itself. What a terrible way to treat him in return! She should have protected him. Let Dixon find out on his own, if he could.

She walked toward the beach. Her whole world had turned sour. She might be leaving Tahoe soon. How could she get a worthwhile job, when the vacation season was almost over? They'd be letting people go in September instead of hiring more. She was dismissed from Starr Enterprises just as her goal was within her grasp. And now she'd set forces in motion that could ruin Clifton.

She regretted having talked to Dixon. She had acted impulsively, without thinking of all the ramifications. She should have consulted Justin or Lyle and let them take the responsibility. What would happen to Clifton now? But it was too late to stop Dixon from acting. If only she had become engaged to Clifton when he first proposed to her, she would never have been so disloyal.

Barrett turned and looked back at the resort, glimmering like a jewel in the midday sun. It was glorious. The sunlight sparkled more brightly because of it. The building rose proudly in the air, cars crowded the parking lots and people swam in the pools and swooped like white doves on the tennis courts.

Finally she straightened her shoulders and blinked back her tears. She didn't love Clifton. She would not marry him. If he were part of the underworld trying to get a hold on all this, he deserved whatever punishment he might get. Nothing was more important than Starr's Tahoe Resort.

CHAPTER

24

While sitting in the cardiologist's waiting room, Eunice glanced through a pile of magazines on the table beside her. Justin was having a complete examination so that the doctor could evaluate the extent of his recovery. Nervously, Eunice waited for the verdict.

It was August 24, seven weeks since the heart attack. She thought of that first week in the hospital, when Justin's life had hung in the balance. Then of the second week, when he'd begun his slow recovery, which led to the five weeks of convalescence at home. He had recovered most of his strength, but only the cardiologist could determine his true condition.

For Justin's sake, Eunice hoped he would show permanent improvement. It had all been her fault. If he were definitely better, she could put the whole ugly memory of his collapse behind her and be rid of much of her guilt. Also, the doctor's faith in her resolve to nurse him back to health would be vindicated. She had been all too aware of the cardiologist's doubts, but she had shown him!

Reading a blurb on the cover of *Vogue*, "America's Leading Aristocrats—Women of Involvement," she wondered who they were. She had been out of the social mainstream for so long that she wouldn't know. Most of the issue was devoted to ten society women who had been chosen from various sections of the country. As she turned the pages, it gave her a feeling of satisfaction that she had known, or at least met, most of them.

One of the women featured had been one of her best friends during her Bellingham years, Marjorie Davidson. The caption read, "Mrs. Wallace Emerson Davidson, philanthropist and community leader of San Francisco."

Fascinated, Eunice looked at the color photographs of her friend. A page of pictures showed Marjorie in various rooms of her condominium apartment, which looked out on the Golden Gate Bridge and the northern part of the Bay. She was beautiful and appeared surprisingly young, although she, too, was in her fifties. She was a widow now, but she lived a busy, fulfilling life. There were pictures on another page of her working with handicapped children, serving on the county board of supervisors, and attending the opening of the opera in a long, sweeping gown. One illustration showed her with friends on a yacht, cruising down the coast toward Acapulco, and another at her country club, playing golf, and at a charity luncheon.

As Eunice looked at the pictures and read the text, she substituted herself for Marge Davidson. If Andrew had managed the Bellingham fortune differently, she, too, would be in San Francisco, enjoying the same luncheons, opera openings, and cruises. She'd be with her own kind, where she belonged, in a city she loved. She thought of the flower stalls along the streets, the cable cars clanging up the hills, the golden doors of Grace Cathedral, the azaleas and cherry trees in full bloom in the Japanese Tea Garden, and the necklaces of lights across the bridges at night. She could smell the roasting coffee from the great mills, the spices being processed, the sandalwood and herbs in Chinatown, the crabs boiling in big pots at Fisherman's Wharf. She recalled the dinner parties in elegant Georgian mansions on Pacific Heights.

Her reverie was so deep that the nurse, standing in the doorway to the examining room, had to speak to her twice to gain her attention. "Mrs. Starr, the doctor wants you to come to his office."

"I'm sorry, I was daydreaming."

Justin was seated across the desk from the doctor. Eunice took a chair next to him, and the cardiologist said, "I have a good report for you. I'm very pleased." He pointed to the tracings on the cardiogram and compared them with the tracings right after the attack. "In fact, this is much better than I dared hoped for. You've made a remarkable recovery, Mr. Starr." He explained Justin's condition at length and summarized by saying, "You can lead a normal life from now on, if you will be very careful."

"Can I go back to the office?"

"Yes, but start with just two hours in the morning and gradually increase the time. For the next month, put in only half a day, at the most, and rest in the afternoon."

Justin slapped the arms of his chair. "Good! I'm mighty anxious to get back in the harness."

"One thing I want to warn you about. You must be careful for the rest of your life. Do everything in moderation. If you want to go on a trip, take a cruise instead of tearing around Europe as you did. If you want to have friends in, have just a few. Don't try to entertain on a massive scale anymore. When you exercise, stop and rest frequently. Remember, fatigue and overexcitement are bad for you and always will be."

Justin nodded. "I'll watch it."

"You must take your medication faithfully, too. This is most important; it's an anticoagulant to help prevent another attack."

Eunice spoke up, "I'll see that he does, Doctor."

The doctor turned toward her. "I'm sure you will. The smartest thing I ever did was to put him in your care. You did a magnificent job, Mrs. Starr. I wasn't sure that you were strong enough to do it."

Strong enough to stay sober, you mean. Well, I showed you, she thought.

"She watched over me like a hawk," Justin said.

The doctor laughed. "I heard about the timer. The governor himself told me he was allowed just fifteen minutes, and when that timer went off, he had to hustle out of your sitting room."

"She was hard-nosed, all right. I believe she'd of kicked out the president of the United States, too. That's how strict she was."

"Well, in all seriousness, I want to congratulate you, Mrs. Starr. I know very well your husband would never have carried out my orders on his own."

"You're right. A lot of 'em seemed like nonsense," Justin said, patting Eunice's arm. "But this girl didn't think so. She did everything you told her to do. Never missed giving me my medicine even once. During the night or if she was going to take a nap or something, she always set the alarm so she'd give it to me exactly on time. Best nurse in the world."

"Well, she saved your life, Mr. Starr, and I mean it."

On the way home in the limousine, Justin repeated the words, "You saved my life."

She smiled at him. "And I'm going to go on saving your life. We're going to live quietly, and you're going to take everything in moderation, darling." She squeezed his hand. "But I will enjoy having small dinner parties with our favorite friends. We'll cut out the bashes with the belly dancers. Your gambling friends will understand." No more big parties. What a relief!

"God knows we've entertained 'em all plenty."

"When we receive invitations to affairs that might be too taxing, I'll send our regrets."

"Let Lyle or Barrett represent us."

"That's a good idea. Or one of your executives. Hank Brenner would be delighted to be Starr's official glad-hander."

"I'll do whatever you say, my girl. You pulled me out of a pretty deep hole, so I'll let you be the boss— just so I can go to my office."

"Beginning tomorrow, you can go at ten and stay until noon. Fred and I will pick you up at twelve."

"You don't have to bother. Fred can come alone."

"No, I'll be there, too. You can intimidate Fred, but not me. If I have to, I'll haul you out by the ear, darling; so you'd better behave."

"I'll behave, but I'll be glad to have some time in the office." There were a lot of things he wanted to look into. Something was up with Lyle; he felt it in his bones. The boy was too damned evasive lately. And this business with Clifton McMillan that Al Dixon had reported. Could the resident manager really have an underworld connection? It didn't seem likely, but he'd seen a lot of funny business in his life. Nothing surprised him anymore. Well, Dixon could handle it better than he could. Seems that Clifton turned informer to save his hide. Dixon had called in other authorities, and they were pumping him good.

By the time they were home, Justin was very tired; so Eunice sent him to bed for the rest of the afternoon. In no time he was sound asleep, so she changed into a swimsuit, went to the pool and stretched out on a chaise. It was very hot, and her mind went back to San Francisco. She thought of its cool sea breeze and the fog creeping over the city at night, then dissipating in the morning, to leave the buildings washed with dew and sparkling in the sunshine.

The pictures of Marjorie Davidson flashed through her mind in a haunting kaleidoscope. The luxurious apartment was just like one she would want. She thought of the full, exciting life, with interesting, cultured people who talked about concerts, plays, the ballet, and the latest books, instead of gambling and business. She ached with envy. It wasn't that she didn't deeply appreciate what Justin had done for her and Lyle and her mother. She did. The past fifteen years would have been impossible without him. But would she ever be able to live the way she wanted to? The future with Justin seemed to stretch on and on forever, never ending.

When it was time to give him his medicine again, she went into the house and awakened him. Then she showered and changed into a long, pale-blue caftan trimmed in silver. She had considered dining downstairs but dismissed the idea when she saw how the examination had tired her husband. They ate in the sitting room, watched the news on television and then sat quietly in the twilight.

Justin took her hand. "I keep thinking about what the doctor said, about your saving my life. You did, too."

"I'm so glad, Justin. Now I can tell you how guilty and ashamed I've felt all these last weeks, about causing your heart attack." Her voice faltered. "If I could only undo that wrong. I've felt terrible about it."

"You have? Hell, I should've told you a long time ago that you didn't cause it. It was coming on anyway. All that damn tearing around in Europe is what brought it on. I got way too tired, that's what."

"Really? Are you telling me the truth?" She desperately wanted to believe him.

"Of course I am. That's why we came home early. I had to skip that stay in New York. I knew something was wrong with my heart and I'd best be getting home. Then, when we got to Paris, I had to stay in bed at the hotel so I could make the flight."

"I didn't realize——"

"Oh, I admit I got awful sore when you didn't meet me or send Fred. I had to take a cab and all. I'm sure my temper put the attack ahead a few hours, but that's all. It was coming on anyway."

Eunice sighed deeply. "Oh, Justin, you can't imagine what a relief it is to hear you say that. I've been castigating myself."

He raised her hand and pressed it to his cheek. "I'm sorry, Eunice. Listen, you should have no regrets about anything. You've given me fifteen of the happiest, most beautiful years a man could have. I married you because I wanted a swell for a wife, but I've grown to love you." His voice broke. "You can't imagine how much—how I feel about you."

He was silent for a while, then said, "I want to give you a present—in appreciation for all the years you've devoted to me and for taking care of me these last weeks. You heard the doctor say that I owe my life to you. He's right."

"Oh, Justin, you don't have to give me a present. I have all the jewels and furs I could possibly use. Remember, we're going to live quietly from now on."

"No, I want to do something for you." There was a stubborn firmness in his voice. He pulled his recliner to a sitting position.

"All right, you can take me on a Caribbean cruise this winter. It will be wonderful to get away for a couple of weeks when it's so cold and horrid here."

"We can do that, of course, but I have something else in mind for you, something you deserve after fifteen years of putting up with me. It hasn't been all beer and skittles for you." He kissed the palm of her hand. "But I've appreciated your devotion, don't think I haven't."

"Well, you've been awfully good to Lyle and me. And think of what you did for my mother. I don't know what I would have done without your kindness."

"You deserved every bit of it." Justin took a deep breath, as if he were steeling himself. "I want to give you something that you've earned, something that will be very important to you."

"What?"

He barely whispered, "Your freedom."

"My freedom! What do you mean?"

"Exactly that. You're free to leave me. I'll buy you the finest apartment in San Francisco, like some of your friends have in those fancy condominiums. You'll have your trust fund now, instead of waiting until I kick the bucket. You can take your furniture and servants and be one of those society swells again."

"Justin, I'm shocked! Surely you don't mean——"

"I mean every word of it. My lawyer can come tomorrow and make all the arrangements."

"But I thought you love me."

"Eunice, I didn't know it was possible for a man to love a woman as much as I love you." His voice shook. "That's why I want you to have this chance, while you're still young enough to enjoy it."

"But——"

"If you're worrying about how this will affect Lyle, forget it. He will always be my son and heir."

"Oh, Justin!"

"I'll admit that I'm thinking of changing my will some. I'm going to add a codicil so Barrett will inherit something, too. She's the only blood relative I give a damn about."

Almost in a trance, Eunice got out of her chair and walked to the window. She grasped the curtain and stared into the garden, darkening in the twilight.

Justin was offering her her freedom. She could hardly grasp the implications: an apartment as lovely as Marjorie Davidson's, a trust fund. She could live in San Francisco for the rest of her life and be with her own kind again. She could be free. Everything she wanted would be handed to her on a golden platter.

She looked at Justin in his recliner. But who would give him his medicine? Who would supervise his activities, so he would do everything in moderation? Who would go to his office and insist that he come home before he became tired? Who?

For the first time she realized how necessary she was to Justin, how badly he needed her. In spite of everything, she had been very content these last weeks of his convalescence—happy, really, doing her needlework and being a companion to him. He'd be so lonely without her. Amazingly, she no longer wanted to drink. She had kept herself alert to take care of Justin. She had saved his life. Even the doctor said so, and he had meant it.

She had been responsible for someone's welfare. Not even Lyle had been so dependent on her. He had had nurses from the time he was born; he would have lived without her. But not Justin. Even now there was still danger. He would overdo and get too tired. He would drink too much and stay up all night and gamble. He would work too hard. He would forget his medicine. He could easily have another heart attack. Who would look after him if she were in San Francisco?

Her thoughts went back to when he was telling his life story into the tape recorder. About the nine-year-old Justin who wasn't chosen by his mother. About the little boy who traveled with a carnival, when all the time he wanted to live in a brick house and have a bicycle and a paper route. About the fourteen-year-old Justin who had ridden the rails west on a freight train to find his mother. The young man who fought off the crossroaders, the con men, and the hoods to save his little saloon and cardroom. She thought of Justin in a foxhole in Italy, afraid, but so brave, and dreaming of home. Then there were his disappointing marriages and his seeking her out because she had "class."

Justin Starr—so complex: difficult, stubborn, crude, irritating. Tears ran down her cheeks. But so *vital*, so remarkable in his success, so human with all his foibles, generous, good, strong—a real man, one in a million, and she loved him. She *loved* him!

She turned toward him and brushed the tears away with her hand. Her voice trembled. "I don't want my freedom, darling. I want to live here with you."

"Eunice!" Justin got out of his chair and gathered her in his arms.

She laid her face against his chest and whispered, "I love you, Justin."

"Oh, Eunice. This is the first time you've said that! You've never told me so before. All these years I've longed to hear you say so."

"I just realized it now. Darling, you're such a wonderful man." She held him close. "And you've got class—the real kind."

Tears ran down Justin's cheeks and into her hair. He hugged her to him as if he could never let her go.

They stood together in the darkness, until she asked, "Justin, how could you offer me my freedom? The apartment in San Francisco? The trust fund? I might have accepted. I'll be honest; I was terribly tempted. I almost said yes. Why did you take such a chance?"

He didn't answer for a long time. Then he said, "Because I'm a gambler, a real gambler. I always play my hunches."

CHAPTER

25

For days, Otto Schroeder haunted the parking lots around Starr's Resort, trying to spot Judith Davenport's car. She was likely to have a big one, and chances were that it would still have a California license. Still, that gave him many to choose from. Most of the cars at the resort were from California, and many were the luxurious kind that she would drive.

There was nothing to do but hope to see her coming in or out of the resort and find out where she parked. If she was an employee, she might use the lot assigned to them. But the notice said she was a trainee. What did that mean? Trainee for what?

Late one afternoon he drove to the resort from his room and was about to turn into the employees' parking entrance when he saw a long white Cadillac convertible pull out of the area reserved for executives. He got a glimpse of a girl who might be Judith, but the car ahead of him stopped suddenly and he had to concentrate on what he was doing. The last thing he wanted was an accident, where he'd have to show his driver's license.

He parked his car safely, got out and walked to where the VIPs had their specially reserved spaces. There were three with names: J. STARR, L. STARR, and McMILLAN. Well, Judith seemed mighty chummy with the young Starr, and he may have told her to use one of the spots. There was nothing to do but wait and see.

Otto found a place in the shade, behind a panel truck, sat down on the curb and leaned against the building. He was almost hidden from view but still could see the spaces where the big shots parked. In less than an hour, the white Cadillac turned into the employees' lot again and pulled into the executives' area. Sure enough, it was Judith Davenport who got out and went into the resort. As soon as she was out of sight, he strolled by the car and made a note of its license number.

Later, he drove to the north end of the lake and called for Rita. Instead of a dress, she wore tight blue pants and a tube top that showed her bare midriff. What a figure!

"We're going back to Stateline," he told her. "Then I want us to make a trial run to the sawmill so we know what we're doing. We can't make any mistakes. I spotted the dame's car, and I want you to see it."

After they had a few drinks in a bar and some pizza and beer, they returned to the resort and drove into the parking lot. Judith's car was under an overhead light.

Rita sucked in her breath. "What a car! And look where's she parked. L. Starr. Isn't that the guy who owns this place?"

"Yeah. She's his girlfriend. That's how come she can park here."

"Oh? We'll use her car, won't we? I can drive a Cad."

"Yeah, I guess we will." It would be safer in her car, and no one would take his license number. "Come on, we'll go into the lobby so you can see her." As they walked by the gift shop, Judith was showing a turquoise necklace to a customer. "She's the dame in the green smock," Otto whispered, "the one with the brown hair."

"She's sure cute. I wouldn't want anything to happen to her."

"It won't."

"What's her name?"

He hesitated. "I'll tell you later. Just look her over and make sure you can recognize her."

When they got back to his car, Rita asked again, "Who is she? I ought to know, if I have to ask for her or something."

"Well, her name's Judith Davenport."

"And you used to work for her father? Doing what?"

"He's got a lot of cattle ranches." Otto started the car and backed around. He didn't like all these questions. That was the trouble with having someone else along: they had to be told too much. "I'm going to run you out to the sawmill so you'll know just where to drive. The less talking we do in front of that dame, the better."

"What I can't figure out is how come, when she drives a big Cadillac like that and is Mr. Starr's girlfriend and her father has a lot of cattle ranches, she's working in that gift shop?"

"Doesn't make sense to me, either. Hell, her father's loaded. A big shot, too—lieutenant governor." What was the matter with him—blabbing away like that? Fortunately, Rita wasn't too smart. To get her mind off his slip, he said, "Now, pay close attention to where we're going. When you drive out of the resort, turn north and go back to Highway 19; then turn right." The car lights illuminated the highway and the trees on each side.

"I've been this way lots of times."

"Look for the snow markers. Then there's a sign: HELP PREVENT FOREST FIRES. See it there—with the cross through the burning cigarette?"

"Yeah, I see it."

"The minute you get there, be ready to turn again. Otherwise you may not notice the road, with all this growth."

They turned in the obscure lane and drove slowly over the corrugated surface and through the brush, which scraped against the car. When they came to the clearing, Otto stepped on the high beam of the headlights to illuminate the sawmill. "There's where we're going to put her."

"It's *spooky*. I'd hate to be left out there all alone."

"Nothing'll happen to her."

She looked at the sawmill again. "You sure?"

Was Rita getting cold feet—trying to chicken out? She'd better not, because she knew too much about the plan.

"When are we going to do it?" she asked.

"Next Tuesday night. That's my night off, so no one'll expect me at work. That OK with you?"

"Sure. One night's the same as the other to me. Except Sunday. That's when Mr. Big sends his goon for the payola."

"It's a lousy shame you have to pay him, but this Sunday'll be the last." He drew her to him. "I'm anxious to cut out of here. You'll be packed and ready to go, won't you?"

"Of course I will." She laid her head against his.

"But you be sure and have the money ready for me."

"I will." He stroked her leg. "We'll have a ball together, Rita."

"I'm glad you're taking me with you. I'm crazy about you."

"Well, I've fallen for you like a ton of bricks. You're the cutest broad I've known in a long time. There'll be just the two of us, you and me, after Tuesday night."

The closer the time came, the more nervous Otto became. It would soon be over, he kept reassuring himself; then he'd have his revenge. Lea and the Davenports—that would close the books. He could go away with Rita and live it up. They could find some land on the edge of a town and build a garage and a beauty shop next to each other at the front, and a house where they could live at the back. If they got along all right, they could even get married and have some kids.

As the time shortened, he got down to business. He swiped some dishtowels to use as a blindfold and a gag. On Tuesday morning he went to Carson City and bought fifty feet of clothesline, batteries for his flashlight, a pair of enormous dark glasses, and a roll of wide adhesive tape. Then he got his footlocker out of storage and put it in the trunk of his car. Returning to the lake, he drove onto a side road, pulled over and counted his money. It was all there. He took two packets for Rita, which still left him $98,000— plenty of bread for both of them.

When he returned to his room, he carried his belongings to the car and stacked them around the footlocker in the trunk. He was ready to move. As soon as Judith was taken care of, he and Rita would be on their way. They'd head straight for Reno and pick up Interstate 80 for Salt Lake City. Then they could decide whether to go north to Idaho, Montana, or Wyoming, or south to Arizona or New Mexico, or east to Colorado. They could even get a camper and travel around until they found just the right place.

About seven, he drove to Rita's place. She was loading her belongings into her van, and she pointed to a suitcase. "That's what I'm going to take with me. You can put it in your car. The rest of this stuff goes in my van."

"You sure got plenty of crap. What are you going to do with the van?"

"Well, I told my landlord I was going to give up this apartment and go visit some relatives for a while. He was real nice and said I could store my van at a trailer court he owns at Stateline. I thought later on, when we get settled, I could take the bus and pick it up."

"Sure. Nothing to stop you."

As he helped her load the van, he kept glancing at his watch. "We'd better shake a leg. It's almost eight o'clock and that gift shop closes at nine. We do have other plans, you know."

"Now, just cool it. It'll only be five minutes more."

"You got the gun?" he asked.

"Of course. Here, you take it." She handed him the gun and gave a final look around before she locked the apartment door.

He followed her van to Stateline, where she parked under a pine tree at the back of the trailer court. When she got in his car and he headed for Starr's, he went over his instructions again. "Be sure you wear gloves so you won't leave fingerprints anyplace. And don't call me by name—remember that. In fact, keep your trap shut as much as possible. Just drive.

Be careful you don't flood the carburetor or get stalled or anything like that."

"I won't. I'm not that stupid."

"You remember how to get to the sawmill, don't you?"

"Of course I remember. We went there just the other night," she said crossly. She hitched up her tube top, which she wore under an embroidered denim shirt. "You've been crabby all evening, and nervous as a cat."

"I *am* nervous. I'll be glad when this is over."

"So will I. It's no fun for me, either."

When they got to the employees' lot, Otto parked the Chevy in its usual place.

"Where's my money?"

"You can at least let me turn the motor off, for Christ's sake!" She was really getting to him. She'd never got on his nerves like this before. He took the two packets out of the glove compartment. "Now, you watch while I count 'em." When he finished, he stuffed the bills in his pocket. "They're yours the minute we're through."

"OK. I'm going to get Judith Davenport now."

"You remember what to say? You backed into her car and want her to come out to see what damage you've done."

"I remember. We rehearsed it enough. Gee, you must think I'm awfully dumb."

"Well, do it right, and be sure she brings her car keys. You better go now; it's almost closing time. I'll be waiting near her car."

He put the gun in his jacket pocket, then put on a pair of gloves and the dark glasses. He reached in the back seat for the bag with the cut-up clothesline, the tape, the towels, and his flashlight.

With his hand in his pocket, ready to draw the gun, he stood in the shadows against the wall, near the white Cadillac, his heart pounding against his chest. No one drove into or out of the lot, and soon Judith and Rita came hurrying out of the employees' entrance. The dame was toting her shoulder bag, he noted. That was good; it meant she'd have her car keys.

"I'm awfully sorry, Miss Davenport. Here's where I hit you." As she talked, Rita slipped on a pair of gloves and led Judith to the side of the car so that her back was to Otto, who stepped out of the shadows and poked the gun between her shoulder blades.

"Don't make a sound or I'll kill you. Get in the front seat. Give your keys to the girl."

Judith gasped but opened the door and slid into the seat.

Otto got in next to her, with the gun pressed into her side. "The keys!" Her hands shook as she got them from her bag and gave them to Rita. Rita started the car, drove out of the lot and turned left, drove to Highway 19, then turned right. There was no traffic. She pressed the floor button to high beam so she could find the lane to the sawmill.

Her voice trembling with terror, Judith cried, "Where are you taking me? What do you want?"

"Just shut up! Do exactly what you're told and you won't get hurt." Otto poked the gun into her side. He was surprised at how calm he was, how forceful his voice sounded.

The car jounced up and down and sideways on the rough surface, and as the brush scratched the sides, Otto winced. It hurt him to abuse a car like this.

At the sawmill, Rita walked ahead, with the flashlight cutting a path through the darkness. Judith followed, with Otto right behind.

"If you want money, I can give you some right now," Judith said desperately. "Then take me back to the resort, and I'll get more for you."

"Shut your trap!"

When they were in the back room, Otto gave the gun to Rita, took a towel from the bag and tied a blindfold around Judith. Then he took off his glasses. Because she started to struggle, he tied her arms behind her back with a length of clothesline. He put another towel between her teeth, knotted it behind her head and strapped adhesive tape across her mouth. Then he tied her ankles together and eased her to the floor.

They adjusted the sagging door in a closed position and hurried back to the car. Rita got back in the driver's side, and Otto slid in next to her.

"You were great, sweetheart! It went like clockwork."

She put out a gloved hand. "My money. I want my two Gs right now."

"OK, OK! What's the big rush?" He took the two packets of bills from his pocket. "Here." She shoved them into her purse and started the car.

All the way back to the resort, Otto was jubilant. "We got the breaks all the way. No one was in the parking lot! And practically no traffic! It couldn't have gone better."

"I didn't stall the car or flood the carburetor, either, smarty."

"That's right. You were great!" She might be a dumb broad, but she sure carried out his orders.

"And I never called you by name."

"No, you didn't. You held up your end of the bargain." He could hardly believe that it was over. "When we get to the parking lot, drop me off at my car. I'll turn it around while you park the Cad in its usual spot. Leave the keys under the seat. If her car's where it belongs, everyone'll think she's still at the resort." He pounded his fists on the seat. "God, we pulled it off without a hitch! We'll be out of Nevada before anyone finds out about it!"

Rita drove into the employees' parking lot, stopped near the Chevy, and Otto jumped out. Then she turned the Cad around so it was headed toward the road. "I can't go with you just yet," she said. "There's something I got to do first. I'll be back about five in the morning and meet you right here. Be sure and be here, at five o'clock."

Astounded, Otto stared at the white Cadillac as it dashed from the lot and into the street.

CHAPTER

26

Otto drove toward the parking lot at five the next morning, nearly insane with fury and panic. He'd spent the night in his room, pacing back and forth, wondering what to do. Should he start without her? If he did, she might blow the whole deal; she knew too much and could tip off the cops. Where did the dumb broad go? Surely she didn't have a customer. Even she wouldn't be that stupid—not when every minute counted. They should have been out of Nevada by now. What was the big idea, anyway?

Would she even be there, after he'd waited all night? Had she taken her two Gs and skipped? But her suitcase was still in his car. It made no sense at all, after everything had gone so smoothly. He cursed her again.

When he arrived at the lot, Rita was standing in the driveway, holding an elongated package wrapped loosely in newspaper. The Cad was back in place.

"You better have a damn good explanation!" he snarled. "Plenty good, or I'll break your neck!"

"I have." She was unimpressed with his fury, but she seemed tired and had dark circles under her eyes. "I'll tell you all about it."

Otto turned the car around, spinning the wheels in anger. He tore through the entrance and turned left. "Well, finally we're on our way." It was barely light, so he turned on the headlights.

"We're not quite on our way. There's something else we got to do."

"What are you talking about?"

"Drive to Squaw Rock."

"Squaw Rock! For Christ's sake, why?"

Something bruised his ribs. It was Rita's Smith and Wesson .38. "Just drive to Squaw Rock."

This was unreal! What was going on?

"Turn here!" Rita commanded, poking him with the gun.

As Otto turned into the fire lane, he thought he must be having a nightmare. The fire lane widened into the meadow, where a brown-and-tan Chrysler was parked alongside Squaw Rock.

"Turn to the right and stop, so you can see the end of the path. Then turn off your motor. We're waiting for somebody."

"What's the big idea?" he snarled, but he did as he was told. If she didn't have the gun, he'd have grabbed her by the neck and choked her.

"Well, I decided that if Judith Davenport drives a big Cadillac and has Mr. Starr for a boyfriend and her father's lieutenant governor, she must be pretty important. Maybe somebody would pay me for telling where she's hid. And I was right."

"You *told* someone?"

"When Max came for the payola Sunday night, I told him about it; he does the dirty work for Mr. Big. Max is sitting over there in that car. He's got another goon with him."

Panic washed over Otto. He wanted to leap from the car and run. Everyone knew about Max, the most feared man in Nevada. He was the same guy that he and Kirt turned the heroin over to five years ago. No one tangled with Max, not if you wanted to go on living.

"Max knows you. He says you're Otto Schroeder, not Owen Shulman. You got out of prison three months ago, and you served time for smuggling heroin."

"Max talks too much." Otto's throat was so tight that it hurt.

"He's got a score to settle with you, because you botched the job and got caught. They lost a bundle."

"It wasn't my fault." His voice was shrill with fear.

"Anyway, he says you must've come back to get even with the Davenports. That's why you wanted to kidnap Judith. You'd have let her die." Rita's eyes were accusing. "Well, she's not going to. We got her last night, and she's in a cabin with a guard. They're going to make her boyfriend do something before they let her go."

"You double-crossing. . . ." Otto lunged at her, but she leaned away and pointed the gun at his face.

"That's the way the cookie crumbles. I'm not going away with you, either, because Max paid me *three* grand to carry out our plan. Now I got plenty to start on my own."

"You lousy——"

"You can throw away my suitcase—there's nothing in it but old clothes, anyway. I just had you put it in your car so you'd think I was going away with you."

He stared at her in astonishment. And he thought she was dumb!

"I'm going to get out of the car now, get my van

and drive someplace where you'll never find me. Neither will Max."

She slid toward the door and laid the package against the seat. "There's something you got to do for Max before you leave, though—to pay for messing up that other job. In a little while a man will come down that path. He's a squealer, a ratfink. That's one thing Mr. Big don't like, a guy that shoots his mouth off to the fuzz. When he shows up, you're to kill him with this rifle."

"What!"

"Yeah, and I'm warning you: don't try any funny business. You can't shoot Max, because he's in that bulletproof car. It can go a hundred and twenty-five miles an hour, so if you try to get away, he can run you down so fast you won't know what happened. Besides, he's got a submachine gun trained on you right now." She opened the car door. "When you're through, you're to toss the rifle out on the ground. He wants it back."

Almost in a trance, Otto unwrapped the package and stared at an Armalite AR-18 assault rifle. It was semiautomatic, short and light, and had a straight-line stock and elevated line of sight. He looked at the Chrysler. So they'd been out a bundle, had they? Well, *he* had spent five years in prison.

There was no use begging for mercy; he'd just get a round of ammo in his gut. He looked around the meadow, back at the fire lane, and ahead at the path from the resort. He knew how an animal feels when it's caught in a trap. His only chance—a slim one—was to carry out Max's orders. Whoever came down that path was doomed anyway; it didn't matter who the hit man was. Mr. Big had spoken. Blabbermouth would be rubbed out.

Otto picked up the rifle, aimed it toward the path and pulled the trigger when Clifton McMillan came into its sights. He heard the deafening explosion in his ears, felt the recoil against his shoulder and tasted vomit in his mouth as McMillan fell to the ground. He started the car, swung it around and headed out the fire lane, followed by the brown-and-tan Chrysler and shaking so badly that he could hardly drive.

He got back on the highway, with the Chrysler close behind him, and headed for Carson City. At the end of ten miles, Highway 50 ended at Interstate 395. He turned to the left, and so did the Chrysler. He didn't try to lose it—what was the use? There was no place to hide, no way to escape.

Angry tears welled up in his eyes, and he swore and hit the steering wheel with a fist. If only he'd taken his hundred grand and headed for Idaho or Montana instead of trying to get revenge. Lea was dead, but that didn't bring Kirt back to life. And Judith Davenport would be free as soon as Lyle Starr agreed to dance to Max's tune.

What a fool he'd been, right from the first, even to want revenge. And he must have been out of his mind to trust Rita, that double-crossing bitch! If he hadn't lost his head over her, he'd have been all right. In the first place, he should have got a gun of his own. His second mistake was that he didn't buy a fast car.

In frustration, he stepped hard on the accelerator, and the Chevy leaped ahead. But so did the Chrysler. Mile after mile, as he headed east toward Salt Lake City, he watched the rearview mirror and saw the relentless brown-and-tan Chrysler right behind him. Then, to his astonishment, the Chrysler pulled off the highway, let a car pass, made a U-turn and headed back to Reno. Otto shuddered with relief. He couldn't believe it! Apparently Max was just making sure that he was getting out of the state. Well, he was, all right—the farther the better.

* * *

When the Chrysler reached the outskirts of Reno, Max growled to his driver, "Get off the freeway and find a phone booth."

The driver stopped at a service station with a glass-enclosed booth, where Max dialed the sheriff's number. "I just want to give you a tip, so listen good," he told the sergeant at the desk. "An ex-con named Otto Schroeder just killed the manager of Starr's Tahoe Resort. You'll find a rifle with his fingerprints near the body, at Squaw Rock. He's been working in the kitchen at the resort, using the name Owen Shulman. Also, ask him how he bumped off Lea Turner. He's driving east on 80 in a green Chevy. Here's his license number. . . ." He gave the number, hung up and walked back to the car. "Now we'll get some breakfast and head back to Tahoe."

Otto kept glancing at the rearview mirror. He could see for miles, but the Chrysler was not behind him. His spirits rose. It was going to be all right after all. He thought of his money, back there in the trunk. He could do about anything he wanted with that much bread. First chance he got, he'd buy a camper and travel around until he found a place where he wanted to settle down.

Driving across the desert, he began to relax. It was getting hot, but he didn't mind. He hadn't had anything to eat, but he wasn't hungry. It was too bad about McMillan, but the poor devil was a goner anyway.

Everything was going to be all right. It would be great to own a camper. He visualized one with just about every comfort imaginable—a shower, air conditioning, a galley and a bed. Of course, he wouldn't want it too big, because he'd use it in out-of-the-way places when he went fishing and hunting.

At first he didn't notice the sheriff's car far behind him, followed by one from the highway patrol. Then, in his rearview mirror, he saw the blue lights on top go around and around. They drew closer and closer. They didn't pass. Were they after him? As if in answer, a siren wailed.

CHAPTER

27

As Barrett drove from Starpoint to the resort to begin another day, a sheriff's patrol car and an ambulance passed her, going in the opposite direction. She glanced in the mirror and saw them turn into the fire lane to Squaw Rock. How strange. Why would they go there?

As of today, she had exactly six days left at Tahoe, she told herself sorrowfully. Lyle had made it very definite: her job terminated next Tuesday. Although she knew Justin wanted her in Starr Enterprises, she had heard nothing from him. Perhaps he had decided not to pursue the matter and cause a rift with his son. Her heart sank; she felt hopeless and beaten.

Just the thought of leaving the resort filled her with despair, for she loved everything about it. Now that the vacation season was ending, her chances of finding another job at Tahoe were remote. She wondered whether to go back to the East Coast or look for a job in California. After this glorious summer, no other place seemed right by comparison. This was where she belonged.

However, she would not marry Clifton as a solution to her problems. She had enjoyed her affair with him, and he would be a wonderful friend, but she was not willing to devote the rest of her life to him. Actually, she had seen very little of him lately, as he always seemed to be in conference.

She parked her car and went to the reservation desk. It was one of her favorite assignments, because she enjoyed dealing with people. After she had been working about thirty minutes, a deputy sheriff came into the lobby and spoke to the bell captain, who pointed to her. The officer approached the desk and asked, "Miss Starr? May I speak to you in private?"

"Of course." Barrett led him to Clifton's office. "I don't know where Mr. McMillan is, but I'm sure he won't mind."

"No, I'm afraid he won't. I'm sorry to have to tell you that Mr. McMillan's body was just found, at Squaw Rock. Apparently he was murdered early this morning."

"Murdered!" The color drained from her face, and she sank into a chair. "Who would murder him?" she whispered. "Who would do such a thing?"

"A suspect has already been apprehended and an investigation started. I have some questions I want to ask."

"Yes, of course. I'll help you all I can." She was trembling, and she hoped she wouldn't faint. "First, may I call the head office in Reno? Lyle Starr should know about this at once."

Barrett's voice broke when she was connected with Lyle, but finally she managed to tell him what had happened. "Oh, Lyle, this is so awful. Can you come right away?"

"I'll leave at once, as soon as I tell Dad."

The officer had his notebook ready when Barrett replaced the receiver. "First, do you know anything about a kitchen helper here named Owen Shulman?"

"No, I don't, but I can send for his personnel records."

"Please do."

She called for the folder and then asked, "Was he the one who killed Clifton?"

"At this point I can't answer that question. Did Mr. McMillan have any enemies that you knew about?"

She thought of the man with the brown-and-tan Chrysler at Squaw Rock. "Perhaps." Her heart sank as she wondered if she had caused Clifton's death by informing on him. "The one who can help you the most is Al Dixon, an agent from the gaming board. He's been conducting an investigation."

"Good. I'll send for him in a moment." The deputy looked around. "I'll use this office, if I may. There are several people I want to interrogate."

"Of course. Mr. McMillan's secretary can assist you."

He asked a few more questions, then said, "I'm sure you have arrangements to make, so I will question you again later."

"Has anyone called Mr. McMillan's parents?"

"Not that I know of. Would you take care of that?"

She nodded and walked to the door. "If you need me, I'll be in the executive offices on the eleventh floor."

When she walked into the outer office and saw Shirley, Clifton's secretary, Barrett started to cry. "Something terrible has happened—Clifton has been murdered!"

The two women clung together. "I can't believe it," Shirley sobbed. "Why would anyone want to kill such a wonderful man?"

Finally Barrett said, "We've got to pull ourselves together, Shirley. There's so much to do. As soon as word of this gets around, we'll be swamped with calls."

Shirley nodded and wiped her eyes. "I guess you're in charge now."

"Well, at least until Mr. Starr comes. I'll go to his office and wait for him. And I must call Clifton's parents. Oh, God, how I dread that."

Barrett kept her composure as she talked to the assistant manager and put him in charge of the resort. "It will be up to you to keep things going this weekend. I'll help you all I can."

"I'll *need* your help, Miss Starr. It's about the biggest weekend of the year," the young man said.

There were others in management who had to be told, and Judith, who could help her bear this grief. But the gift-shop manager shook her head. "Judith hasn't come in yet. It's strange, because she's usually so prompt, and she knows we have a lot to do to get ready for the Labor Day crowd."

"Maybe she overslept. When she reports, tell her to call me at Mr. Lyle Starr's office. I'll be there for the rest of the morning."

As she rode the elevator, Barrett fought for control. This was all her fault. She had informed on Clifton, and the underworld found out about it. As Dixon had warned her, there were spies everywhere. The agent had called in the authorities, so perhaps Clifton was killed to keep him from telling too much. Or was it for revenge? She ached with regret. She should have told him that she was reporting his visits to Squaw Rock so he could have protected himself.

The phone call to McMillan's parents in New Jersey was shattering. Barrett offered to have someone meet their plane and bring them to Tahoe and told them to call her back when their plans were made.

Then there were several calls from newspaper reporters that had to be handled with tact. At least, the tragedy hadn't occurred at the resort, she thought; Squaw Rock wasn't on Starr property. But still, the victim and the suspect were employees of the resort, which wasn't good. Besides, it was right on the heels of Lea's death, which would add to the bad publicity. She was still worrying about the resort's public image when Lyle arrived.

Shaken and distraught, he greeted her, then nodded at a nearby chair as he sat at his desk. "Now, fill in the details for me."

Barrett began with Clifton's mysterious telephone calls and told how she had followed him to Squaw Rock at five in the morning and had seen the burly man grab him and threaten him. "It seemed incredible, but I realized that morning that Clifton might be the one who's been directing the underworld's activities here. So I told Mr. Dixon about it."

"Why didn't you contact me?"

"Because you refused to believe that a gang was ripping off the resort. You said I was witch-hunting to impress Uncle Justin."

"I know, I know." Lyle put his elbows on the desk and buried his face in his hands. "I've botched up a lot of things."

"I feel terrible that I didn't warn Clifton—didn't tell him that I'd seen him and reported it. Perhaps he could have done something about it."

Lyle raised his head. His face was white and haggard. "No, he couldn't have done anything. Once you're in the clutches of those boys, you've had it."

"At first I couldn't imagine what connection there could be between Clifton and the underworld—he was so refined and cultured—but Mr. Dixon thinks that, a long time ago, Cliff was chosen and specially trained so he could supervise their racket at a Starr resort."

"I'm sure that's true."

"But Clifton was the last person you'd think of as a gangster. He wasn't the type."

"That was his best asset. Their perfect front man." Lyle got up, thrust his hands in his pockets and began pacing the room. "His death is a tragedy, but it was inevitable. If he talked too much to Dixon and the other authorities, he was finished."

"That's just what happened, it seems. But the officer said that a man has been arrested."

"He wouldn't be one of the inner gang. Those guys don't get caught. They hire a hit man or set up some sucker to do their dirty work for them."

Barrett watched him pace back and forth, his face drawn, his manner agitated. She had never seen Lyle like this. Had Clifton's death affected him so deeply? Had they really been that close? She expected him to be sad, but not so upset.

He sat down behind the desk and rubbed the back of his neck. "This may be just the beginning."

"What do you mean?"

"I'm in a mess, Barrett." His voice quavered. "When you phoned this morning, I realized how serious it is. They'll stop at nothing—nothing."

"Are you in some kind of trouble, Lyle? Something connected with Clifton?"

He looked at her, his eyes naked with worry. "*Am* I! You can't imagine. When I think of what Dad will do. . . ."

"What is it?"

"You know that property I bought at the lake?" She nodded.

"Remember how offhand and casual Clifton was

when he told me about it?" Lyle laughed bitterly. "There was nothing offhand about it. It was the most carefully planned operation you ever saw. I was set up as the perfect pigeon, and I fell for it."

"In what way? Was there something illegal about the way you bought that property?

"No, there's nothing wrong with the property or the way I bought it, but those purchases were used as a come-on to soften me up. I bought them for about half of what they're worth. I should have suspected something was fishy. The property belonged to the syndicate, through some front. They took a loss on it so they could go after bigger game."

"What did they do? What did *you* do?"

"We worked out a capital venture with various people. We have a limited partnership, like the one in Hawaii—but that's on the up and up. This is for an illegal operation. I didn't realize it at first. It's too complicated to explain right now, but they've got me in a vise. It's the first time that Starr's has ever been part of an underworld racket."

"Can't you withdraw?"

Lyle shook his head, got out of his chair and paced back and forth again. "There's no way. They've got me. They'll have a hold on Starr's."

"But we can't let them!"

"You saw what they did to Clifton. They mean business, and there's no way out! I'll have to go along with them or else." He sat down again and put his hands over his face.

"Does Uncle Justin know?"

Lyle shook his head. "No, and when he finds out, he'll disinherit me. It's exactly what he's cautioned me against, right from the beginning."

"Oh, Lyle, why didn't you consult him before you got in so deep? Was it because of his heart attack that you didn't want to bother him?"

"Hell, no! I was sore at him. He made me so mad when he didn't consult me about making you a vice-president that I blew my top. I just went ahead and acted on my own, without realizing all the ramifications until it was too late. On the surface, everything was fine, but I soon found out what was really going on."

"Oh, Lyle, I'm sorry if I——"

"It wasn't your fault, Barrett. Dad had been riding me about a lot of things. He was on my back every day. Then you came along and insisted that something funny was going on up here—a big rip-off—and Dad chewed me out for not getting wise to it on my own. He said I should be on top of things more. Well, it all got to me. When this deal came along, which looked so great, I rebelled and said to hell with him. He didn't consult me, so I wouldn't consult him. I got into it on my own."

Barrett understood how the front men could maneuver Lyle and use him, how they would act when Justin was away. She had sensed Lyle's naïveté early in the summer, as Justin had many years before. The men would flatter him, then set him up in ready-made deals where he'd think he was very astute and could impress his father by increasing the fortune. And he fell into the trap, just as they had planned.

Ashen and sick, Lyle looked at her in desperation. "Barrett, what shall I do?"

CHAPTER

28

Barrett put her hand on Lyle's shoulder. "The only thing to do is to come clean. Tell Justin the whole story. He'll understand your mistakes, because he's made plenty himself. He'll understand your anger, too, because he's got a temper of his own. He can have the legal department——"

"What do you think *I've* been doing? I've already consulted a private lawyer, but they've got me hogtied. On the surface, it's all legal. It's only when you get to the nitty-gritty—to the kind of people who are involved—that you find out what's really going on. And proving it is another thing."

"Of course, racketeers are experts at covering up their operations. They've had years of practice."

"Have they ever!" Lyle thumped his fist on the desk. "Dad will disinherit me!"

"I doubt that very much. Let's send for him. We can say that it has something to do with Clifton's murder. I'll help you, and the three of us can talk it out."

Lyle shook his head. "No, he'll never forgive me."

"Of course he will. Your father loves you very much."

"I know he does, and I love him. He drives me up the wall sometimes, but I still love him. I don't know anyone I admire more. Think of him—starting out with nothing and ending up with millions. All *I* have to do is take care of his money, and I can't even do that!"

"There's always the last resort—Mr. Hightower. I remember the number: 987-6050."

"Call Mr. *Hightower?* You don't know what you're saying!"

"But Uncle Justin said they won't harm us."

"Look, there are lots of things they can do to you besides murdering and kidnapping. And you'll wish they would kill you before they're through. No, I'm not calling Hightower."

"Then, come clean with your father."

"I just can't. He's so damned proud of me; he thinks I'm the greatest just because of my background. I can't disillusion him. I don't want him to find out what I really am—a stupid, inept fool!"

"Oh, come on, Lyle. You're not stupid *or* inept. You're a well-trained, capable businessman. You have everything going for you. It's just difficult to deal with the gambling world, that's all."

"But Dad expects me to deal with it, because he sent me to Stanford. He thinks the university provided all the answers, but it didn't."

"Of course not."

"I love Dad, but I hate his world. I hate gambling. I hate this resort and the atmosphere. I hate it in Reno, too. And all the maneuverings with the politicians. I hate dealing with the racketeers, the prostitutes, the underworld goons. Even the entertainers with their egos and hang-ups. God, how I loathe them all!" Hard, wrenching sobs shook his body.

Barrett didn't try to stop him; she wanted him to release his emotions, fears, and frustrations. At last, as Lyle's sobs subsided, Barrett went into the bathroom and ran the cold water. "Here, put this towel on your eyes."

"I haven't cried in years," he said. "I'm so embarrassed."

"Don't be. Everyone should blow his cool once in a while. Now, let's decide——"

The telephone rang, and the secretary in the outer office said, "A Mr. William Smith to speak to Mr. Starr." Barrett gave Lyle the phone.

"Lyle Starr speaking."

"Listen, Starr, and listen good. We've got your girlfriend, Judith Davenport."

"No!"

"Nothing will happen to her if you cooperate. We want Barrett Starr out of Nevada. She's to take the next plane to New York and never come back. As soon as she leaves, we'll release your girlfriend. We'll know when. We have a man at the airport."

"How can you prove you've got her?"

"She'll tell you herself."

"Lyle!" Judith cried.

"Judith, are you all right?"

"Yes, but please do as they say!"

The telephone receiver clicked at the other end.

Lyle turned to Barrett. "Did you hear? They've kidnapped Judith."

"Yes, I heard."

"You've got to go to New York at once, on the next plane. Call for a reservation, and I'll drive you to Starpoint so you can pack your things. Then I'll take you to the airport. Lord, will this nightmare ever end?"

"I'm not going, Lyle."

He stared at her in disbelief. "Not going? But you've *got* to!"

"No. I'm not dancing to their tune!"

He grabbed her arm. "My God, Barrett, look what they did to Clifton. They'll kill Judith, too. If anything happens to her. . . . I love her and want to marry her. You've got to go."

"I'm staying here."

"Be reasonable, Barrett! We've got to get Judith back. Then I'll manage, somehow, to cope with my situation. I'll think of something so Dad doesn't find out. I'll———"

"Lyle, I'm staying right here at Tahoe. *You* go."

"Me? Go to New York?"

"No, to Hawaii! That's where you belong. Take charge of Starr Enterprises there and build it up. You're a round peg in a square hole here, but you'd be great over there, handling that end of the operation. It should be expanded."

"If I only could!"

"I'll take charge here. You can't defy the underworld, but I can."

"But what about Judith?"

"I'm going to call Mr. Hightower, and he'll have her returned safely. She can join you in Hawaii and you can get married there. I'll get you out of that limited partnership, too."

Lyle slumped back in his chair. "Barrett, are you sure?"

"Yes, but you have to leave right now. Get out of their clutches. Take some money from the cash reserve at the casino, drive to San Francisco and take the first flight you can get. Don't even come back on a visit—not for a while, anyway."

"But Dad———"

"Let me handle him. I'll look out for your interests.

I know how much he cares for you and your mother, and I'm too smart to try to undermine either of you. There's room in Starr Enterprises for all of us. You take care of Hawaii, I'll be here, and Justin is able to look out for the rest."

"Barrett, I'll never forget this, never!" Lyle grabbed her and hugged her. "I *will* go to Hawaii. I'll go right now."

"Leave a key for your apartment so Judith and I can pack your things and ship them over."

He took a key from his chain, gave it to her, then kissed her. "Thanks for everything. And take care of Judith for me."

"I will. We'll meet you in Hawaii for the wedding."

After Lyle left, Barrett gazed at the telephone. Did she really have the courage to call Mr. Hightower? Talking about it was one thing, but actually doing it was another. Was she brave enough to try to hassle the head of underworld operations in Nevada? A man who was probably affiliated with a worldwide crime organization? A powerful and feared man, who would stop at nothing to gain his ends—torture, kidnapping, murder? Look what had happened to poor Clifton this very morning. And now Judith. Could she call him?

She thought of the stranglehold the underworld was trying to get on Starr's, how they had been skimming and cheating the casino ever since it opened, how they had maneuvered Lyle to get him under their control. They had to be stopped. She dialed the number.

"I wish to speak to Mr. Hightower."

"Who's calling?"

"Barrett Starr, Justin Starr's niece. I want to speak to Mr. Hightower at once."

When another man spoke, his voice was distorted, as if by a mechanical device. "Yes."

"Mr. Hightower?"

"Yes, Miss Starr."

"I have a favor to ask of you." She kept her voice calm and polite but very firm. "Someone is detaining Judith Davenport, and I want her released immediately. In fact, I want her here at Starr's Tahoe Resort within the hour. Would you kindly arrange this as a special favor to Justin Starr and me?"

There was a long silence. Finally the voice said, "I don't know what you're talking about, but——"

"But you have so many resources at your command, Mr. Hightower. I'm sure something can be arranged within the hour. In fact, I strongly advise it."

Mr. Hightower said nothing, but Barrett could hear him breathing. She waited. At last he said, "I'll see what I can do."

"I have every confidence in you. By the way, I am now in charge of the resort and our other Starr interests at Tahoe. There will be several changes in our personnel, effective immediately."

"I see."

"Mr. Lyle Starr will no longer be in Nevada. He has business commitments elsewhere. From now on, Justin Starr and I will be in complete control. Am I making myself clear?"

"Yes."

"Then, I can expect Judith Davenport to be back here within an hour?"

"Yes."

"Thank you."

"You're welcome, but I may ask a favor of you someday."

Barrett replaced the receiver, already dreading the time when Mr. Hightower might ask that favor of her. She hoped it would not be too difficult, but she would deal with that problem when the time came.

In the meantime, there was so much to do. She

must explain Lyle's sudden departure to Justin and Eunice, truthfully but in the best light. She must hire a new resident manager as soon as possible, for the assistant was not sufficiently experienced to take over permanently. And Carl Rhodes and his gang had to be fired and replacements found and trained. In spite of everything, the resort must run smoothly. It was her responsibility.

As the enormity of the recent events dawned on her, she sat back in Lyle's chair and again admired his sumptuous office, which would be hers from now on. The secretary in the outer office would work for her. Her name would be displayed in gold letters on the door: BARRETT STARR, VICE-PRESIDENT.

She would take over Lyle's bedroom and bath and the two other rooms, make them into a kitchen and a living room, and turn the suite into a luxurious apartment for herself. She stood up, opened the glass door, stepped onto the balcony—the eagle's nest—and grasped the railing. Next to Justin, she would have the power. She would be one of *the* Starrs. She would be in charge here, and recognized and respected in every casino. From now on she would have to show her money so the other operators would know that Starr's was prospering.

As time went on, she knew, Justin would delegate more and more authority to her. She was the heir to the throne. He would train her to take over the vast empire. And someday she would find a mate, a real man like Justin, someone strong and vital, who could help her.

With a sigh of regret for Clifton, Barrett looked out over the lake, smooth as glass, not a ripple disturbing its surface, reflecting the deep blue of the sky and surrounded by majestic, serrated peaks. The jewel of the Sierra. In spite of its present serenity, however, she knew that it, like her future, could be storm-lashed, forbidding, and dangerous. But today nothing was more magnificent than Tahoe.

Then she looked down at her immediate surroundings. The parking lots below held thousands of cars from all over the country. Throngs of people were arriving and leaving, and she could picture the Andromeda and Orion rooms, crowded with guests milling around the slot machines, the roulette wheels, the crap layouts, and the 21 tables. All weekend the Celestial Room and the entertainment lounges would overflow with customers.

Barrett looked at all this, and a thrill of triumph ran through her. "It's mine now," she whispered, "all mine!"

**WE HOPE YOU
ENJOYED THIS BOOK**

OTHER SELECTIONS
FROM
PLAYBOY PRESS

THE DRAGON AND THE ROSE   **$1.95**
ROBERTA GELLIS
When Henry took the bloody throne of England, he
pledged to marry Elizabeth, daughter of his most
bitter enemy, in order to keep peace in the land.
Theirs was a match of convenience, laced with mis-
trust and fear, but from this unlikely alliance, there
grew a love so strong and a passion so fierce that it
changed the course of history.

HUNTER'S MOON   **$1.75**
NORAH HESS
Widowed at nineteen, the passionate Darcy Stevens
knew only one way to survive—by selling herself to
men. When the chance came for a new life, however,
Darcy decided to move to the isolated Kentucky hills
and leave her sordid past behind. But violence pur-
sued her, and soon Darcy was caught between the
bold and dashing Delaney brothers—two fierce mountain men, each determined to make her his own.

THE REPORTERS   **$1.75**
LARRY SPENCER
Two investigative reporters on the Washington beat
plan a flattering series of articles on the late beloved
president, lauding his great contributions to the country and world peace. But, as they probe, an ugly
portrait of a corrupt and ruthless leader emerges.

FLOWERS OF FIRE $1.95
STEPHANIE BLAKE

From the Irish revolution to the American Civil War, from the slave plantations of the South Seas to the Wild West, this sweeping love story follows the tumultuous life of beautiful but strong-willed Ravena Wilding, who is torn between twin brothers—one whom she hates but is forced to marry, the other whom she loves but cannot have.

THE PRESIDENT'S DOCTOR $1.95
WILLIAM WOOLFOLK

Alone, brooding, the president of the United States plots in his Oval Office. Paranoid, plagued by mysterious violent tempers, he gets ready to press the nuclear trigger. The secret behind his tormented behavior is locked in the mind of one man.

THE CLOSED CIRCLE $1.75
BARNEY PARRISH

By day, Lila is quietly religious; by night, she is lewd and possessed of a strange psychic power that enables her to witness events a continent away—weird events, diabolic orgies, and a cult of evil that calls itself The Closed Circle.

THE DEATH CONNECTION $1.50
ROGER BRANDT

When the newly appointed assistant chief inspector of the U.S. Border Patrol tangles with one of the most ruthless alien smugglers in the country, all hell breaks loose and the bloodbath begins.

THE FIVE-MAN WAR $1.50
CHUCK BELANGER

Chicago was the target of random terrorist attacks. The police had no clues or suspects. Was there any way to avoid panic and chaos? A cliff-hanging novel of five men who bring a city to its knees.

A NORTHERN SAGA $1.75
STEVEN C. LAWRENCE

Bound for Russia with a cargo of guns and ammunition, the brave crew of the S.S. *John Mason* were carrying out their most dangerous mission, knowing that one hit from a Nazi bomb or torpedo would blast their ship sky-high. A story of courage aboard the Liberty ships during World War II.

FROGS AT THE BOTTOM OF THE WELL $1.75
KEN EDGAR

Molly Reagan is a beautiful, dedicated policewoman who puts her life on the line when she infiltrates a terrorist organization made up of revolutionary feminists who would kill in cold blood to dramatize their cause.

MASSY'S GAME $1.75
JACK OLSEN

A thriller about an eight-foot-tall pro basketball player who is determined to succeed no matter what the price. When reporter Sam Forrester begins to dig into the past to find out why Massy insists on playing out the drama that could cost him his life, he uncovers the most bizarre series of plots in his career.

THE CANDIDATE'S WIFE $1.75
BURT CARRICK

A blockbuster of explosive political blackmail! In the eyes of the nation she was the symbol of the perfect wife and mother—but concealed behind the virtuous image was a promiscuous woman with insatiable sexual needs.

HURRICANE OF ICE $1.95
H. L. PERRY

A howling inferno of a storm descended with crashing force. The mighty Trafalgar Bridge surged and thrashed like a bucking bronco, and the ultraplush Tallifaro Inn—with its curious microcosm of guests —shook to its very foundation, pitted against nature in a harrowing test of survival.

NIKKI $1.95
ALLAN NIXON

Everyone in the world knew Nikki Eckstrom as the most beautiful, exciting Hollywood love goddess of all time. What they didn't know was how she got there and the heavy price she paid for success. Obsessed with fame, Nikki uses everyone and everything to claw her way into the spotlight and stay there. Husbands, lovers—even her own daughter— fall victim to her insatiable needs. Until one day, her beauty fading, she strikes out in total desperation and is destroyed.

WOLF MOUNTAIN $1.95
PETER LARS SANDBERG

To Matt Whittaker, retired Vietnam pilot, it was a sanctuary where he might heal the wounds of his disillusionment; to Kate O'Rourke and her climbing club of teen-age girls, it was a playground for adventurous fun—until two psychopathic killers made them the targets in a macabre shooting gallery.

BIG NIGHT AT MRS. MARIA'S $1.95
BARNEY PARRISH

Everyone who was anyone was invited. And everyone came: the Hollywood starlets, the politicians, the superjocks, the society matrons, the rich and the celebrated, the gifted and the damned. But it was an orgy that would turn into a night of terror.

ELISHA'S WOMAN $1.95
NORAH HESS

Bold, passionate, willing, Rachael Jobe came as a stranger to Devil's Ridge. She was eager to begin a new life, hungry to find love and determined that no man would hold her cheaply again. When she met Adam Warden, she thought she had found her match, but Adam believed she was Elisha's woman and contemptuously called her a whore. Insulted and enraged, Rachael resolved to teach him a lesson about women that he would never forget.

FREE BOOK OFFER!

ayboy Press wants to bring you the type of books you enjoy. For
is reason we are asking you to fill out our questionnaire so that
e can learn more about your reading tastes. For your effort we
ill send you FREE any one book of your choice advertised with-
these pages.

Are you_____female_____male?

What is your age?
_____Under 15
_____15 to 24
_____25 to 34
_____35 to 44
_____45 to 54
_____55 or over

What is your level of education?
_____Currently Jr. High_____H.S._____College_____
_____Some High School
_____High School Graduate
_____Some College
_____College Graduate

What is your occupation?

_____

What is your income level?
_____Under $10,000
_____$10,000 to $14,999
_____$15,000 to $19,999
_____$20,000 to $24,999
_____$25,000 and up

Where did you buy this book?
_____Bookstore
_____Drugstore
_____Chain Variety Store
_____Supermarket
_____Department Store
_____Discount Store
_____Newsstand
_____Bus or Train Station
_____Airport
_____Other

_____
Please Specify

Please turn page

7. How many paperback books have you bought in the last six months?
_____1 to 3
_____4 to 6
_____7 to 9
_____10 or more

8. What types of books do you like best?
_____Softcover editions of hardcover best sellers
_____Romantic Novels
_____Gothics
_____Historical Novels
_____Mystery and Suspense Thrillers
_____Westerns
_____Science Fiction
_____Self-Help and How-To Books
_____Biography and Autobiography
_____Other _____

9. Why did you buy this book? _____
(You may check more than one answer)   Give Title
_____Recognized the title
_____Author's reputation
_____The book's cover
_____Price
_____Friend's recommendation
_____Newspaper or magazine ad
_____Radio ad
_____TV ad
_____Store display
_____Saw author on TV, or heard him on radio
_____Book review
_____Subject matter
_____Other _____

If you do not wish to include your name and address, please do indicate the name of your town and state.

Please return your questionnaire and coupon to:
Mary Williams, Playboy Press, 919 N. Michigan, Chicago, IL 60611.

Please send me a free copy of: (Give title and number)

1st choice _____

2nd choice _____

NAME _____

ADDRESS _____

CITY_____ STATE _____ ZIP_____

THIS OFFER EXPIRES DECEMBER 15, 1977

Book Number 408